MW00794915

BLOWNUP IN PARADISE

PARADISE SERIES

BOOK 14

DEBORAH BROWN

BLOWNUP IN PARADISE
All Rights Reserved
Copyright © 2018 Deborah Brown

ISBN-13: 978-0-9984404-5-3

PRINTED IN THE UNITED STATES OF AMERICA

BLOWNUP IN PARADISE

Chapter One

"We're being followed," Fab said in a hushed tone as we headed down the Overseas Highway from the top of the Keys, her eyes alternating between the road in front of her and the Hummer's side mirror.

I turned in my seat. "The sports car?"

"The Harley. It's been moving up, then hanging back, and now it's almost on my bumper." Fab pulled her Walther out from under her skirt, where she had it holstered. "Madison, wait," she exclaimed after a minute. "It's not us... It's the Ferrari the Harley is interested in."

I craned my neck around the back of the driver's seat, in awe that she could identify the make of a car with a quick glance. "That's Bordello!" I struggled to keep from shrieking. Now on my knees on the passenger seat, I kept a tight grip on my Glock, which I'd also had holstered under my skirt. "Mostly certain." I climbed into the back seat to double check.

James Bordello was a man with unsavory family connections, and I'd long suspected that he would stoop to violence to get what he wanted in a business deal but hadn't been able to prove it. Much to my dismay and despite my attempts to talk my brother out of it, Brad had formed a real estate partnership with the man. To say Brad's taste in women and business partners was terrible would be an understatement; they were invariably either crazy or criminal. *But did he ever listen to his sister? Oh, heck no.*

"Don't look now," I instructed Fab, which she promptly ignored, turning her head towards the driver's side window. "You don't listen very well."

"What already?" Fab asked in exasperation.

"Bordello just pulled up alongside us. Wonder where he's going?" I scooted to the middle of the backseat on the off chance that he might see me. Probably not, since I'd chosen the darkest tint I could get for the windows.

"It's Bordello, all right," Fab said, her disgust coming through loud and clear. "Judging by the way the Harley is dogging the Ferrari, plus the cannon tucked under that leather jacket, I'd say the rider likely gets a shot off and kills Bordello. Are we getting involved, or am I turning around and heading for my appointment? Your call. Personally, I vote for being do-gooder citizens, but only because I want to know what's going down."

"Follow him." It was probably a bad idea, but like Fab, I wanted to know what was going to happen next. "We have a few extra minutes before we need to hit the Turnpike to make your appointment on time."

The bike rider hunkered down and sped after the car, remaining a discreet distance behind, not ready to make it known that their only interest on the road was the Ferrari.

"Maybe whoever it is has a good reason to want him dead," I said, my face almost pressed to the glass.

"I'm a bad influence." Fab snorted. "That would be my rationale."

First, the Ferrari changed lanes, pulling in front of us. Next the bike slid in, cutting it close to the bumper and forcing Fab to hit the brakes.

"What's the plan?" I asked.

"Get back up here," Fab ordered. "Rider reaches for the gun, I'll clip the back tire. Hopefully, their speed won't get back up to what it was because this isn't without a certain amount of risk. Might scratch up the Hummer." She patted the dash.

I sighed. The SUV was the coolest car I'd ever owned and an amazingly good deal, and I was tired of taking it to the auto body shop, hoping to get it back in near-new condition.

"Do you think Bordello knows he's being followed?" I asked, climbing back into the front.

At that exact moment, Bordello pushed hard on the accelerator. The shiny silver sports car took off with a roar, speeding past the Tarpon Cove city limits as he rocketed down the highway heading south.

"He knows now." Fab eased down on the gas in hot pursuit of the two, but hung back, leaving plenty of room.

The bike accelerated and was about to run up on the car's back bumper, but several seconds later, the brake lights flashed and the motorcycle skidded, the back wheel swinging around ninety degrees. The rider hit the pavement and rolled, coming to a stop lying face down on the asphalt, not moving. The bike continued its skid, the crunch of the frame as it wrapped around a pole ensuring a mangled mess.

I let out a loud groan.

Fab slowed and pulled to the side of the highway, leaving a couple of car lengths between us and the accident. The two of us jumped out and ran to the rider.

Struggling to move, the rider managed to turn over, grunting and groaning all the while.

"I'm calling 911," Fab said, just as the sound of screeching tires redirected our attention.

Bordello had also pulled over and now put the Ferrari in reverse, backing up, blowing dust and dirt in our direction, and coming to a squealing stop. He barreled out of the car and raced the few feet to where we were. He did a double take at seeing Fab and I standing on the roadside and glared.

"Don't touch her," he bellowed at the two of us.

I stood, having already bent down to offer

assistance until an ambulance arrived with the hope that once Fab got an operator on the phone, they'd tell us what to do.

Bordello threw himself down next to the rider, unbuckled the helmet and slipped it off gently, cradling her head in his lap. "I'll take care of this," he snapped. He pulled his phone out of his pocket, punched in 911, and reported an "accident," telling the operator an ambulance was needed. All the while, he ran his hand over her long blonde hair, which had tumbled out and over her shoulders.

The woman blinked several times in an attempt to focus. A long-legged, willowy blonde, her bright blue eyes brimmed with pain as she drifted in and out, her fingers clawing at the dirt. The woman made an effort to sit up, but didn't get far before Bordello eased her gently against his chest.

"Just relax. Help is on the way," he said softly.

I wasn't sure what the heck I was witnessing, and Fab appeared to share my sentiments as we stood rooted on the side of the road. Bordello was practically cooing at the injured woman; the only tones I'd ever heard him use were sarcastic and demanding.

Bordello's brown eyes, now black pin dots, turned on Fab and me. "If it isn't Madison Westin and Fabiana Merceau. What the hell are you two doing here? F'ing following me?" he ground out. He'd recovered from his brief brush

with being nice and his true self was back—
arrogant and full of himself.

"Apparently you know this damsel in
distress." I glanced down at the woman. "Did
you know she planned to shoot you?" I cut my
eyes to the pavement a few feet away, where the
Smith & Wesson lay.

He ignored me, focusing on comforting the
woman, murmuring words neither Fab nor I
could hear. Fab had the nerve to step closer.

"You two need to get the hell out of here," he
ordered, a snap of his fingers in his tone, along
with the expectation that we would obey without
question. "I'll handle this. The only recitation of
the facts the cops need to hear is mine."

"A thank you would be nice," Fab huffed.
"Instead of you comforting your shooter, you
could be getting dragged out of your car and
bagged off to the coroner about now."

"I told you to leave. I'm not telling you again."

Fab's Walther made its second appearance of
the day, and she aimed it between his eyes. "If I
don't, what are you going to do about it?"

I smiled when he flinched, but I grabbed hold
of Fab's arm and gave it a gentle tug. "Next time
we see one another, let's pretend that we've
never met—ever." I nudged Fab toward the car.

Bordello's glaring eyes followed us as we got
back in the car.

Fab put the car in gear, and we both watched
as Bordello leaned over and picked up the

woman's gun, shoving it down the back of his pants. As Fab pulled out onto the highway, flashing lights could be seen approaching in the distance, and by the time we made a U-turn at the next exit, a cop car and ambulance had pulled into the space we vacated. We slowed for the drivers in front of us, most with their necks craned out the windows to get a glimpse of the accident.

"What just happened?" I asked in sheer confusion as Fab sped by the lookie-loos and back up to the posted speed limit.

"As long as that woman's face doesn't appear in the weekly with the word 'dead' in the headline, I'm erasing this from my memory."

"Bordello knows I'd never keep my mouth shut if that happened."

"I'd sure like to know what that was about. Don't suppose we'll ever find out." Fab handed me her phone. "Call the client and make some excuse to reschedule for tomorrow."

"You're the owner of the company; that's your responsibility."

"I'm delegating."

"How does a flat tire sound?" I caught her eye roll. "The truth would also sound made up."

Chapter Two

It was early morning, and I was the last to come downstairs and join my two roommates and boyfriend for coffee. I'd inherited the two-story Key West-style house from my aunt and became friends with Fab not long after. One day, I came home to Fab's announcement that she'd moved in. Not long after that, she met her boyfriend, Didier. It wasn't long before, unbeknownst to him, she packed his belongings and moved him in, too. Now that Fab and Didier were engaged, they'd probably want their own house, and I hadn't spoken up about how much I hated the idea that they'd move. There was a certain chaos that came from living with three, sometimes four high-energy adults under one roof. To me, it had become the norm, and I wasn't looking for a change.

My boyfriend, Creole, turned at the tapping of my heels on the floor as I crossed the entry and went into the kitchen. Six foot and muscled, he leaned back on his stool, cobalt eyes locked on mine before slowly perusing me. I could almost feel the warmth of them as they traveled up my bare legs and over my short turquoise dress.

While out shopping, Fab had tried to steer me to the same dress in black, and I'd had to remind her that I wasn't the one afraid of color in my wardrobe. Now I was happy that I did.

Creole had been a proud detective for the Miami police department until an undercover sting erupted into gunfire, leaving him shot and his partner dead. Since that day, he'd been on medical leave, undergoing a long recovery. During that time, the two of us had spent the majority of our time at my house. Now that he was back in fighting shape, I suspected that his status might change after his meeting with the chief today.

Jazz and Snow made their way single file into the kitchen, meowing that it was time for something better than the dry food that filled their bowl. You'd think that the two oversized felines hadn't had a meal in forever. Didier opened the refrigerator, handing Creole a can of gourmet something. He had the food dished out and sitting on the floor in moments, bringing the howling to a stop.

"Another meeting?" Didier asked, running a finger down Fab's cheek. His blue eyes twinkled as he checked her out from head to toe. "You both look *très belle*." In her black suit, Fab looked professional, not a hair of her brown, almost waist-length hair out of place.

Beautiful, that's what a woman likes to hear. I nodded and smiled at him.

"You didn't say how yesterday's meeting went." Creole's eyes shifted between Fab and me. "You get a new client?"

Fab arched her brow at me, as if to say, *You tell them.*

"Neither of you asked," I weaseled. That was the wrong tactic. Creole's easygoing smile disappeared and both men began frowning, alternating between Fab and I. "We... well, I... as part of my new duties, I called and rescheduled that meeting for today."

"You might want to get to the point," Fab directed, a slight smirk on her lips.

"We got delayed... sidetracked, might be a better word." At the sound of both men growling, I blurted, "We were doing our civic duty. Helping our fellow man."

The second round of growling was much louder and had me stepping back, but I didn't get far, as Creole hauled me to his chest and raised my chin. "You okay?"

"We both are." I pushed a lock of his black hair that had fallen forward back behind his ear.

"I'll tell them," Fab said with a shake of her head. She hit the highlights, leaving out Bordello's oddly tender behavior toward his would-be killer—not that I blamed her; after all, who'd believe that anyway?—and ended with, "What do you suppose Bordello's motive was for keeping his potential killer out of jail?"

"He doesn't want the publicity," Creole said.

"He does a good job of staying out of the public eye and wants to keep it that way."

"What if the woman ends up dead?" Didier asked.

"Then he's going to jail. No matter how connected he thinks he is," Creole said with the authority of a man that had dealt with the worst kinds of criminals.

"What are your plans for the day?" I eyed Didier's tousled dark hair and his Euro casual attire: dress pants and a shirt with the sleeves rolled up.

Each of the men in this house used just one name. "Creole" was my boyfriend's undercover moniker, and I hadn't heard any mention of him going back to his birth name should he decide to leave the department. And then there was Didier, the ex-model turned real estate developer.

"Meeting the architect down on the docks to go over plans for the new development."

I'd brought Didier and a longtime Tarpon Cove resident, Butch "Corndog" Randall, together for a real estate deal. Corndog owned dock-front property and was being pressured to sell. Having no desire to do so, he eventually decided that he wanted to develop it himself and needed a partner. Didier hadn't been looking for a big project, but after his initial meeting with Corndog, they'd hit it off and agreed on a few ideas for the historical area... which didn't include razed and rebuilt.

All of it made possible by Bordello, who had first approached Corndog about buying out his interests, with plans to demo the area and replace it with a large glass-and-steel office building in homage to himself. After rejecting the deal, Corndog was beaten up and ended up in the hospital. And then several fires were started on his properties. That was how I ended up meeting the man. He hired me to run a background check on Bordello, so he'd know what he was dealing with. Unfortunately, it revealed nothing more than that the man had a clean background. Most of what was known about the man's unsavory side was whispered about under the protection of anonymity.

Under Corndog and Didier's partnership agreement, I was offered a small piece of the action, and in return, I'd handle public relations, which was code for problems. I'd already hooked them up with a friend of my aunt's from the building department, who was helping to coordinate interactions and approval from several different agencies. Thus far, he'd been invaluable in wading through the many regulations that had to be addressed so that the project went smoothly. I'd put in a request for a small corner retail location, which they both agreed to after I pitched my plan for an upscale dive bar to be named "Tropics."

To my knowledge, neither Bordello nor my brother knew that the partnership had been inked, and I didn't look forward to the day they found out that Corndog had not just refused to sell the property but was moving forward with plans of his own. Another surprise that awaited them was our purchase of another building in that same area. They had put in a bid on it, but Fab snagged it for her private investigation firm and Didier's real estate office. She'd offered Creole and I space, but we'd turned it down, as neither of us had any use for a large office. I told her that, on the few times I came to the office, I'd find my own space, even if it meant using the conference table or sharing her desk, which would be more to my liking.

"Just remember, if I can be helpful, you know where to find me," I reminded Didier. "Forgot to tell you, I met Hazel from the city council at Jake's the other day and schmoozed her, set her and her husband up with free lunch, beer, and an available pool table."

Jake's was a tropical dive bar that I owned on the main highway that ran through town. It shared the block with two other buildings I also owned: an antique garden store and a lighthouse-turned-office.

Didier flinched. "Wasn't that kind of obvious?"

"I didn't hide that I was kissing up. She knew it and so did her husband; he even winked at me."

"That's my girl." Creole hooked his arm

around me, kissing my cheek.

"You know I'll do anything you ask?" Fab told Didier.

"And everything I ask you not to," Didier said, and he and Creole laughed.

"You know I've been really *good* lately?" Her seductive smile didn't go unnoticed by anyone.

Fab and Didier were perfect for one another. If Fab could calm the voices in her head telling her she might screw up the relationship, they'd get married before they were both old and grey and probably still a hot couple.

Creole leaned in and squeezed my cheeks, kissing my lips. "Try and stay out of trouble." He kissed me again. "You see Bordello, ignore the man. He gets shot, he can call 911 himself."

Having already checked the clock on the microwave, I looked at Fab and tapped the non-existent watch on my wrist. If we left now, we could stop at the bakery.

"I'll walk you out." I looped my arm around Creole's. "We can make out by the car while these two smooch it up in here." Before we walked out the door, I said over my shoulder, "Don't dally."

Chapter Three

"How much farther?" I whined, having sucked down the last of the caramel latte I'd gotten via the drive-thru window at one of our favorite coffee places. It hadn't taken long for me to figure out that one cup of extra-strength caffeine wouldn't be enough for this day. Fab ignored me as she rocketed across the Causeway. I fished change out of the ashtray and handed it over for the last of the tolls. "If you're going to take clients up here in North Miami, I suggest you get a toll sticker."

"Put that on your list of things to do." She flashed a fake smile.

"I'm your partner, not an assistant that you get to boss around. Or whatever they're called. You're going to need one. I suggest someone a little shifty, like yourself. You'd scare the heck out a straight arrow, who'd probably call the police on you as he/she bolted out the door."

"I'm a straight whatever that is."

I made a choking sound, which earned me a glare.

"I'm going to hire Mac."

"Over your dead body." I glared back at her. "I'm the best boss ever, and you're an unknown. If I get wind that you so much as even suggested Mac leave my employ, I'll beat the snuff out of you."

Mac Lane managed my beachfront cottages. On paper, it would seem like an idyllic job, until you met the tenants and discovered not a one of them was operating on all cylinders. For the most part, she managed to herd them along in an orderly fashion and keep the cop calls to a minimum.

"As long as I have you to order around, I'm not in any hurry." Fab took a turn that put us parallel to the coast. "Do you know where we're going?"

I turned my head to stare out at the waters of Biscayne Bay; its number one feature the view of the rippling waters running off to the sides. I briefly contemplated having her drive in circles, but figured she'd kick me out of the car once she figured it out. "That sign—" I pointed as we drove past. "Couldn't read it."

"I don't know who's more annoying, you or that woman on the GPS."

"Turn right in two kilometers," I said in a snooty tone that accentuated my words. "Here." I jabbed my finger at the approaching corner.

"You don't know your distances very well."

"You made the turn, didn't you?"

The Venetian Islands were a string of islands

connected by bridges from the Miami mainland to Miami Beach. The sun beat down on the aquamarine water, making it a perfect day for sailing, and a few boats were out on the water doing just that.

"All you told me is that it's a case of boats and trailers stolen from a storage yard at some upscale condos. How about filling in the blanks?"

"Two boats were stolen over the last couple of weeks, with a third attempt, two nights ago, thwarted by a condo owner out walking his dog. He told the cops and condo management that it was four males; two, he swore, were teenagers."

"There's no way to solve this case, if that's what your client wants, without staking out the place." I groaned inwardly.

"Today, I'm here to make security recommendations. We talked about several different options, and surveillance was included. He balked at the cost."

"I take it the property doesn't have a security guard. There's always that option," I suggested.

"I'm surprised he hasn't already done that. I got the impression he wants to stop the thefts but not spend a lot. He did say he'd need board approval to implement any suggestions."

"Do you even remember the *client's* name?" When she didn't answer, I said, "You need to get better at remembering. 'Hey you,' isn't professional."

"It's on my phone."

Fab pulled into the driveway of a fifteen-story building... or maybe more; all the floors looked the same. The six-foot-tall white cement sign read: Venetian Palms. She took the circular drive around to the back side of the property, parking in front of a trailer with glass doors labeled "Business Center." The development would appeal to most every type of boat owner, offering water slips and inside and outside dry storage.

"I'm assuming we're not here to shoot anyone, so what do you want me to do? Stand around and look pretty, perhaps?" *Gotcha!* I thought as Fab almost laughed.

"Check out the area and do what you do best—chat it up with a boat owner or two, and maybe they'll tell you something no one else could get out of them."

We'd barely gotten out of the SUV when an older man in boating clothes—deck shoes, shorts, and a shirt advertising the Venetian Palms, his beer gut covering any evidence of a belt—pushed through the doors. He had a wide smile plastered over his face; beady eyes on Fab, he completely ignored my existence.

"Hoskins Crisp," he introduced himself, taking Fab's hand in his and kissing the back, gobbling her up as though she'd been served up as the entrée on his dinner plate.

Oh, ick! Spit on her hand. I moved my hands behind my back after tapping Fab's arm and nodding, letting her know I was off to snoop around. It didn't take long to find a man off by himself, leaning on the jack of a trailer, inhaling as much as his lungs could hold from the cigarette hanging out of the side of his mouth.

I introduced myself, and instead of offering up a name, the man said he was the maintenance man for the property. I didn't press, thinking he was a better choice than a slip owner, who might or might not know anything more than the latest gossip being spread around.

"I'm here with my partner to investigate the boat thefts." I looked over my shoulder to where Fab and Hoskins had been standing, but they'd disappeared.

"Stolen from the outside lot." He pointed. "Must have had some kick-ass chain cutters. Thickest we could get and an even more impressive lock. Broke in twice and hauled the boats off in the dead of night."

"Not much of a gate; looks more like a crossing arm."

"We've never had any criminal activity in this area until about a month ago. Now it happens on a regular basis. According to the cops, we've been discovered as the newest hot spot. Started with stolen car parts, twice. Car thieves jacked up a sports car and hauled-ass with the tires." He half-laughed, as though he still couldn't believe his own story. "No break-ins, no one ever hurt – at least, not so far. These latest thefts have all happened in the early morning hours."

"Anything special about the boats that made them a target?"

"Both boats were twenty-six-foot Regals, neither one that old. New, you'd pay 100K. Top-of-the-line trailers, too. Not sure what they're worth, but an easy resell."

"Is there a market for stolen boats with no title?" I knew some buyers weren't picky about buying cars and such without proper paperwork, which I'd never understood because as soon as you got pulled over, you'd get arrested for grand theft auto.

"With a boat like that, you've got a few choices. Take it to a remote area for personal use, someplace there's not a state agent checking for current tags. Another way to offload would be to sell the motor—they're hot right now—or sail it to Mexico for a fast sale."

"Across the Gulf?" I squeaked. *Not me!*

"A trip like that wouldn't interest me, either. Boat's a little small for the long haul, and if bad weather came up, you'd be screwed."

"Thanks for your time," I said. "I'm new on the job, and the info you gave me is going to make me look good to my boss. Speaking of…"

Fab and Hoskins were walking the storage area. Fab had her camera out, and Hoskins posed for a couple of pics.

"He's a magnet for the ladies."

At a loss for words, I smiled lamely.

"Just remembered. One of the penthouse owners stopped the last heist before the thieves could get the gate open. Heard he got pictures and a partial plate of the getaway car. It might not be very helpful. Heard the cops tracked down the car, and it was stolen."

Working with Fab for so long, I always had cash in my pocket, and more often than not, it came in handy. I handed the man money.

"You don't have to do this."

"I'll bill my boss." I left unsaid, *and she'll bill yours*. I waved and started toward Fab, who'd finished snapping pictures and appeared ready to leave. A couple of men walked off the docks and hailed Hoskins, who hustled over and stood locked in conversation.

"There's no security here," Fab huffed. "Minimal inside the warehouse, but it would take a lot more work to steal a boat from there. And as far as the gates go, they're do-it-yourself stuff."

I gave her the highlights of what the maintenance man told me. "How did this Hoskins character get your number? He didn't take his eyes off you; think he thought you'd be his next tasty morsel."

"Referral from an old client," she answered vaguely.

"This is a straight-up job and nothing illegal… or did I miss that part?"

Fab walked back to the car, waving at

Hoskins. "I promised Didier no more grey-area jobs."

"I promised Creole nothing grey or illegal."

"What Hoskins wants is the boats found, which I tried to tell him politely 'good luck' on. I'm certain these weren't random thefts. The thieves had an order to fill, and they're long gone. Hoskins would also like the men caught in the act. I reminded him that would require a stakeout, which I wanted to discourage. I told him his money would be better spent beefing up security."

"Good luck if *you* have to tell Didier you're doing a middle-of-the-night stakeout. I'm telling you now, Creole won't go for it." I should have felt bad about making Creole the bad guy, but I didn't. "In the spirit of full disclosure, if the trail leads to Mexico, I'm not going."

"Hoskins wants me working this case personally, but I'm already thinking about outsourcing."

I bet he does.

Chapter Four

KABOOM!

Fiberglass and debris flew into the air, and the pieces spread out across the water in Biscayne Bay. It was followed by another explosion, not as impressive as the first, and more flying wreckage.

Flames leapt into the air.

"What just..." Fab hunched over the steering wheel, staring out the windshield.

"That's a first." I stared open-mouthed. "At least, I think so. Don't recall any news stories of boats exploding."

We'd left the condos and were waiting at the stop sign to turn back onto the Causeway, where we wound up with a ringside seat for the explosion.

"Judging by the size of the debris field, I'd say it was probably a yacht." Fab reacted to a honk from the SUV behind us by hanging a U-turn and then another before pulling to the side of the road. "My guess is that wasn't an accidental boat malfunction we just witnessed." She grabbed up her phone, hung her head out the window, and snapped a couple of pictures.

"I hope whoever was on board had a chance to get off." I pointed at the approaching Coast Guard boats and helicopter hovering overhead. "You have to be impressed by the response time. Hopefully, there will be rescues."

With a parade of Coast Guard boats responding, it didn't take long to put out the fire.

"I'd love to know what happened here." Fab put the SUV in gear.

I pointed to the right at the approaching corner.

"I think I could have figured that out, since this is the way we came in."

"Just trying to be helpful." I did my best not to laugh, enjoying the moment of being annoying.

Fab hit the gas. "I'm going to see if I can break a record getting home."

"You race in your Porsche," I snapped. "In my car, you stick somewhere close to the speed limit."

"Yes, ma'am." She saluted.

"I need to go by The Cottages." At her groan, I said, "I'll call you a cab. That way, you won't have to hang around."

"Sometimes, you can be so annoying."

"Another reason this is the perfect friendship—we're both annoying."

* * *

Fab didn't break her driving time record, which

my stomach would thank her for if it could. About to turn into the driveway of The Cottages, she hit the brakes. It was completely blocked, not by a couple of cars but a mammoth motor home.

Fab backed up into the driveway of the yellow house across the street. The house had been aptly named long before I moved to town, and I suspected it would retain the name even if it were painted blue. My manager, Mac, and her childhood bestie, Shirl, had bought the duplex and each claimed a side. We had carte blanche to park in the driveway and use the porch to watch the police drama when they showed up. Police calls were at an all-time low lately, since we had our own sheriff's deputy living on the property.

"What is an RV doing in the driveway?" I demanded. You'd never know from my current vantage point that a ten-unit, u-shaped beachfront property sat behind the mammoth vehicle.

"If you're expecting an answer from me, you're going to have to wait for me to investigate, and by that time, you'll have your answer. My best guess is that it belongs to one of your guests."

"It's got to go. There's a city ordinance against parking recreational vehicles and boats in plain view on residential property." I glared at her chuckle. "Since we're on my turf, that means I'm boss and you're sidekick—you need to figure out where it can go."

The laugh, if that's what it was, was enough to raise the hair on my neck. I got out and walked across the street, inspecting the planter to make sure it hadn't been run over yet again. It had escaped mutilation. This time. I skirted along the side of the vehicle, taking a right to the office.

Mac must have had her head hanging out the window again as the door opened and slammed shut before I got halfway there. Her ample hips swung from side to side in a short pink skirt and bedroom slippers and today's t-shirt, stretched across her chest, read, "Guess what?" with an arrow pointing to a chicken's butt.

"The Denvers booked in advance," Mac said in exasperation. "As you can see, they left out a few things. I can't be held responsible when these people are less than honest."

"Liar is a more succinct word," Fab told her.

Mac shot her a drop-dead look. "Today's not the day for your helpful comments." She held up her hand. "Before you ask, I found it a parking space over by Spoon's place; a seedy area, I know, but it was the only one with open spots. Mr. Denver's mad because it means he's going to have to pony up extra cash, but I made it clear it was that or hit the road."

Jimmy Spoon owned an auto body shop down in the docks area, not far from Fab's new offices. He catered to a select clientele with high-end vehicles. In addition, he was married to my mother, who'd snagged herself a boy toy. I was certain that the ten-year age difference didn't really qualify him as such, but it was fun to tease her anyway. Anyone with the nerve to say it to his face would have their head ripped off and used as a bowling ball.

"Word's going to get out that customer service is nonexistent here," Fab said.

Mac harrumphed. "Shows what you know. We're always booked." She jerked her t-shirt down and fisted the bottom in a nervous gesture.

Fab stared. Not sure what she was expecting to see happen—the seams splitting, perhaps.

"Ignore her." A Golden Retriever barreled to a stop in front of me. "What is that?"

"A dog."

Mac and I rolled our eyes at Fab.

I held out the back of my hand to test the waters. The dog licked my hand and wagged his tail at the same time.

"Prince here is one of the things they forgot to disclose. Actually said they 'didn't think anyone would notice.'"

"Get an extra deposit," I said in exasperation. "I'm afraid to ask if anything else needs my attention." I glanced over at Miss January's porch and was surprised not to see the woman passed out in her chair. "How's Miss January doing? I haven't seen her very much since the boyfriend moved in. What's his name again?"

"Nestor. And according to her, he keeps her busy." Mac crossed her fingers.

Fab made a gagging noise.

There was something to be said for a younger boyfriend... except he wasn't; they were the same age. But after years of hard living, she looked twice his age. The fact that she was terminal also factored in, but she thumbed her nose at the grim prognosis and moved through life without a care.

"And Nestor, is he getting rave reviews?" My opinion of the man wasn't high, as the few times I'd seen him, he'd been less than cordial.

"Rarely see him unless the lovebirds are going somewhere. Don't worry, I'm keeping an eye out."

A scream tore through the air and a grey-haired woman came into view, yelling a string of epithets you seldom heard a woman her age repeat. She paused for a breath and wound herself up for another volley, ending in "bastard."

Mac looked at her watch. "That didn't take as long as I thought."

The bastard in question rushed headlong around the corner from the pool, adjusting his tighty-whities, which he'd pulled on backwards, and wearing his signature rubber boots, his white hair standing on end. I made sure to keep my eyes focused on his face. I should've known that this out-of-control woman would have something to do with the whorey retired college professor.

"Baby." Crum held out his hands in a conciliatory gesture.

The woman, who had already half-turned, her eyes angry, black slits, turned the rest of the way and charged, arm back, fist clenched for a right cross. The only reason she didn't connect was that Fab twisted her arm up behind her back.

Crum stepped back several paces.

"Calm down," Fab said in a no-nonsense tone. "You can't damage the goods for the rest of the ladies." She cut off the woman's whiny retort. "If you didn't know his history, then shame on you. Next man, do your homework."

"You owe Fab," I hissed at Crum, motioning for him to go back to his cottage as Fab walked the woman to the end of the driveway. "You better have a good excuse for not stopping that whole drama before it got started," I said to Mac. "Don't bother pleading ignorance—you just admitted that you knew something."

"Forget about me breaking up fights. Not getting this pretty face bruised." Mac preened. "It's not my fault he books the women a little too close together. I warned him, but he ignored me."

"Please, tell me he's not selling his... uhm... services." I was relieved when Mac shook her head. "He's eighty. How is he able to—"

"Stimulants," Mac said, as though it was a no-brainer.

"He's been told that underwear alone is not

suitable attire. The next time he forgets his skirt, towel, or whatever covers him up, it's a twenty-five dollar fine, and he pays up or moves."

"You can't do that." Mac threw her shoulders back and huffed. "You know I have a hard enough time scheduling entertainment as it is, after your boyfriend ixnayed most of my ideas. Besides, the tourists like him, and the returning ones enjoy a little flash."

"It was only the illegal activities that Creole banned, the ones that could land both of us in jail." I shook my head. "I stopped to get the paperwork for my accountant, and then I'm leaving before something else happens. Oh, don't want to forget Joseph. He okay?" Another terminal tenant that did as he damn well pleased and, most of the time, holed up in his cottage with his inflatable girlfriend, Svetlana, and a 12-pack, the television blaring.

"He's still alive. I took him to his doc appointment and forced my way into the exam room. He didn't seem to mind. After taking his blood pressure and a few other things, the doctor clapped him on the back, said he'd see him next time, and reminded him to call 911 if he had an emergency."

"Just when I think you're a complete nutjob, you do something so sweet." I smiled. "Joseph probably wouldn't say so, but I bet he was happy you were there."

"He actually thanked me and offered up a beer."

Fab joined us as we walked toward the office. "Next time, I'm going to let Crum get his face rearranged."

Chapter Five

The front door banged shut, and since Fab and Didier had gone out to dinner, that left the possibility of either Creole or an intruder, and I was certain the latter wouldn't make that much noise.

I'd positioned my chaise to give me a view of the pool area and outside dining area. Anyone entering the backyard from the house or the side path, I'd see them before they saw me. I shoved my book down beside me, tucking it under a pillow, and smiled when Creole appeared in the patio doorway. He'd left the house this morning in a suit and returned in shorts and a black t-shirt that fit snugly over his abs and left his powerful arms exposed.

In a couple of strides, he straddled the chaise, sat down facing me, and brushed my lips with his. "We all alone?" He wagged his eyebrows and handed me an envelope. "This was stuck in the door."

I glanced at it and tucked it inside my book, knowing it came from GC. Anyone else would ring the doorbell. GC was short for Gunz's connection (Gunz being a friend of Fab's), and he'd never offered up another name, real or otherwise. I knew several people who thought knowing their birth name was overrated. I'd gotten a phone introduction via Gunz, and after a short conversation, it was decided that we could tolerate one another for favor-doing purposes.

"The lovebirds went to dinner. I tried to interest them in takeout, but they both turned me down." At the mention of food, my stomach growled.

Creole leaned over and kissed my stomach. "I'll cook."

"I don't want Pop Tarts for dinner," I whined.

"I'll do the next best thing—order from Jake's and have someone there deliver." He fished his phone out of his pocket.

I licked my lips.

After he placed the order and hung up, I asked, "How was your day, honey?"

"Flunked my psych evaluation." He grinned.

"I thought today was just about meeting with your boss."

After being shot several times in the ambush, Creole had suffered a host of injuries, and it had taken months for him to heal, in part because he was the worst patient. He had put off making a decision as to whether he would be returning to the force or not.

"Chief Harder had the psych appointment set up and even walked me over to the doctor's office."

"The chief knows you well. He knew you would've gotten lost along the way. Or had some other creative excuse you came up with for not showing up."

"I did briefly entertain the thought of just running. Instead, I spent over an hour dodging questions about my feelings and how I was coping."

"How did you leave it?"

"Come back, Mr. Creole," he imitated a high-pitched voice, "when you're ready to participate in the mental health plan that is required for me to release you back to your job."

I bit back a laugh. "Mr. Creole?"

"Another bone of contention—I refused to reveal my birth name."

"I'm surprised it wasn't in your file." His closed-off look told me he was done with this subject, but I had one more question. "Harder must know how your visit went. What did he have to say?"

"Grow the hell up," Creole barked, sounding just like his boss. "Make up your mind, or I'll make it up for you."

The doorbell rang.

Creole got up, and before he disappeared inside the house, I called out, "Gun in the junk drawer." He turned, and at his confused look, I added, "Just in case."

His laugh drifted back out the door.

Creole came back, shopping bag in hand,

along with silverware, a beer, and water. He put everything down on the oblong patio table, which was big enough to seat my entire family. Although, ever since Mother moved to Tarpon Cove, the bulk of the entertaining had moved to her condo. Creole came over to the chaise and scooped me up in his arms, carrying me back and setting me in a chair at the table.

He pulled two containers and plates out of the bag, filled my plate with a chicken enchilada and rice, and set it down in front of me. He did the same for himself and sat next to me.

I picked up my bottle and toasted him: "To the best boyfriend ever."

"Hmm…" he said over the rim of his bottle. "You do something today you forgot to tell me about?"

"You're so suspicious. My declaration was heartfelt." I guzzled down my water. "We had front row seats for a boat explosion. You know anything about that?"

"Biscayne Bay? Marshall Sacks was blown to bits on his luxury yacht, according to what I heard at headquarters. It's rumored that were three other people on board, but that has yet to be verified. Gossip has it, his mistress was on board."

"As in the mega-rich Sacks family? Accident?"

Creole shrugged. "I just got the bits and pieces that floated around the office; nothing definitive had been decided before I left."

"It was pretty darn spectacular as explosions go. Sorry to hear people died. I had hoped that anyone on board managed to get off in time." I hesitated and then told him about the boat thefts. "The HOA manager can't seem to make up his mind regarding a stakeout, but that has more to do with the cost. If they want to catch a group of thieves that strike in the middle of the night, how else can they accomplish it?"

Creole shook his head and finger at the same time. "I know you hate stakeouts. That said, I also know that you won't let Fab go by herself. If she's planning on sneaking out of the house, tagging you, and then telling all afterwards, she can forget it. I'll tell on her."

"That's so rude," I sniffed. "We need to make an agreement that anything we say to each other can't be used against other people."

"I agree. Starting with the next job, certain stipulations will apply and will most likely need to be renegotiated on a regular basis."

I squinted at him. "Have you thought about getting your law degree?"

"I'm not cut out for a suit and tie all day… or defending guilty people." Creole stood.

"Will you bring me that envelope? We can find out what's inside together."

"I did want to know, but wasn't going to ask."

"If Fab had been the one to find it, it would have been opened before she handed it to me."

Creole shook his head, retrieving it off the

chair and handing it to me.

"Have a seat." I ripped open the envelope, taking out one sheet of paper. "This is from GC. I asked him to check on the highway incident and make sure that no females turned up dead under suspicious circumstances." I smoothed the sheet out between us.

"Nice letterhead." Creole harrumphed at the blank top of the page and lack of signature.

"He's a man with many idiosyncrasies, and I just follow his rules. And he delivers, no excuses." I didn't bother to confide that I didn't care what his name was and it didn't bother me to not know. "I mind my own business because he's the best information go-to person we've ever had, and I don't want to lose him, as they're impossible to find."

"This is interesting." Creole nodded absently and tapped the first paragraph. "According to the accident report, the biker woman was a friend of Bordello's—a Jane Jones."

I snorted. *She's probably related to Jane Smith. Neither one could come up with a better phony name?*

"This is a shock," he said sarcastically. "A background check on her came back as 'no such person.' One of them paid cash at the hospital for services rendered, and she was released the same night."

"I thought you had to produce ID upon checking into a hospital," I said.

"Here's another good one: a private tow

company was called to pick up the bike—Al's Tow—and guess what? No report on file of any such hookup." Creole slapped his hand down on the paper. "Stay away from Bordello. It appears that one phone call from him and he can make anything happen."

I folded the report and stuffed it back in the envelope. "I'm going to leave it on the island for Fab. She can read it to Didier." I leaned forward and kissed Creole. "Jane Jones, or whatever her name is… as long as she's breathing, I'm happy. If he went to all that trouble, maybe she'll stay that way."

"Enough business." Creole stood. "I'll clean up here, and then let's go for a walk on the beach."

Chapter Six

The house cleared out early the next morning. When Fab found out I had an early meeting at Jake's, she turned up her nose and accompanied Didier to the office. Creole went back to his house, where he was working on a super top secret project. I'd have to wait on the exact details, but he promised that I'd be the first to know.

The parking lot of Jake's was empty as I pulled in. It was the only tiki-looking bar in town, with a thatched umbrella at the roofline and palm trees scattered across the front. Glancing around at the other businesses on the short block, I saw they all had one thing in common—they were closed. The lighthouse was now a hot tourist attraction, thanks to a little advertising and the picture-taking opportunities it offered. The one tenant, Fab's associate, Gunz, used it as office space and was rarely seen. Junker's, an antique garden store, was open by appointment only. How he managed to pull that off was unclear, but his inventory turned over on a regular basis. The brightly painted roach coach, Twinkie Princesses, never opened at all. I'd never asked about the women's lack of entrepreneurial spirit, just accepted the rent check that always arrived on time.

"This better be good," I said to Doodad as I came through the front door. The six-foot older gentleman was behind the bar, finishing up the liquor inventory. I'd gotten to Jake's early enough that none of the morning drinkers had shown up yet. "Where are you holding this meeting?"

The inside was quiet, the jukebox turned off, and the doors to the back deck were open, the ceiling fans and outside lights turned on. In addition to a miniscule dance floor, there were two pool tables, a couple of arcade games, and my favorite: the half-court basketball machine.

Doodad, aka Charles Wingate with a number after his name, slammed his hand down on the bar top. "Right here." He set down a coaster and a glass of clear bubbly liquid.

"Cherries." I hopped up on a stool, indicating the toothpick in the glass. "You're buttering me up for something." I picked one off and devoured it.

"Calling this meeting to order." He banged a spoon on the bar.

"Too much drama. Reassure me, please, that you're not quitting."

"You're going to be pleased. I want a promotion and a raise." He gave me a toothy grin. "Promote me. If I deliver on what I'm about to outline, then you can raise my pay."

"I'm going to need a double." I pushed my glass across the bar and watched as he filled it with more soda. "Don't be stingy on the cherries."

"As you know, we tripled the revenue over the holiday season, and I attribute that to my amazing idea of holding theme nights." He brushed his knuckles on his shirt. "In that vein, I'd like to continue doing them at least once a month."

I winced, remembering how much Creole disliked those events. "You do remember that fights broke out and there were one or two where the cops showed up?"

He shook his head, conveying *no big deal.* "I also want to take over the gambling den, rental room, or whatever you call it. It has untapped potential and the ability to add more to the bottom line."

"You're forgetting one thing—that's my mother's brainchild."

"Except Madeline doesn't show up anymore, and her poker buddies have started to complain that the level of service has gone down. My thought is to hire a part-time bartender on the days the room is booked—someone exclusive to them and in charge of both drinks and food. I'm thinking a limited menu, a few steps up from chips… or resurrect the buffet."

His ideas were good, but I wasn't forgetting

I'd have to run this by Mother. I wanted to climb up on the bar and take a nap, but didn't think that would project the right image. "You do know gambling is illegal in this state?" I raised an eyebrow.

"Did I say gambling?" He smirked. "I meant game room. Card games are perfectly legal; as long as there's no cash on the table, it's all good. I suspect whatever scheme those old coots have going can continue as long as they keep it in their tight circle." He held the drink hose up for a refill. I shook my head and covered the top of my glass. "I read all the state regulations before pitching the idea." He smiled in satisfaction.

"The job promotion?" I already liked all of his ideas, but thought it prudent to hear him out.

"Manager. I want the title and the freedom to run this place without having to check with you on every detail... within reason. I wouldn't use it to harm the business or you in any way."

"How about a trial period?" I tried to keep from laughing—of course he was getting the promotion.

He paused and squinted at me, his mouth quirking on one side, letting me know that he knew he was being jerked around and the job was his. "I'm going to need another full-time bartender and a couple of part-time people." He looked down at a piece of paper he'd pulled from his pocket. "I've got a couple of people I'm calling in for an interview. That was the plan if you said yes. You're not going to regret this."

"I'm sure not, or I wouldn't agree. Just know I'll still be around like usual. Any problems, and that includes cop visits, I want a call." I pointed to his list. "The kitchen is Cook's domain, and I don't want anything upsetting him." Since my first enchilada, I'd given him the authority to run it any way he wanted, and he did his own hiring—all family members, no matter how remotely related. "I'd like you to continue to use the relatives where possible; they're reliable and have the same easygoing attitude."

"Me and Cook are *simpatico*. Like this." He held up crossed middle and index fingers. "As for using them, no problemo—they're all hard-workers. I'll start a couple out in the game room, and if they work out, I'll make it permanent."

"Before you start that project, you'll need to break it to Mother and get her on board with you being in charge." That was cowardly, but Mother wouldn't have a hard time telling Doodad if she hated the idea. "I'm thinking that she's been busy with her newish husband and probably won't mind, but be sure to run your ideas by her—they could be the selling point. If I'm wrong and she flips, then you can be the bad guy."

He laughed. "I'll call and set up an appointment with her, have a Jack Daniels on the rocks waiting, and charm the heck out of her."

"You'll only get away with that last part if Spoon's busy that day and doesn't come along."

"Maybe I should invite them both, so I won't come off as a scammer."

"Something tells me that you're ready to put your plans into action immediately. So, when's the next theme night?"

"Next weekend. Still deciding on a theme. I'll get the flyers printed and hire a couple of kids to deliver them." He scribbled a few notes.

The front door opened and a busty blond walked in, her double D's preceding her.

"Hey Kelpie." Doodad waved to the woman, who paused to check out the interior of the bar. She was every bit of six feet, with an ass-kicker physique, in a knee-length full skirt and matching purple stilettos, the material of her partially unbuttoned shirt straining at the seams. "Remember when I mentioned interviewing for a new bartender? Here's our first interviewee."

"You'd hire someone who could kick your butt?" I whispered.

He frowned. "Not happening."

"Hey, baby," she said to Doodad.

My brows shot up. *You sleeping with her?* written on my face. He shook his head.

"You Madison? I'm Kelpie Reese, your new bartender if you hire me. Named after my granny." She stuck out a good-sized paw.

Instinctively, my hand shot behind my back.

"Sorry, forgot. Doodad told me you weren't into hand shaking. You know I spit on both of them and wiped them on my butt right before I got here." She laughed, loud and guttural. "Not really, but I did see a guy at the bus stop do that."

Ick! At a loss for words, I asked, "You have experience bartending?"

Doodad waved her to a stool.

"I've got beer-serving skills. I'd have to brush up on the fancy drinks."

Her only serving beer had me wondering if she'd worked at Custer's, a rathole bar on the other side of town. It had lost its liquor license and now sold only beer and screw cap wine. I wasn't impressed with her answer but kept it to myself, lest Doodad remind me that he'd been short on experience when he interviewed and had turned out to be a good hire.

"I'm telling you, I've got a few tricks up my skirt—I can bartend, handle the rowdies, and bounce them out the door on their asses. And men like me... These keep them happy." She smooshed her breasts together. "I've heard there's been a shooting or two in this joint, and I'll admit I'm not all that accurate with a pistol, but I am pinpoint accurate with this..." She raised her skirt and displayed a Bowie knife in a leather-and-lace garter around her thigh.

Fab would be so proud, and she wasn't here to enjoy the moment. "I'm fairly certain carrying a concealed knife that large is illegal, and if you get the job, you'd have to agree not to wear it to work. Is that doable?"

"I can maintain law and order without it. I'm a big gal, and it's all muscle. Mostly, anyway." She winked.

"I'll talk this over with Doodad, and he'll get back to you."

"You'll need to decide quickly, or someone else will snap up my skills," Kelpie said. She jumped up with a smile and a wave and flashed a "call me" with her fingers at Doodad.

When the door closed, I asked, "How many other applicants?"

"Zero."

I stared at him.

"I know what you're thinking, but if we don't hire someone with a certain amount of brass and unconventionality, the customers won't like them and the feeling will be mutual. What you see is what you get with Kelpie—no games—and she's loyal."

I sighed. "You're the one being promoted to manager, so you can hire and fire whoever you want... sort of. Just know that if Creole comes storming in here, shouting she's got a criminal record a yard long or some such thing, it's on you."

"Deal."

Chapter Seven

It turned out that Didier and Marshall Sacks were friends from back in the day when Didier lived in South Beach. He'd heard about the explosion and called Marshall's wife, Alta, to offer his condolences, and she asked that he attend the funeral.

"Drink, anyone?" Fab yelled from the patio door to where Creole and I floated in the pool.

Creole nodded, and I yelled back, "One beer and something with a cherry." Which was code for non-alcoholic.

Didier carried a platter of drinks out and set them on the side of the pool, then retrieved two inflatable chairs and tossed them in the water.

"I don't suppose the coroner made a mistake and Marshall's still alive?" I asked, as that had happened once at our local funeral home.

Fab made some inappropriate noise, judging by the peeved look Didier shot her, and said, "If a mistake was made and he was still alive after being declared dead, he's not anymore. Cremated."

"Do rich-people funerals have better food?"

"None of those fancy sandwiches you like." Fab winked. "I would've stuffed one in my pocket for you."

The three of us laughed. Probably, like me, the guys weren't able to conjure up an image of her doing such a thing.

"Any talk about who would want to see Sacks dead?" Creole asked.

"Alta invited everyone back to the house. It was more of a casual get-together than a celebration of Marshall's life. I didn't hear his name mentioned once," Didier said. "You'd never know that everyone had just come from the memorial service."

"Isn't the spouse always the first suspect? What's she like?" I asked.

"Alta put on a helpless act. She even suggested Didier handle her affairs." Fab faux swooned, sighing in dramatic fashion.

Didier pulled Fab's floater to his side and leaned over, kissing her cheek. "Remind me to thank you again for extricating me from that situation without my having to come off as a bastard."

She whispered something that tinted his cheeks pink.

"You'll never guess who else was a friend of Marshall's..." Didier practically snorted. "Unbeknownst to me, I want to add, as I don't remember ever meeting him back when we socialized more frequently."

"Let me tell them," Fab said.

Didier flourished his hand in a gesture to go ahead.

"The one and only Brick Famosa." She ended it on a high note. "He didn't appear to be as surprised to see me as I was him. We also met Mrs. Famosa."

"I don't suppose you remember her first name," I said. "What's she like?"

"The woman was insufferably rude," Didier answered. "She ran her eyes over us, deemed us unworthy of her notice, and flounced off. She did mumble something in Spanish that I didn't quite catch, but I answered, 'Have a nice day,' in Spanish. I'll admit I enjoyed watching her shoulders stiffen. All the while, Brick gazed after her with a stupid-ass smile on his face."

I clutched my chest and said in a horrified tone, "Language." Didier was a stickler for manners, and it wasn't often I got a chance to tease him.

Didier laughed.

"Here's the nervy part: Brick told Alta that he, personally, would be investigating Marshall's death. Then included me in the conversation by saying it made sense to use my services, since we were all friends." Fab made a face. "Didier, ever the gentleman, didn't correct him." She grabbed hold of Didier's raft to prevent it from floating away. "Turns out Mrs. Sacks has employed the services of lawyer extraordinaire Cruz Campion, and Brick outright lied and said that Cruz and I had a working relationship."

That was a whopper. There was a time that, when criminal trouble reared its ugly head, Fab and I had had Cruz on speed dial and he took our calls. It had been a long time since we needed his services, and we both hoped it stayed that way. Now the only calls Cruz took were Mac's, and that had to do with booking cottages and entertainment for his relatives.

"Brick pushed me into such a corner that rather than responding with a knee to his groin-" Fab demonstrated from her slightly prone position, and Creole and Didier winced. "I reluctantly agreed to offer my services."

"I suspect Brick will start burning up your phone line and soon," I said. "If it's not about Alta, it will be something else."

"Didier and I got a break from Alta and Brick when we were surrounded by old friends of Didier's and snuck off. You should've been there," Fab said to me. "I tried to morph into you and get people to talk." She sighed. "Sucked at it. So I played to my strengths, sought out the oldest man in the room, and flirted away."

I tipped my glass against hers. "Probably the most enjoyable time the man's had... well, ever. What did you find out? You get his number? Just in case. What am I saying? Of course, you did."

"I gave the man my card... You know, just in case he might need my services."

Creole laughed and, when he stopped, said, "You get anything good out of the old guy? Spill."

Fab smirked at him. "He said the gossip is that Sacks had a mistress on board, along with two other friends, who blew sky-high along with him. I did try to get out of the old guy where he got his information, but got back a 'here and there' answer."

"Whoever shared that tidbit wasn't law enforcement," Creole shared. "My sources tell me that the body count may be exaggerated, as they've only recovered one body."

"Your sources confirm that the yacht was rigged to blow?" Fab asked Creole. "Also heard that the malfunction hinted at in the news was a total ruse. Getting on a high profile murder case would be good for my business."

"It's too bad anyone died," I said.

"You need backup, I'm available for the next month," Creole offered.

I stared at Fab. "If you avail yourself of the services of my boyfriend," I said evenly, "you *will* disclose *all* the details *ahead* of time. Got it?"

"Oh, all right," she said dramatically. "There is something I should probably mention."

I groaned.

"Hoskins Crisp from the Venetian Palms called, and he's insistent about finding the culprits. The priority is getting the boats back."

"How many times does he need to be told that

those boats are gone and he's not getting them back unless they're the stupidest criminals ever? Which wouldn't be a first," I conceded.

Fab ignored me and turned to Didier. "Hmm... Hoskins wants me to do a stakeout," she said hesitantly.

"I already knew that would be a possibility," Didier said, which surprised Fab.

"I thought we had a promise," I snapped at Creole.

"We did." He pushed his inflatable closer to mine, and I paddled backwards. "I wanted to make sure that you two weren't going to be sneaking out in the middle of the night to do this job. What I did was crappy, and I'm going to make it up to the both of you. I'm going along on the stakeout."

Fab turned away from Didier and flipped Creole the finger.

"I'm going, too," Didier said.

"What happened to the fancy security report you had *my* employee put together for you?" I wanted to smile, seeing that Fab was surprised I knew she'd asked Mac.

"Hoskins totally ignored it. He thinks his idea is better."

"I think this is a waste of time," I said. "You should call GC and see what he can find out about boat thefts."

"Why haven't I met this guy?" Creole grouched.

"Maybe because you're a badass cop and he's allergic." I laughed at his disgruntled look. "Before you ask *again*, I don't know his name. You should know from his stationary that he isn't forthcoming." I traded a slight smile with Fab.

"When is this stakeout going down?" Creole asked.

"Tomorrow night," Fab said.

Tomorrow? I suppose I should be happy it's not in the next five minutes.

Creole stared her down.

"Hoskins says there's been activity around the boatyard the last couple of nights. Claims he got a tip about another attempt planned for tomorrow night and wants me on the job." Fab put her hand up. "Before you ask, I did try questioning him and he clammed up."

Creole and Didier exchanged silent guy talk. I'd have to ask for a translation later.

"These jobs are usually manned by two people. You've got a four-person stakeout team; that should cover any and all problems," Creole said.

I hated when people said, "no problem." It was a red flag, in my opinion.

Chapter Eight

My phone rang in the middle of the night, and everyone knows that means bad news. Before answering, I wondered briefly who'd been arrested and needed bail and/or a ride home from jail. No bus service after ten, and that was only helpful if the person was booked with change in their pocket.

"Hello," I answered groggily.

Creole rolled over, throwing one arm across my body. "Who is that?" he growled.

I wished I'd thought to hand the phone to him, but I didn't think he'd ever met Corndog and it might be weird.

"Cops are on the way," Corndog said in a low voice. He had meant to be a short-term guest at The Cottages while recuperating from getting beat up, but he'd made it long term. "It's like staying in a home setting with weird people," he'd told me.

I scooted to the edge of the bed, putting my feet on the floor. "What's going on?" I rubbed my eyes, crossed to the armoire, and pulled out a pair of crop sweats and a long-sleeved t-shirt. I dressed quickly and corralled my red hair into a hair clip.

"The RV people provoked a fight with Crum, Joseph jumped in the middle of it and got knocked on his backside, and it's unclear if he hit his head. One of the other tourists called the cops."

"Don't get involved; I don't want you getting arrested. I'm on my way." I disconnected.

"Arrested? Let me guess, The Cottages?" Creole sniped. "Toss me a t-shirt." He stood up, pulling on a pair of sweats that he retrieved from the floor. "Doesn't matter what the threat level is; you're not going by yourself in the middle of the night. Or the day."

"No reason for both of us to lose sleep."

"You ready?" He caught the shirt I tossed him and pulled it over his head.

We got downstairs and in Creole's truck in under five minutes. He gunned the engine, turning out on the Overseas.

"If Didier hadn't been asleep, I'd have kicked their bedroom door on our way out. Give Fab a taste of her own humor."

I laughed. "She's a light sleeper and knows we left the house. I'm surprised she hasn't called, wanting details."

"Speaking of… what's going on?

I related what Corndog had told me. "I forgot to ask where Mac was, but knowing her, she's partying it up somewhere."

"I thought her and the bartender hooked up?"

"How did Mac put it... 'We like doing it.' She refused to commit to anything more than hot sex."

He barked out a low laugh as he sped down the darkened highway.

By the time he pulled into the driveway, a cop car blocked one side. Her arms crossed, Mac hadn't ventured far from the office door—just enough to see everything going on.

She wobbled over, unsteady on her feet, which I assumed had more to do with the heels she'd paired with a very short pleated skirt than having drunk one too many.

A scowl on her face, she ranted, "I could've handled this. Number three called the cops, claimed she was scared by the violence, but not so much that she went inside her cottage and pushed a chair in front of the door. No, she's out on her stoop." She took a deep breath and acknowledged us with a smile. "Sorry, just got here."

"Which cop got the call?" Creole asked.

"Kevin."

Kevin Cory was a local sheriff's deputy who lived at The Cottages. He complained about the tenants but never followed through on his weak threat to move.

"I thought the RV problem was dealt with. Why isn't it gone?" I demanded.

"Guess they thought I wouldn't notice." Mac rolled her eyes.

"And tonight's drama?"

"All I know is Crum told the new people to knock off the noise and take their cigarette smoking inside the RV. He then snatched the pack and threatened to break it up so they could chew it instead. The smell and all." Mac wrinkled her nose.

Creole snorted. "I'll go find out what's going on." He took off down the driveway.

"Joseph hurt?" I asked.

"He's tougher than he looks. My opinion, he's milking a non-existent injury." Mac shook her head. "What was the dumb lug thinking anyway, jumping into the middle of an argument to spout his two cents? Got knocked on his backside, then started whining, and that's when one of the guests called 911. I'll be talking to her about that in the morning."

"Is Kevin going to haul everyone off to jail?"

"Kevin showed up and read everyone in hearing distance the riot act. Then ticked off the rules, which included the times for raising a ruckus without getting jailed, ordered everyone inside, and said he better not see their faces until daylight. The new guests weren't happy when he told them he lived here. He had the last couple of days off and went fishing or something."

"So, you've got everything handled?"

"Kevin wanted me to call you, and I told him you were on your way. I didn't tell him Corndog called you. He's the only smart one here; he went back inside his cottage and stayed there. It's refreshing to have a tenant with common sense. The only other tenants that don't have their noses caught up in the drama are passed out drunk. Kevin wants you to know that you owe him for handling the situation in an orderly manner."

"Did you happen to mention to Kevin that that's his job as a deputy sheriff?"

"Noooo," she huffed. "I thanked him for not dodging the call and promised snacks later, when he's off duty."

"If that RV isn't gone by tomorrow morning, then they have to go," I said. "If they don't cooperate, let me know and I'll have someone big and burly deliver the message."

Mac grinned. "I know a couple of guys that would do it for a small credit at Jake's."

"It's getting so we know the same disreputable people."

Chapter Nine

Tired from being awoken by Cottages drama the night before, and with no time for a nap, I put my head in Creole's lap, stretched out across the back seat, and nodded off most of the way to North Miami.

It was past midnight when Fab pulled into the parking lot of the Venetian Palms. The boat storage yard had two gates, and she parked under a tree in a space across from the gate closest to the road, which afforded her a view of the entire driveway and any approaching traffic. The thieves couldn't use either exit without being seen.

"If the thieves show up, do we shoot to kill?" Didier asked in a stern voice. He almost pulled it off but glanced over at Creole and started laughing.

"We round them up and call the cops. *No one* gets hurt, especially not you." Fab fisted Didier's shirt and pulled him towards the console, kissing him. "Got it?"

He saluted. "Now what?"

"We hurry up and wait." I yawned. "This is the exciting part."

"Let's go over this one more time," Creole said. "Fab and I are the front men, Didier is backup, and you—" He yanked a strand of my hair. "—get it all on film."

I reached down and took out a special video camera Fab had gotten that took night shots. Which she then gave to the least electronically minded of us to get the goods. I asked how it was even possible to take pictures in the dark and got back such a technical answer that my eyes crossed and I almost fainted. Close anyway.

"I still don't understand how that HOA guy knows tonight's the night," I said. The only good thing about all this was having Creole for a pillow.

"It better go down tonight," Didier grouched. "You two are not going to be doing this night after night."

"Stakeouts are boring," I said. "But we've never been shot at... or have we?" I nudged Fab's arm with my foot.

"There was that one time..." she started, and at Didier's growl she added, "Just kidding."

Fab and I laughed. Judging by the silence, the guys weren't amused.

I dozed off again while the other three stayed busy on their phones.

"We finally got a car coming this way," Fab announced. "Two cars."

Creole pushed me to a sitting position and stared across me as the cars pulled into the driveway of the boatyard.

Unsure of the time, I checked my phone and saw that almost two hours had gone by.

Two Miami police department units pulled up, one directly in front of the Hummer, the other off to the side, both activating their emergency lights. A third patrol car arrived. Several officers converged on the SUV from behind, stopping one or two lengths back.

"Did you call the jurisdictional police to advise them of your assignment and give a description of this vehicle?" Creole asked.

"Didn't think about it," Fab answered with a shake of her head.

Fab would have to make a change to her usual off-the-cuff work style if she planned to go completely legit, as she claimed.

"Maybe the HOA convinced someone to drive by," Creole said.

"You'd think Hoskins might've mentioned that," Fab huffed.

One of the officers got on the vehicle loudspeaker, announcing, "City Police," and, "Roll down your window and throw the keys to the vehicle out."

Fab powered down the window. Grumbling under her breath, she followed instructions. "Officer," she said, throwing her badge folder along with the keys, "I'm a private investigator on surveillance for a boat thief."

If the officer heard her, he didn't respond;

another officer scooped up the credentials and returned to his vehicle.

"Stay calm and do everything they tell you. No creative answers," Creole said. "We're not doing anything illegal. Give them the straight truth; there's no reason to be hedging here. Is there?" He didn't wait for an answer. "If none of us lie, then our stories will match. Answer the questions, short and sweet."

Fab shook her head. "You know everything I do about the job."

I hope so. I caught movement out of the corner of my eye—Fab started to pull her gun out of her waistband and changed her mind. I stashed mine in the camera bag and would disclose its location when I handed over my carry permit.

"Driver, exit the vehicle; the rest of you stay put until instructed," came the next command over the speaker. "Face front and raise your hands, then walk backward toward the officers."

"Follow directions; keep your hands where they tell you," Creole told Didier and me.

I watched out the side mirror as Fab reached a spot near the front of one of the police cars and knelt down on the ground. An officer stepped forward and handcuffed and then searched her. He removed her handgun from her waist holster and handed it to another officer, then assisted her to stand, walked her to one of the police cars, and helped her inside.

The officer then called out to Didier, "Front

passenger, get out of the car," and went through the same procedure.

Creole squeezed my hand. "You need to breathe. It's going to be the same for you and me. We'll be out of here before you know it, and I damn well intend to find out what the hell is going on."

The officer called me out next. Creole brushed a fast kiss on my cheek.

It looked to be the same process as with Fab and Didier. After searching me and taking my weapon, the officer said, "Hands behind your back." He read me my rights, cuffed me, and led me to the back of a separate car, pushing my head down and assisting me into the back seat.

Another officer stuck his head in the door and asked, "Name? What are you doing here?"

I answered politely and told him what I knew. "Why are we being questioned?" I asked.

"You're trespassing for one thing. This is private property," he answered.

"I'm sure the HOA manager can clear all this up."

"He's not in his office."

Of course not, it's the middle of the night. Did Fab have an after-hours number for the man? "I'd like to call my lawyer."

"You can do that after you're booked."

There was no time to ask any more questions as the cop closed the door. I'd been in this position before—in the back of a cop car, my wrists cuffed behind me. It was damn uncomfortable, and I didn't like it. Also, like the others, I couldn't help wondering what the hell was going on.

"They think *we're* the boat thieves," I whispered to myself.

It went slightly different for Creole. After handcuffing and searching him, his identification got closer scrutiny and another officer got called over. The conversation went on for several minutes. They had him sit on the ground as they met with the other officers, and a conversation ensued that even Creole wasn't close enough to be privy to.

In the end, no one got arrested, our weapons were returned, and we were promptly released.

* * *

Creole was the last person to get back in the car. He'd stood outside a few minutes longer, talking to a couple of the officers, and they'd had a good laugh over something.

"Let's hope that Creole is finding out what the heck happened here tonight." Fab stared over the steering wheel.

"Hoskins gets a tip. The thieves are a no-show. The cops show up, ready to arrest… you?" I said to Fab's reflection in the rearview mirror.

After handshakes all around, Creole climbed back in the SUV.

"Stick to the speed limit," he told Fab. She nodded, pulling out of the driveway and heading back to the Causeway. "Apparently, Fab, you're a dead ringer for one of the suspects in the boat thefts. You checked out as a licensed PI with a clean criminal record—a few arrests, one of them snickered, but no convictions—and that's the reason you're not headed to jail for a lineup."

"The description I got from Hoskins was that there were four men involved. Nothing about a woman, and certainly not anyone that looked like me," Fab said indignantly.

"911 got an anonymous call about persons lurking in the driveway, one a woman carrying a weapon," Creole informed us.

"That's ridiculous..." Fab said and went silent.

"Thank goodness you were here," I said to Creole. "We might otherwise need bail money."

"Probably not. Your story would've checked out, and it would have ended the same way," Creole reassured me. "They're not going to waste their time with a bogus arrest." He hugged me to his side. "I knew the drill and was smart enough not to jump out of the car and show a badge. Reaching for my ID folder could've gotten me killed if it were mistaken for a gun. I just waited out the situation and followed their directions. No need to argue with street officers, as they were just doing what I would do in their shoes. As I was being cuffed, I identified myself and told the officer where he could find my identification. Shamelessly threw in that Chief Harder was my boss. There's no way he wasn't going to find out about tonight anyway. He won't be happy."

With a little luck and no traffic, Fab soon had us back on the Turnpike headed home.

"I watched while the officers congregated in the driveway," Didier said. "What was that all about?"

"I suspect the officers were comparing our stories and found them reasonably similar. They realized that they'd detained a group of PIs. After I told him I was a Miami PD officer, the officer that cuffed me asked, 'What the F is going on here?'" Creole laughed. "I told him. Not long after that, the same officer told me that no report would be written and the officers would simply clear the stop as unfounded."

Chapter Ten

Later that week, Creole and I returned to my house after a couple of days at his beach hideaway. Fab had called about a job and practically ordered me to come home and change into something other than a bathing suit, all the while mumbling something about freebies and Brick.

When we came through the door, Didier held up a glass with something liquidy and orange in it, setting the blender jar down on the counter. It didn't look any more appetizing than his green concoctions.

I made a retching noise in response.

"I'll have a double," Creole said, then whispered in my ear, "That's not nice."

"But truthful." I reached in the refrigerator and took out a bottle of water, sliding onto a stool next to Fab.

"We're already going to be late." Fab pointed to the clock on the stove. "You need to run upstairs and make yourself presentable. To that end, I hung a dress on your closet door and even chose the shoes."

"Not so fast, sister," I said in a tone that had her glaring. "I'm not moving until I get some details. What cheap, tightwad client did you offer a freebie to, breaking your own rule of never, ever doing it? Since I also heard you utter the Brick obscenity, I'm telling you now, I won't do jack for him for free."

"It was my idea. Or so I thought," Didier said, then turned to Fab, looking confused. "Brick? I hope he didn't manage to get himself involved."

Creole downed his drink, barked out a laugh, and sat down across from me.

"I was about to update you," Fab muttered.

Sure you were.

"You do know that if this case in any way degenerates into shots fired, you get billed triple," I said to Didier before Fab could *entertain* us with the rest of the story.

"You're not to shoot anyone. That isn't what this case is about." Didier pointed at me for emphasis.

"No worries, I only shoot to maim. Your girlfriend, on the other hand…" I clutched my chest. "Dead."

Both guys laughed.

"I can't stand much more of your antics," Fab said.

I pouted.

Didier cut in. "Alta is afraid that, since law enforcement always suspects the spouse in cases of murder, it won't be long before they're knocking on her door. My thought is that you two could do some investigating of your own and see what you can come up with."

"And if she's guilty?" I asked.

"I'm certain she's not. They were a happy couple."

"He was so happy that he acquired a mistress." I tried to dial back the sarcasm and failed.

"Alta claims that's all malicious gossip; the woman in question was a friend of the family," Didier said.

"And Brick?" I asked. "How did he manage to sleaze his way into this story?"

Fab shook her head at me. "The good part is that Brick is picking up the tab. Since he was a family friend of Marshall and Alta's, he wants all avenues investigated, and that includes Marshall's associates. Anything that might lead to the killer."

"If you two need backup, I'm available," Creole offered.

"Guess I'll get dressed." I slid off the stool, slowing to pet the cats on the way to the stairs.

* * *

Fab's choice of a dress for me was a little black number that would be better suited to an intimate dinner for two in a restaurant with china and silver. The shoe heel length had me cringing, and I hadn't even tried them on. Not happening, which I felt certain Fab was expecting.

I sorted through my closet, coming up with a hot-pink linen spaghetti-strap dress with a slit on the side and pairing it with low-heeled sandals.

Creole must have heard the bedroom door open; he was waiting at the bottom of the stairs, giving me an appraising stare. I twirled around, lifting my dress and wiggling my hips.

"You're naughty." He smiled.

"Yes, and you'll see how much later on, but only if you don't kill yourself during your run." Both Didier and he were dressed for a punishing beach workout.

He hooked his arm around me.

Didier and Fab appeared in the entry.

Fab also checked me out, and although she didn't say so, the wardrobe change clearly met with her approval.

"Where are we going?" I asked as Fab picked up our purses off the bench in the entry, handing me mine.

"Fisher Island," she said as Didier opened the door for us.

"Nooo," I whined. "That's where rich people who've gone nuts live."

Creole held out his arms, enveloping me in a big hug and feeling up my back.

"I strapped it to my inner thigh," I whispered.

"You've got one minute to smooch it up and then out to the car," Fab ordered, and she and

Didier went out the door, banging it behind them.

Creole's mouth pressed against mine, and he whispered, "You be careful." The second kiss was hotter than the first. When the kiss ended, we were breathing hard and staring at each other.

I was barely able to murmur my agreement. At the sound of a horn, he chuckled and walked me outside.

Didier stood by the driver's side, shaking his head.

As Creole reached to open the passenger door, I said, "Have fun getting all sweaty."

"Yes, ma'am."

One last kiss and I slid into the passenger seat. "The driver is impatient."

Creole closed the door, and he and Didier waved as Fab backed out of the driveway.

Chapter Eleven

"I realize we're late, but there's a speed limit for a reason." At Fab's look of annoyance, I added, "Just sayin'."

"I lied," Fab said flatly. "We have plenty of time, but only because I had the forethought to build in extra time, since you have a tendency to be difficult and drag your feet." She glanced over and smirked. "I knew you wouldn't wear the stilettos."

"Well, at least I won't have to call Alta Sacks with some lame excuse about why we're late. Since I'm sure that would be one of my duties as your..." I almost laughed when she didn't say anything, staring intently at the road. "Did Didier set up this meet and greet?" At her nod, I said, "Can't wait to see how you handle what I'm sure will be an uncomfortable meeting. I suggest you save, 'Did you kill him?' until last."

"We'll do a friendly girl thing."

"You know how to do that?"

"How hard can it be?"

Once again, I wanted to laugh, but she was serious.

"It's my hope that you'll ask a bunch of

snoopy questions in your charming way, get something useful out of her, and we can be on our way."

I knew she found it annoying that I could talk to most anyone and often did. "Once we're seated, no manspread." At her confusion, I demonstrated and spread my legs.

Fab did a double take and laughed. "So that's what it's called." She continued to laugh. "I've never… and neither have you," she tried to say sternly and failed. "You were saying?"

"I've a great opener for you: 'We're here to get the dirt on Marshall and ask if you know who might want to blow him to bits.'"

"You can stay in the car."

"You know the edict from the boyfriends — no splitting up. In all seriousness, you've met Alta Sacks; what do you think?"

"I met Marshall and Alta several times socially and didn't interact enough to form an opinion, except that they were one of the 'it' couples and she hung all over him." Fab tapped the steering wheel impatiently, waiting for a slow driver to get out of the way.

"Did you get a read on her at the funeral?"

"For someone you'd expect to be overcome with grief, she flirted heavily with Didier. Didn't matter that I was standing next to him or that I'm wearing his engagement ring. I wanted to poke her eye out with my diamond, but wouldn't risk damaging my ring."

You'd have to be blind not to notice the several-carat diamond ring.

"Didier ignored her antics, which is one of the many things I like about him; he doesn't see the need to respond to every simpering glance sent his way, of which there are too many."

I tugged on a strand of her long brown hair. "I'm sure there were just as many men staring at you."

"You know you made the right choice when you have zero interest in any other men."

I smiled at her, happy for her and Didier. "I'm surprised Alta's lawyer would sanction this meeting, especially since he won't be present. Or will he?"

Fab shook her head. "In addition to never saying no to Didier, the chance to work for Cruz was the reason I didn't try to get out of this job. Brick informed me when he called this morning that Cruz sanctioned his involvement in the case, and although he didn't say so, my guess is that Cruz doesn't know about my involvement, which is why he didn't return my call. Brick danced me around — he's so good at it that you don't realize you've been played until you hang up. He also mentioned Didier's call to Alta, which annoyed him; he told me to pass on the message that if the widow needed anything, he'd take care of it."

"Sounds too personally involved. Wonder if he's forgotten he has a wife. How did you end the call?"

"He started to lecture me on inappropriate behavior, and I cut him off and barely remembered to say good-bye."

"I'd bet he meant my behavior." I grimaced. The man had ordered Fab to find another partner on more than one occasion. "I think you should give GC a call, get him started digging into Marshal's life. You'll end up knowing more about the man than he did himself."

"You call him. You relate better to weird people. Besides, he likes you better."

Great! Weird-people rapport. "What do you want, besides a detailed background report?" I pulled my trusty notepad from my purse.

Fab had clearly been thinking about it, as she responded quickly. "The remains of the boat, where are they? Probably in some government building we can't get into, and no, I'm not suggesting that we sneak in," she said in response to my lifted brow. "Pictures will do, although, I like the sneaking-in part better. A copy of the police report—find out what investigators think happened. Include Alta on the list. The mistress? Or supposed one, anyway."

"For a faithful husband, if he was, his name is linked to a few too many women." I told her, having researched the social columns online. "Gossip that doesn't go away generally has some truth to it."

"Brick insisted on a thorough job and reassured me he wouldn't complain about the bill."

"Is this coming out of his pocket?" I'd never known the man to do anything out of the goodness of his heart.

"Had the same thought but didn't ask. He's going to be racking up some hefty expenses for the woman."

Fab turned onto the Causeway, where the traffic was light heading east over Biscayne Bay. We got to the end and in line for the ferry to take us to the island. Another picture-perfect day — blue skies, white fluffy clouds, the sun shimmering off the water, and sail and powerboats headed out toward the Atlantic.

"This might be the first time we're coming out to Fisher Island as guests instead of trespassers," I said as the SUV rumbled onto the ferry that was docked and ready for the return trip, a guard guiding us on board with no waiting.

"You make it sound like all my cases are illegal." After a minute of sulking, she said emphatically, "Well, not anymore."

The test would come when one of her clients offered big money and the thrill of climbing through a window or picking a lock to retrieve information that generally showed the client to be a dirtball.

"Sacks blowing up in these waters could've caused more deaths." I powered the window down and hung my head out, enjoying the fresh air on my face.

Fab couldn't complain; in fact, for once, she powered her side down, too. All engines were required to be shut off for the ride, and we could hardly arrive at the client's house dripping in sweat.

It was a short ride across the water. Fab exited the ferry and looped around on the main road around the island, pulling up in front of the security gate of a cream-colored gazillion-square-foot two-story Mediterranean mansion. She stuck her hand out the window, pressed a button, announced herself, and within seconds, the gates rolled back.

"Wow," I said, looking around the massive brick courtyard. Palm trees and tropical flowers lined the driveway, an artificial waterfall giving it a lush tropical vibe.

"It's only seven thousand square feet, a bit small for this area."

"I'm sure it must have been hard for two people with so little space. They must have always been bumping into one another."

Fab hated to encourage me by laughing and instead turned away. Unsure where to park—not that there wasn't plenty of room, but there was no assigned visitor parking and nothing about deliveries, which I was certain weren't encouraged through the front entrance—she pulled the SUV up to the front door. We got out, and I wanted to take a moment to admire the landscaping, but an impatient snap of Fab's fingers had me following her up a couple of steps and under the portico. Before we could think about knocking, one of the massive doors opened, and a dour-faced butler in what looked like an uncomfortable monkey suit stared back.

Or maybe I was feeling uncomfortable for him. I wondered how he tolerated the black suit and bow tie on hot days without melting into a puddle. I got my answer when he ushered us into the entry and it was easily twenty below zero. Alta Sacks must have been purebred polar bear.

"This way." The butler extended his hand, directing us to follow. One step down, he led us into a wide-open space—easily over a thousand square feet, it hadn't been set up to be cozy and inviting—and directed to us to the smaller of two conversation areas. Unlike the other, it didn't have a couch, but instead had six chairs arranged next to the fireplace.

"Mrs. Sacks will be right down," the butler intoned.

He offered us a drink, which we turned down. I smiled at him. He ignored me and strode across the room to stand ramrod stiff at the bottom of the circular staircase.

Fab and I seated ourselves in the pale pink modern tufted chairs with no arms—nice to look at, but horribly uncomfortable. It was impossible for a short person to put their feet on the floor. Dismissing the idea of putting my feet on the square cocktail table in front of me, I repositioned the pillow so I wouldn't slouch. Neither Fab nor I spoke as the butler stared with a benign expression in our direction. Maybe he thought we'd pilfer a trinket.

It was all I could do to sit without fidgeting. My bottom ached, and I wanted to ask Mr. Prim if he could scare up an iced latte but kept quiet. I don't know how long we were made to wait on Alta Sacks, but it was too damn long; worse than a doctor's office. The woman certainly had no respect for our time. I wondered if she'd have had her butt in one of the uncomfortable chairs across from us as soon as we arrived if we were society matrons.

Finally! A statuesque blonde, easily six foot in her red stilettos, appeared at the top of the stairs. Alta, I assumed, as she made her way regally down to the first floor. Fab stood, and they exchanged hellos and air kisses.

"And who's this?" Alta asked, her intense blue eyes roving over my dress, lingering on my shoes and dismissing me.

"My partner, Madison Westin," Fab introduced.

We exchanged phony smiles, and she blew a kiss; unsure how to respond, I managed a bigger smile.

Alta settled into a chair on the other side of

table, straightening her black high-waisted dress. This area wasn't set up for intimate conversation; the woman sat at least eight feet away.

"I'm an open book," she said to Fab. "Ask me anything you want." To my surprise, she didn't have to shout to be heard.

"Are you aware of anyone who wanted your husband dead?" Fab asked. "Did Marshall have any enemies that you know about?"

I bit back a smile at Fab's directness.

Alta's mouth formed an 'O' and she let out a short giggle. "Of course not. Everyone loved Marshall," she cooed.

Fab wasn't impressed with her answer. Judging from her body language, she'd already written off this trip as a time-waster and was ready to leave. I'd apologize later for not contributing more to the conversation, but I knew Alta wouldn't be impressed by anything I had to say.

Glancing at the staircase, I saw that the butler had disappeared. I wanted to get up and go find him and ask for a tour, but I didn't think that would go over well. While checking out the rest of the room, I heard Fab ask Alta to relate the events of that fateful day. I forced myself to listen to the answer.

Alta sighed. "I'll never forget that day. I was sitting right here," she said with a wave of her hands, then pointed to the dock that ran the length of the property. "Our boat, *In Cahoots*, was sitting right outside. Marshall and I had plans to go out on the water, but I had an upset stomach and stayed behind at the last minute. Fate, I suppose, that we didn't die together." She ended on a soft sigh.

Fab asked about other passengers that may have been on the boat. Thus far, no other bodies had been fished out of the water.

"The rumors ran rampant that first day. Several business associates' names were bandied about. It wasn't unusual for Marshall to conduct business meetings on the boat." She produced a tissue from the pocket of her dress, dabbing at the corners of her eyes. "Thank goodness for Brick. He investigated and found that each man mentioned was indeed alive. It took a while to check off Denise Rossi, one of Marshall's financial advisors, as she was out of town at the time." The syrupy sweetness of her tone didn't match the irritation in her eyes.

"Besides Marshall's, are you aware of any other bodies having been recovered?" Fab asked.

"Oh, thankfully no. I'm not sure if the search is still ongoing or has been ended. I'd hoped for Didier's support in getting through this."

If I hadn't been observing her, I'd have missed the glare she shot Fab. Fab noticed, stiffening in her chair.

"I realize he's a busy man," Alta purred.

To distract Fab from jumping to her feet to strangle the woman, I asked, "Did anyone other than household staff have access to your dock area?"

Alta either ignored me or didn't hear the question. She not only didn't glance in my direction; I got no reaction at all.

Fab asked her the same question and got the name of the company that serviced the boat.

I stood, and at Alta's raised eyebrow, I asked, "The ladies room?"

That apparently was worth a response. She pushed a button on the side table, the butler reappeared, and she snapped her fingers and pointed to me.

"This way, ma'am." He led the way to a door under the stairs, which he opened and stepped back, ushering me down the hall. He finally came to a stop outside a closed door, his arms across his chest, adopting an air of supreme boredom, telegraphing that he planned to stand outside the bathroom. So much for a quick sneak around. Opening the door, I stepped inside and my eyes bugged out in awe at the half-bathroom. It was the size of a small bedroom with all high-end finishes.

I locked the door, trailing my finger along the marble countertop. "Well? What now? Besides wanting to go home," I asked my reflection in the mirror. Not getting an answer, I counted to one hundred, flushed the toilet, and ran water in the sink, not wanting the butler to figure out that my bathroom run was a ruse.

"You need a Plan B," I told myself. The first one that popped into my mind Fab and I had used in the past with great success. I rummaged in my purse and came up with a hundred-dollar bill. Tucking it in my hand, I opened the door, coming face-to-face with the butler, who was staring with raised eyebrows. My cheeks burned at whatever he thought I'd done.

Giving myself a mental shove, I held out the money. "Were they a happy couple?"

He sniffed at the cash, but took it anyway. "Fought all the time. The only time the staff got any peace was when neither of them was home." He started towards the living room and stopped, turning back. "Tuesday, 10 a.m. Meet me at the Coffee Café. Ten more of these for the short version, and five times that amount for the long version." He continued along the hallway.

Highway robbery. "We'll be there," I said to his back.

He nodded.

I shuffled across the living room, wanting to take in everything I couldn't see from the other side of the room.

Alta stood, her tight-lipped glare focused on me. "I'm sorry to cut this short, but I'd forgotten about a charity luncheon that I've scheduled. I can't let the little children down." She grasped Fab's hand in hers, patting the back of it. "If you have any further questions, you've got my number?"

Happy not to have to sit back down, I fought back the desire to run and forced myself to walk calmly to the front door, where the butler stood, hand on the knob. I rolled my eyes and his lips quirked ever so slightly. Efficient fellow.

Chapter Twelve

Fab gripped the steering wheel, radiating supreme aggravation as she flew around the island and once again caught the ferry just as it was ready to leave the dock for the return trip, making it back to the Turnpike headed south in record time.

Both of us had been lost in thought since leaving Alta's.

Fab broke the silence. "What did you think of Alta Sacks?"

"Politely evasive and wasn't particularly good at it," I said. "She's not the least bit interested in your help and didn't mind wasting your time as well as hers. The big question is, why did she bother?" I looked out the window; the old man next to me honked and I waved.

"Stop that," Fab admonished.

"If I weren't taken…" I laughed. "Although, he's a little old for me." It annoyed me that we'd wasted the entire morning of this beautiful day.

"Alta didn't appear worried about being accused of the crime; she didn't even bring it up. My guess is the 'poor me' act was an attempt to cozy up to Didier. The last thing she expected was to deal with me."

"What do Didier and Brick expect of you?"

"Didier is too nice; he just wanted to be helpful and doesn't have high expectations, like bagging a murderer. He only wanted to offer peace of mind. I'm not sure what Brick's game is. He wants every scintilla of evidence he can get and made it clear that it's his decision what happens to the information."

"What if it turns out that Alta is involved; does he want it covered up?" My radar now on high alert, I wondered if Fab had been hired to make any evidence that made the woman look guilty disappear.

"I've done a lot of questionable things for Brick; covering up murder isn't going to be one of them."

"If he pressures you in any way, I expect to be the first to know." I stared at her until she gifted me with a short nod. "We've only just begun, and this case already has the feel of a joke that we're not privy to." I pulled out my notepad. "Background reports, talk to his associates..." I paused. "Get a list of them from Brick. No one's going to be helpful on their own. Who wants their name associated with a murder? No one." I didn't blame them—being too helpful often came back to haunt you.

"On the way out the door, Alta forbid me to speak to the neighbors or anyone else without her express permission," Fab huffed, concentrating on the traffic backing up.

"Almost forgot, there's one person willing to talk." I went on to tell her about my short chat with the butler and the meeting scheduled for Tuesday, not leaving out the eye-raising amount of cash he'd demanded. "You won't get reimbursed. Alta's hardly going to pony up bribe money to pay her own butler. You could pitch it to Brick that you've got some sources who'll gossip on the condition of anonymity and cash. If you rat the butler out, he'll lose his job."

"Everything I can think of that would be the least bit useful in this case, Alta doesn't want done. I'll talk to Brick and see what he wants me to do. I'm telling you now, I'm not fronting cash."

My phone began to ring from the drink holder where I'd dumped it. Recognizing the ringtone, I reached for it. "Hey, babe," I said, turning toward the window.

"Where are you?"

"Headed in your direction; about thirty minutes away. Could make it five with the way you know who drives." I smiled at the phone.

He laughed. "Tell lead foot to stick to the speed limit or I'll take the keys away."

I kept my face averted so Fab wouldn't question my big grin.

"No easy way to say this… The docks and slip area burned down earlier today. Arson."

"What?" I almost screeched. "Please, tell me

no one was hurt." Fab knocked me in the shoulder. "Can I put you on speaker?"

"Go ahead."

"Dock fire," I said to Fab.

"The fire destroyed all the slips, along with ten boats, and produced a huge smoke plume, which is how it was discovered," Creole updated us. "Didier and Corndog are over there now, surveying the damage."

"Anyone hurt?" I asked.

"Thankfully, the area was deserted at the time. Whoever is setting these fires is getting more destructive."

"Corndog suspected Bordello of the first two fires," Fab reminded us.

"He suspects him this time, also. Not that Bordello would do it personally." Creole switched to a lecturing tone. "Which is why if either of you want to check the area out, it won't be by yourself."

"Agreed," I said for Fab and me.

"If it is him, he takes sore loser to a whole new level."

"I think it's personal. Bordello was set on having that property and sparred for months with Corndog, claiming it was the ideal spot for the shrine he planned to build. It's probably a huge blow to his ego that Corndog is developing the property himself."

"Had a talk with Kevin and asked him to keep me in the loop."

A voice I didn't recognize called Creole's name.

"Text me when you two get close, and I'll meet you there."

I disconnected and tossed my phone on the console. *What next?*

"Maybe due to our mutual dislike of Bordello, we haven't considered other people," Fab said. "There's always a possibility that it's not him."

"Except that when previous incidents have been mentioned in his presence, he smirks. Innocent people tend to at least *try* to look sympathetic or shocked when they hear about something bad happening to someone. Unless it's all a big game. I agree with Creole about one thing—why isn't Bordello over this already and moving on?"

"A parting shot, perhaps. He knows that Corndog wants to restore the area, and Bordello's gift is to make sure there's nothing to restore. I suggest a security guard for the area," Fab added.

"With the docks gone, there's nothing else flammable—a couple of store fronts, but the majority of the buildings are brick and concrete."

"Looking forward to seeing everything with my own eyes."

I nodded in agreement.

* * *

My phone beeped, alerting me to a message from Creole. "Roads to the dock area closed, blocked with fire trucks and law enforcement vehicles and will be for several more hours."

That there was nothing to see made the decision to go home and change clothes an easy one. Neither of us was dressed for walking in the dock area anyway. Rounding the corner to my street, I saw that Creole's and Didier's cars were parked in front.

By the time Fab parked and we got to the front door, Creole had it open. I kissed him and headed upstairs to change. I kicked off my shoes, threw my dress over the back of the chair, and pulled on a cotton shift dress, then ignored the voice in my head telling me to go back downstairs and instead laid on my bed. That was where Creole found me, eyes closed, pretending to be asleep.

I practically leapt off the bed, screeching, when Creole tickled me.

"You're such a faker." He kissed me.

"You're mean." I mimicked Fab's scary girl stare and then laughed.

Creole pulled me into his arms.

"What's going on downstairs?" I asked.

"Fab entertained Didier and I with this morning's saga. Her story seemed vague in places, but I didn't ask what she was leaving out. I figured I'd get it out of you." He ran his hands down my sides. "No visible wounds. You came home looking as hot as when you left. So, it went well?"

"There's a reason there's not much to tell." I ran down a quick version of the morning, spending extra time on my disappointment at not being able to get around the butler.

Creole laughed. "There are a lot of unhappy couples, but the percentage of relationships that end in murder is small. And using a bomb… that requires specialized knowledge and mechanical skill to avoid blowing yourself up. Unless the cops unearth an accomplice, I'd have a hard time believing Alta would chip her fingernails on such a risky venture."

I had a few questions that I hadn't asked Fab, such as how well Didier knew Alta Sacks. Was he really able to glean another's character from attending the same social events? And what was his relationship with Marshall, Alta, or both?

"What did you think of Alta?" Creole asked, cutting off my musings.

"As I've told a few people, you can't dictate how a person grieves. But if she's grieving, she hides it well. Marshall seems to be a dim memory. I'm thinking once Fab dumps the background reports on Brick's desk—case closed."

"You need to get up." He flung my legs over the side of the bed and pulled me to a standing position. "I'm giving a presentation of pictures and commentary regarding the dock fire, and you wouldn't want to miss it." He flashed a grin.

Creole tucked my hand in his, and instead of being cooperative, I did my best to hang back and slow our walk back downstairs. He tugged on my hand, and when that didn't motivate me to move faster, he stopped, picked me up, and threw me over his shoulder. He landed a hard smack on my upturned butt, carried me downstairs, and set me on the floor in the living room.

"My bottom hurts." I scowled.

"Would you like me to rub it?"

"Yes."

"How about a drink instead?" He winked.

"I'll have a double margarita."

He looped his arm in mine and led me out to the patio, stopping to grab a couple of waters. We sat opposite Fab and Didier, sharing the same chair. A margarita was already waiting for me.

Creole shared his story of being on the road, seeing the plumes of smoke, and following the trail. "I thought to myself," he said, "what would Fab do? Oh yeah. I got out and took pictures." He took his phone out.

Fab stood and moved behind his chair, hanging over his shoulder while he flicked through his phone. "You got some great pictures. Forward them to me." She picked her phone up off the nearby table, waiting for them to arrive. "I'm surprised the cops didn't tell you to 'move along.'"

Didier pulled her back to his side and down in front of him and kissed her cheek.

After Creole sent the email, he handed me his phone and I flipped through the pictures. I glanced up and met Didier's eyes, neither of us happy over the setback, not to mention the cost.

"I'd like to drive by the site once it's cleared," I said. "Then go check on Corndog." I planned to call Mac and ask her to check in on him tonight.

"When I heard about the fire," Didier said, "I went over to his cottage to give him an update, but he already knew, having listened on a police scanner. I drove him over and we got as close as we could." He was a man with a million details on his mind. "Now for the cleanup."

"Make getting the debris out of the water a top priority," Creole said.

I scrunched up my nose at the thought of the water turning black and staying that way. "I can deal with the insurance company and adjusters, and handle all the paperwork. I have the patience to deal with the red tape."

"Done." Didier slapped his hand on the side table. "FYI: ran into Bordello and Brad watching the flames shoot in the air. I'd told Brad earlier, when we met for coffee, about the offer to partner with Corndog and that I'd accepted. If he'd shared that information with Bordello, he didn't say a word, and I had no reason to bring it up. I also didn't say a word about your

93

involvement; thought that was for you to divulge."

"I keep telling myself there hasn't been a good time. Now I've stalled for so long that it will be nice and awkward, but I'm doing it in the next couple of days, starting with Mother. Maybe she'll have a good idea for smoothing the way." I didn't want to think about my family's reaction.

"I think it will be fine," Didier reassured me. "Brad's excited about some new project in Miami Beach; kept the details to himself."

"Invite him to lunch," Fab suggested.

"That's a great idea." I smiled at her.

Chapter Thirteen

Creole and Didier both left early. Didier had an early morning meeting about cleanup at the docks. I'd already put in a call to a man I knew in the building department who'd helped us out on the property, apprising him of the latest, in case he hadn't heard. It was great having a connection who could help us get the work done the right way the first time.

The chief had called and summoned Creole for another meeting. He'd received the curt call the previous day and cancelled plans to spend the rest of the day at his house. I wanted to grill him about his "project," but had so far managed to keep from firing one question after another... and I'd never sneak a peek.

I grabbed a notepad and headed toward the patio doors to lounge in a chair and organize a list of things that needed to be done.

"Stop right there," Fab demanded from behind me. I turned in time to see her bang her coffee mug on the counter. At least it was empty; nothing sloshed over the sides.

"You break one of my mugs, you buy me a

whole new set. They have to be seashell and match."

Fab rolled her eyes. "You need to go back upstairs and change into something casual-cute. Show a little leg." She made a shooing motion.

I dug my feet into the area rug, arms crossed over my chest, and glared.

"Oh, all right. Please."

I continued to glare.

Fab blew a loud sigh. "I need you to ride along with me while I find out why I'm unable to contact the cretin at the Venetian Palms. Hoskins has been avoiding my calls. I want answers about the other night and to get paid."

"Couldn't you ask nicely?"

"Hmm... I thought I did." The sides of her mouth quirked. "Lunch is my treat."

I nodded and headed back upstairs.

Halfway up, Fab yelled, "Don't forget your Glock."

It didn't take me long to change into a skirt and top, strap my gun to my thigh, and go back downstairs, where I met Fab standing at the door.

"Why do you suppose Hoskins is blowing off your calls?" I asked as we crossed the driveway.

"We're going to find out, and I don't have a good feeling about this."

* * *

We arrived in the Venetian Islands and at the Palms in record time.

"What am I doing? Bodyguard?" I smiled at that idea.

"Hoskins knows that you're my partner. He saw you at the first meeting, so seeing you again shouldn't be a surprise." She pulled up in front of the office and parked.

A tall, sixtyish man, reed thin, with dyed brown hair and dressed in boat-clothes chic that neither of us recognized from the previous visit stood in front of the glass doors. We got out, and he asked, "What can I do for you?"

"I'm here to see Hoskins Crisp," Fab said with a smile.

Judging by the man's double take, it wasn't one of her more friendly smiles.

"Name's not familiar," he responded.

"The HOA manager."

"That would be me, Harv Levee," he introduced himself.

"I was here just a few days ago and spoke to a Hoskins Crisp about the boat-theft problem. At his insistence, I did a stakeout."

"You're the one!" Harv laughed. "A local officer that regularly patrols this neighborhood stopped by, and we had a good laugh over that one. I had no clue why someone would be staking the place out when the thieves were caught a couple of weeks ago."

"We also talked about tightening the security," Fab insisted.

"You might want to look around. That job was completed yesterday. I hired the company myself."

Fab and I both looked around, and sure enough, the gates to the outside boat lot had been changed.

I took a step forward. "I was with Ms. Merceau when she had her appointment. I also met Mr. Crisp. He had complete access to your office, and I also noticed that he talked to a couple of boat owners as we left. How did this man have access, and why would he lie about the thefts?"

"I don't know you." He hadn't been friendly to begin with; now he wasn't bothering to hide his irritation. "How do I know you're not here to case the place and steal more boats?"

"We're thieves and standing here talking to you?" *Dial back the sarcasm; it's not a good way to get information.* "You can verify our story with the maintenance man; I was the one to speak to him."

"Rog and I were both on vacation, and we got back yesterday. Our maintenance man has his own company and sends out his workers when I call."

"This was all a ruse?" Fab asked.

"I'd be happy to call the police, and maybe you can figure it out with them," Harv said with a sneer.

I was tired of his snotty attitude. He'd made it clear that he didn't believe either one of us. "We're not here to make trouble," I said.

Fab withdrew her PI license from her pocket, showing it to the man, who barely glanced at it. "We were hired to do a job, and we came here today to follow up on the security details that were suggested. You claim not to know either of the men described; don't you find it as odd as we do? Just another day of men impersonating you?"

"You two act legitimate, but this is Florida, and there's a nut on every corner."

Along with an ass. His attitude had me perplexed. Being the suspicious sort, I figured he knew a lot more than he was sharing. But beating the information out of him wasn't a good idea, as the cops knew our names.

"Thank you for your time. Not sure what happened here," Fab said, her tone conciliatory. "I'd like to exchange business cards."

It was clear old Harv didn't like the idea, but he seemed unable to say no. He walked back inside briefly and came out with a card, handing it to Fab, who pocketed it. I noticed she didn't hand one of hers over.

To cover the awkward moment as he waited, I stepped in front of Fab. "Thank you for your time. I believe this qualifies as the oddest job we've had to date." I mustered up a small laugh.

I heard the car door close behind me and hustled to the passenger side, jumping in. I waved through the windshield as Harv stared back, open-mouthed.

"Don't drive out of here like a crazy person," I warned. "Practice being normal for a few seconds."

"What the hell just happened?" Fab almost yelled.

"Take a breath." I kept watch in the side mirror, and Harv didn't move until we cleared the driveway. "We just followed up on what appears to have been a pretend job—both of the men we met with were imposters. The guys will find this one hard to believe."

Fab glared at the road, surprisingly following the speed limit. Tired of the silence, I interrupted her brooding when she turned onto the Turnpike.

"A setup?" I threw out. "Took a lot of planning to pull this one off." Still she brooded, so I continued, "Who was the old client that referred you? A call to him should clear things up."

"I'm thinking the same thing." She pulled her phone out of her pocket, handing it to me. "His name is Victor."

I scrolled down and connected to the number. Before I could ask if it was a home or office number, a woman answered, "Mr. Victor's office."

"This is Fabiana Merceau," I said doing my best to mimic her. "I'd like to speak with him."

"Mr. Victor is out of town. I can have him call you when he returns."

Fab looked at me quizzically.

I shrugged and asked, "Do you know when he'll be returning?"

"Mr. Victor's schedule is fluid. If you tell me what this about, I can make a note for when he returns."

"A file he asked me to look into. Please tell him it's quite urgent."

"Maybe it's something I can help you with."

"Just pass along the message. Thank you." I hung up and handed Fab her phone back. "Another one out of town."

"Why would Mr. Victor set me up? Or anyone else? For what?" Fab asked. "Last job I did for the man went well, no complaints. And the client that originally referred me to Mr. Victor is dead. Natural causes," she said in answer to my raised eyebrow.

"Since I don't like having questions and no answers, I'm going to do some investigating of my own, starting with giving the names of the two men from the Palms to GC. The maintenance man withheld his name on purpose; he didn't want anything traced back to him. I chalked it up to not wanting to get caught gossiping. He's smarter than I gave him credit for." I hesitated for a moment, then added, "I'm also going to add

Mr. Victor's name to the list."

"We're running up quite a bill with this GC character."

"Now that you've said that, the phone will be ringing with some dangerous job he needs us to do." I frowned at the screen. "We need to start paying cash so we're not giving up the right to say no."

"Whatever you come up with, I'm in agreement. What are we going to tell the guys?"

"The truth. Maybe Creole will come up with an angle we've overlooked."

"If I'd shown up by myself for that stakeout, or with just you, we might have been arrested. Creole is the one that handled that situation and made sure it didn't go from bad to worse."

"I don't like this. Who'd want you and me arrested? We need to be careful. If someone went to this much trouble, I can't imagine they'd give up now."

Fab handed me back her phone. "Call Didier and find out what he wants from the grocery store; tell him he's cooking dinner... unless he wants me to do the cooking." She unleashed a devilish laugh.

Chapter Fourteen

I refused to hang up the phone until Brad finally agreed to lunch, and even then, I had to wait two days for an opening in his schedule longer than fifteen minutes. I laid it on pretty thick that we hadn't had any sibling bonding time recently.

Fab was understanding when I told her I wouldn't be going with her to meet the butler. Didier, who'd been listening, insisted he go as backup. It was decided that he'd sit at another table so as not to scare the man off. She'd admonished him, "No guns. Not that show, anyway." Didier kissed her, murmuring something about "owing," and I slipped out of the kitchen.

It was clear that I was Madeline Westin's daughter—booking the lunch reservation at our family's favorite restaurant, The Crab Shack, and arriving early to make sure we got a prime window location that overlooked the ocean. The clincher to me was the restaurant's low-key atmosphere. It was decorated in fake palm trees, and I appreciated that the fish mounted on the walls weren't real.

Ordering a glass of wine, I didn't have long to

wait as Brad walked in precisely on time. I watched as he paused just on the other side of the bar. Looking around, he spotted me and waved. It didn't surprise me that he'd shown up in black suit pants and a white dress shirt, the sleeves rolled up his muscled forearms. It did surprise me that he'd ditched the tie. I watched, amused, as two women sharing a table nearby didn't take their eyes off him until he got to the table, pulling me up into a big hug and kissing my cheek.

"Do you want me to yell to those two women gobbling you up over there that I'm your sister?"

He looked over his shoulder in their direction, and the women giggled.

"What did you do?" I asked as I sat back down.

"Winked." He claimed the chair next to me. "They have such good taste."

I laughed. "I've missed seeing you."

"I figured you were in some kind of trouble and needed my help."

My smile must have slipped. He groaned.

Thankfully, the server interrupted and set a beer down in front of Brad that he must have ordered when he walked by the bar.

"No scotch?"

"I've got a pile of paperwork on my desk. If I throw back a couple of drinks, I'll want a cigar, and then all I'll be good for is kicking up my feet."

"Hasn't anyone had the nicotine talk with you?"

"It wasn't Mother, that's for sure."

We both laughed. She also smoked cigars, hand-rolled ones shaped more like cigarettes.

"This was supposed to be a bro/sis bonding lunch," I said as Mother waved from the hostess stand.

Brad stood, pulling back a chair. "What was I supposed to do when she found out that we were meeting for lunch? Tell her no?" His brows shot up. "*You* tell her to go home," he said, just before she got within earshot.

Brad stood and hugged and kissed Mother. She bent down and kissed my cheek, then clipped me in the back of the head before sitting across from me. "Why didn't you invite me?"

"Because…" I said, "I planned to invite you for a girl lunch, and now, surprise spoiled."

"Separate lunches," Brad said. "She's in trouble," he sing-songed.

I kicked him in the shin.

Brad jumped. "Ouch, dammit. That hurt."

"My foot slipped."

"Children, children." Mother almost laughed. "Don't worry, Brad and I are good problem solvers." She patted my hand.

The server set down her Jack Daniels on the rocks. The Westins being regulars at this restaurant, the bartender probably had it ready as soon as he saw us.

"Frankly, you both have guilty looks on your faces." She took a sip of her drink. "Don't bother to deny it. I have experience with you two."

The server came back to the table, inquiring about our order. Brad scooped up the menus, handed them back, and ordered a platter of appetizers guaranteed to feed eight.

"I'm calling dibs on the leftovers," I said.

Brad nodded. "I have some news of my own, but since I'm the guest, you first," he said to me.

"You both know that I'm friends with Corndog." I left off the part about him now living at The Cottages. They both rolled their eyes. "If you could be patient, this story is best told from the beginning."

"A grown man calling himself Corndog..." Mother harrumphed.

"That just goes to show how long people's memories are. They gave him that nickname after he was named dog-eating champion several years in a row. No one even remembers his real name now."

"That's nice," Brad said sarcastically. "Let's get to the good part."

"I met him when he was referred to me by an old acquaintance to do a background check."

"Here we go," Brad groaned.

"Why don't we agree to stay quiet until she's finished?" Mother suggested.

I sent her a silent thank you. "I was slow getting back to him, and by that time, he'd been attacked, and I ended up visiting him in the hospital. Over time, we became friends, and I helped him out on several occasions."

"This is your fault, Mother," Brad said. "You allowed her to haul home strays ever since she could walk, and now she's graduated from cats to humans."

"Remember, we were going to let her finish her story before interrupting." Mother used her patient voice, as though we were six years old.

Brad wasn't amused.

A well-timed interruption came in the form of our food, which smelled divine. The server cleared the center of the table, setting down the platter and giving us each a plate.

"Drink refills?" he asked.

Mother and Brad got refills. I ordered a soda and lime and helped myself to a stuffed shrimp.

"As you both know, Corndog owns a large portion of the sought-after dock area. Once he firmed up his plans, he offered me a small piece of the project, and I accepted. It was overwhelming at first, but that didn't last long. I jumped at the chance and was excited to be included."

Mother's surprise clearly showed. Brad contained his reaction.

"I requested a particular location for a retail outlet, and he agreed." Now wasn't the time to spring on them the extent of my involvement, which would consist of being a front person, or that my idea was another bar.

"Why did this Mr. Corndog, or whatever, think you had any experience?" Mother asked.

"I asked the same thing, and he cited my real estate background with my ex, but my contacts were the selling point for him. It's not a hindrance to know everyone in town."

"You got Didier involved?" Brad asked.

"When Corndog sent over the prospectus and architectural plans, I showed him, and he was excited about the scope of the project, so I introduced them."

"Can I speak now?" Brad asked Mother with a cheesy smile.

Mother nodded, a chagrinned look on her face. None of us liked being the last to know.

"That dock project was Bordello's deal, and his interest started long before I met him," Brad said. "I'm not sure why he didn't give it up as a lost cause some time ago. I'm well aware of the animosity between Bordello and Corndog and told Bordello to get over it, which he took well." He downed the rest of his beer and held it up. "I've also been apprised that this Corndog fellow, and probably you, think Bordello had him beaten, set the fires, whatever, but I know the man, and he wouldn't sink to a criminal level."

"I thought you wanted this project?" Mother asked Brad, and to me, said, "I hope you didn't use information you got from me when you knew I was trying to help Brad."

Brad brushed a kiss on Mother's cheek. "That project was always Bordello's brainchild. Didn't matter to me. I was just excited about working with the man and learning everything I could. Like my sister, I've amassed contacts of my own that I plan to use when I venture off on my own." All in all, Brad had sold me on the idea that he couldn't care less.

I'd planned to tell them that Fab had bought the commercial property they'd bid on, but she adamantly told me not to, worried her relationship with Brad and Mother would be over. No amount of persuasion would change her mind. I warned her to fess up before they found out.

"Mother, I didn't and never would use you for information. There were things I knew at the time that I wasn't able to divulge. I regret not being upfront from the beginning, but at that particular time, there was a lot of awkwardness between us."

Brad hooked his arm around my shoulders, kissing my head. "There were a few angry feelings in the beginning, solidarity for my friend and all." He tugged on my hair. "Don't spread this around, but we're working on a deal more to my liking. Bordello can build his shrine elsewhere. I told him a Miami Beach address would hold more cachet."

I was ecstatic that Bordello had already found

another piece of property. Something new to focus on was what the man needed, and I hoped it would end the hard feelings all around. Not that I'd ever trust the man.

"So, is that the new plan you talked about?" Mother asked Brad.

"That's it." He flashed a big smile. "Can't give specifics, as it's not a done deal, but we're scheduling the closing this week or early next. I can say it's up in Miami and I'm looking forward to getting started."

"Does this mean you're commuting?" I asked, not liking the idea. Miami wasn't far, but it was nice knowing he lived just across town.

"I'm keeping my condo here and getting a second place in South Beach. Now *there's* a town with never-ending entertainment."

I wondered if his girlfriend was also relocating, but didn't ask and, I noticed, neither did Mother.

"I expect you to attend family events and not beg off with some stupid excuse," Mother said adamantly.

Brad leaned over and gave her a half-hug. "I'll be there."

"I have some news of my own." Mother smiled.

"You're pregnant," Brad said.

"Brad Westin." I shook my head.

Mother laughed. "That would be something. My own business news. Charles... I mean,

Doodad, that bartender of yours. What's with all the nicknames?"

"This town's full of them." I laughed along with her.

"Says he's manager now, is that true?"

I nodded.

"That's probably good. Since his arrival, I've noticed Jake's has gotten even busier. Told me he wants to take over my entertainment room."

It was the first time I'd heard the room described that way.

"Your illegal gambling den," Brad corrected.

Mother shot him a glare without much heat. "I questioned him about his plans and think they're good ones, and I told him that after I talked to you, I'd get back to him. I'm fine with it, and it gives me more time to spend with my husband without feeling guilty for neglecting the den."

She had done an amazing job of transforming Spoon from a curmudgeonly grouch into a great husband.

"I like that you two are not going to be hanging around Jake's that much. You know, sis, it has a seedy reputation."

"With your highbrow friends, maybe."

Mother patted our hands. "We're doing so well, we don't want this to degenerate into a fight."

I expected her to shake her finger at us, but she didn't.

"So, we're all good." Brad knuckle-bumped Mother, then me.

"I'm just happy that both of my kids are happy, and at the same time." Mother beamed.

Chapter Fifteen

"At least, you wore black," Fab said. It was the first either of us had spoken since leaving the house.

"You said it was a funeral. I've also noticed that Raul always calls you for these jobs." I gave her an assessing glance; she too had chosen a black dress. "Maybe you can tell me why people need bodyguards at their final send-offs." I slid my feet out of my flip-flops and into a pair of black heels.

Fab slammed on the brakes for the red light, making me jump in my seat. "You know how the guys are, they go out of their way to accommodate every funeral request." She turned onto Main Street, getting ever closer.

"That's a nice non-answer." How many times had I contemplated jumping from the SUV and running... and never did? Looking down at my shoes, I decided today wouldn't be the day — not able to picture myself going barefoot. "Have you left out any pertinent details?"

Fab pulled into the driveway of Tropical Slumber Funeral Home, backing into a space across from the entrance. Over the years, the old hot dog stand had morphed into a large operation, offering an array of services and even a pet cemetery.

"Just paste a smile on your face. This will be over before you know it." Fab slid out and closed the door on any further questions.

Looking through the windshield, I wanted to laugh at Fab standing there glaring at me, tapping her foot. I got out and joined her. "You can expect my invoice by the morning. I charge by the hour, just so you know."

"You know these jobs are freebies," Fab reminded me. "The good news is that they're serving those little sandwiches you like."

The owners, Raul and Dickie, had done us a few favors in the past, and in return, we never said no to anything they asked. Hopefully this funeral wouldn't morph into a food fight. I liked my dress and didn't want mayo stains on it.

Raul and Dickie were partners. Raul—medium build, bodybuilder physique—was the business brains of the operation. Dickie—tall, thin, and pale—was the dresser of the dead. Both stood in the doorway, waving, looking relieved to see us.

We barely got out hellos before the twin Dobermans, Astro and Necco, beelined around the two men and skidded to a stop next to me. They gave Fab a cursory glance and rubbed their heads against my hand. Both dogs knew who'd sneak them a treat and where to get their necks scratched.

"So happy you arrived before our other guests." Raul had barely completed his sentence when a short bus pulled into the driveway and a dozen or so mourners in an array of get-ups, as my grandmother would have called them, got off the bus.

A man and woman stood out from the rest. He had on black bathing trunks, a black suit jacket buttoned up and covering most of his bare chest, and a red tie. The woman hanging on his arm had donned a form-fitting white dress with a large hole in the back showing her butt crack. It appeared the designer had designed it that way.

Raul and Dickie formed a receiving line to shake each hand.

Dickie whispered to me, "There's food at the bar, but the dogs aren't allowed in the main viewing room with the deceased, Billings Case."

I nodded and snapped my fingers at the dogs, and they stood to follow me.

"Dickie said the dogs need a walk." I knew Fab didn't believe me, but by the time she was certain that I'd lied, I'd be around the side of the building. "Come on, you two. I owe you a sandwich from last time."

* * *

It didn't take long before Raul appeared at the

side of the building, whistling for the dogs. "Thank you so much for agreeing to this and waiving the fee."

"Are you expecting fights? Anything else we should be on the lookout for?" I scanned the parking lot, noticing a few more buses had shown up and the rest of the spaces were fuller than usual.

"No." Raul appeared confused. "Is there something I'm unaware of?"

I shook my head, both of us confused at this point. "Large turnout." I couldn't think of anything else to say.

"Mr. Case specified at least one hundred mourners, and on such short notice, I came up with the idea of approaching a couple of retirement homes in Homestead." He took out a handkerchief, dabbing his face. "First, I had to sell management on the idea, then the oldsters themselves. They perked up at the mention of cash, and that got them onboard for the bus ride to the Keys on what would surely be a beautiful day. I went out on a limb there, but most days here are perfect. Plus, free lunch. I stopped short of an open bar, thinking it wouldn't be a good idea to have a bunch of drunks passed out in their chairs."

"You're telling me that Fab and I are here as professional mourners and not bodyguards?" Wait until I got my hands around her neck.

"Ohhh." His brows shot up. "Fab's such a

sweetie. You know, she never turns us down."

I contained a flippant response, but just barely; his smile reminded me of an indulgent parent with a bratty kid on their hands.

"Ready?" he asked, and I followed him back inside.

Fab was right where I expected her to be, in her favorite seat, the one right inside the door of the main room. It made for an easy getaway ahead of the mourners, and I shoved her shoulder as I squeezed past to sit in the next seat. "What's the going rate for a paid mourner?"

I remembered that Mother had met someone at a funeral who told her it paid well. It could be parlayed into a full-time career, but not here in the Keys; one would have to move north.

"I'm going to make this up to you."

"No, you're not." I waved her off. "I'm holding this over your head until those cows, wherever they are, come home."

"I don't even know what that means."

A short, bald man that could barely see over the podium tapped a bell sitting on the top. He started the service: "Welcome, loved ones..."

I zoned out, pushing my sunglasses down off my head and over my eyes so I could close them without getting caught. I'd forgotten my phone in the car or I'd text Creole and see how his day was going.

My eyes snapped open when the man welcomed the first person to the podium to say a few words. *So, Mr. Case has a few friends in attendance after all.* A few more followed.

"Let us welcome our last speaker, Madison Westin."

I shot up, almost giving myself whiplash, certain I'd heard wrong. But no, Dickie was pointing to me and a dozen pairs of eyes turned my way.

Raul appeared in the aisle, extending a hand. "I want to thank you for offering to speak," he said in a conspiratorial whisper.

The specter of Madeline Westin had me rising out of my seat. I'd never hear the end of it if I made a scene at a funeral, especially if it made the local rag. And even if it didn't, all Mother had to do was find out. Creole would probably die laughing.

I leveled my fiercest glare at Fab and kicked her. Her hiss made me feel only slightly better. "What am I going to say?" I asked Raul. "I didn't know Basket Case."

"Billings Case," he corrected. "That's the beauty of this—most of the people here didn't know him, either."

Beauty. He's lost his mind.

I walked so slowly to the podium that now everyone was staring. I got to the microphone, and taking a calming breath, I said, "Thank you so much for coming; it would have meant so much to B..." I hesitated. "Billings..." That was it. "...to know that you're all here to celebrate his life." I smiled, slowly scanning the room, trying to figure out what to say next.

"I'm so very sorry; he was such a wonderful man." I turned towards the casket, my eyes closed. I did my best to avoid close-ups of dead people. "Billings was a good friend and relative, as evidenced by this turnout. He loved life and will miss you all dearly." *Think,* I told myself. "I want to thank all of you for coming, and I know he's smiling down from heaven in thanks." I reminded myself to breathe and walked away from the podium, congratulating myself for not running. I made eye contact with those staring and pasted a determined smile on my face. Instead of sitting next to Fab, I took a seat on the other side of the aisle.

The gentleman who started the service was back at the microphone, encouraging everyone to file by the open casket for a final good-bye and then directing them out to the patio for food and beverages. It was a fifty/fifty split which way people went.

Two older ladies stopped in front of me. "That was lovely, dear."

They were twins—seventies, I'd guess—and dressed identically, which put the first genuine smile on my face since I arrived.

"We're going to snoop around," one confided.

"The viewing rooms are over there." I pointed. "And sometimes the doors are unlocked.

They both waved and went straight over,

turning the first knob and sticking their heads inside. I wondered if they were related to Fab.

Chapter Sixteen

Fab made several attempts on the way home from Billings' funeral to engage in conversation, and I ignored them all. She pulled into the driveway, and I got out and walked around the Hummer, holding out my palm as I passed her. She dropped the keys in my hand and I jumped behind the wheel, backed out into the street, and skidded to the corner.

I pulled myself together and managed the drive to Creole's in a less hair-raising fashion. As I was parking next to his truck, my phone rang. Without looking at the screen, I turned it off and went into the house, banging the door closed.

Creole stared at me from the couch. Assessing the mutinous look on my face, he didn't ask how the funeral was, instead, watched as I kicked off my shoes, which did a slight summersault before hitting the floor, and came to a stop in front of the coffee table.

"I gave a farewell speech at a funeral today." I poked my chest. "I need to get out of this damn dress." Flustered, I struggled to reach the zipper.

He smiled that sexy, toe-curling smile of his and beckoned me over.

I turned and backed up to Creole, lifting my hair.

He unzipped my dress, and with a flick at the sleeves, it pooled around my feet.

I hooked it with my foot and flipped it up into my hand, then threw it over the back of a chair. I turned, and Creole stared back, a big grin on his face. He held out his arms and I flew into them.

"I'm being a dick. Instead of unleashing my sensitive side and asking about the funeral, I'm rather happy that I seem to have won the grand prize in your bad-day sweepstakes." He nipped my shoulder.

"I know I'm overreacting."

"I've got the cure for that." He growled out a laugh.

* * *

The aroma of coffee woke me the next morning, my first clue that Creole had awoken earlier than me. I rolled out of bed, tugged one of his t-shirts over my head, and trudged into the kitchen, spotting the two large mugs that he had bought off a peddler on the beach, which easily held two cups in each.

In only a pair of sweat shorts, Creole scooped me up in his arms and hugged me hard to his chest. "I thought we'd take our coffee out to the beach. I picked you out some clothes." He nodded to the stool.

I eyed his selection. "So sweet." I wrinkled my nose. "Those are your sweat pants; they won't fit and will probably fall down."

"That's okay." He leered.

"Not if something shows, it isn't." At least his t-shirt would keep me covered.

He grabbed my hand, stopping me from making my escape, and snatched up the pants, turning me around, my back to his chest. "Let me show you." He hiked up my shirt and held out the pants, and I stepped into the legs.

I wadded the material at the waist.

He bent down, rolling the legs up to my knees. He stood, pulled the drawstring as tight as it would go, and knotted it. "See?" He looked so proud of himself.

"I do see, and you're nuts."

He grinned at me, then filled the mugs to the top, grabbed them up in one hand, and took my hand in the other, heading out to the patio and down the steps to the sand.

I had grabbed a towel that I spread out, and we sat, digging our toes in the sand.

He handed me a mug filled with my favorite brew.

We watched as a couple of herons strolled in the lapping water, searching out food; the beautiful white coastal birds not concerned that we weren't sitting that far away.

Creole broke the silence. "I have an update for you."

His serious tone put me on alert. I snuggled closer, and he wrapped his arm around me. I turned my face to his.

"I had another meeting with the chief, as you know, and told him I'm resigning from the force and want to leave with a clean slate. To that end, I saw the psychiatrist."

"That doctor is accommodating."

He half-laughed. "The chief had the appointment already set up. It was my last chance to get my act together. He reminded me that if I didn't complete the evaluation, I could be fired if it were determined I was just being a butthole. His word, not mine."

"Wait until I see him again." I sniffed.

"If we weren't such good friends, I'm certain the meeting would have been more formal. A little name-calling had us laughing." He brushed my lips with a soft kiss. "Since I'd already made up my mind to leave, I had an ulterior motive for wanting to cooperate. If I left without passing the psych eval, I wouldn't be legally allowed to buy or carry a firearm and wouldn't be able to get a private investigator's license. Since I'm signing on for backup duty for you and Fab, I'm going to do it legally."

"You're happy with your decision?"

He nodded. "I won't be around a lot in the next few weeks. To accomplish all this, I need to take a few classes to fulfill the licensing requirements."

"Is this the project you've been working on?"

"I have a few irons in the fire as far as my post-law enforcement career goes. I do know that I'm not interested in being a full-time investigator. Once I've got everything completed, you'll be the first I share my new plans with. The good part is that it will give me the flexibility to keep an eye on you and Fab."

"That right there is a full-time job."

"One I'll be taking very seriously. I'm telling you now that I draw the line at taking part in any of those creepy funeral home jobs."

I sighed. "The guys probably think I'm a hideous person for stomping out of there, not speaking to anyone. I should call and apologize, but so far, I haven't come up with anything that sounds polite."

"That's an easy one. Blame everything on Fab." We both laughed. He took my empty mug, put it in the sand next to his, and slid me over onto his lap. He tilted my chin. "You have anything you need to share?"

"You're pretty up to date on our escapades. Ever since Fab decided to put her name on a business card, she's been running a legit operation. Although, she has a few shady clients. All rich businessmen."

"From what I've been able to get out of Didier, she's always been fearless, not caring about the danger she puts her life in. Guess she figures she's got nine of them, like some cat."

"That changed when she met Didier." *Thankfully so!* I thought. "It didn't happen overnight, but she's no longer accepting every job that comes her way, and now the danger sneaks up on us when we least expect it. Brick's cases are good examples of that."

"It's amazing someone hasn't shot him."

"Oh, they have. It's happened a couple of times since I've known him, but he's too ornery to die."

"I'll be happy when you two sign off the Sacks case. With any luck, it will be a while before you hear from Brick again."

"That's about to happen. It's a case where no one wants to cooperate, and I, for one, will be happy to never hear about the Sacks again. Sorry the man was killed, but thus far, Brick has had us chasing our tails. I'm not sure why and don't care. He's a licensed PI, and it's his friend; he should be the one to investigate."

We stared out at the water, the waves lapping the beach — so quiet, except for the birds, and peaceful.

I tried to stand and didn't get far; Creole pulled me back down. "Where do you think you're going?"

I yawned, patting my mouth and making sound effects, much to Creole's amusement. "I think we need a nap."

"We just got up not that long ago."

"And turn off our phones, so we won't be disturbed."

He pushed me to my feet and grabbed the mugs and towel. "I'd race you, but you'd have an unfair advantage. My hands are full." He crouched.

"It would take more than that." I gave him a hard shove back onto the sand and took off running. I got about halfway back to the house before Creole's arm wrapped around me, twirling me around.

"You think you're getting away from me? Not happening."

Chapter Seventeen

Creole's and my time together at the beach house came to an end the next day, as Mother had planned a dinner party to celebrate Brad's new business venture. Attendance was mandatory, and to ensure that, knowing that Fab and I would have one good excuse or another for not showing up, Mother had contacted Creole and Didier and laid on the charm—some would say guilt—and they both agreed that we'd all make an appearance.

Bordello had inked a deal on a building on Ocean Boulevard in an upscale section of Miami Beach. This was the project my brother was eager to get started on. I was interested to know Brad's buy-in, but since he didn't volunteer it, I didn't ask. Money wasn't an issue for the Bordello family; when the background check came back, it had shown that the patriarch of the family was worth several billion and Bordello himself in the high millions.

Creole whistled as I came down the stairs in a black above-the-knee sheath dress. He held out his arms and twirled me off the bottom step, setting me on the floor with a kiss.

Didier gave me a thumbs up.

"You both look hot." I smiled at them. They were wearing suit pants and dress shirts, Creole in black and Didier in dark grey. "Where's Fab? Do I need to go back upstairs and kick the door?"

The guys laughed.

"I'm right here." Fab stood at the top of the stairs. From the way she eyed the banister, she was giving thought to sliding down.

I was about to point out that she had on a skin-tight dress and would have to hike it to her waist, showing more than she'd want Creole and I to see, when she walked sedately down, antic-free.

Fab eyed me curiously, and I knew she wanted to know if I was still mad.

As much as I might enjoy dragging out the drama, I was putting an end to it right now. "You owe a big thank you to Creole," I told her. "He pointed out that it would end up being a funny story in retrospect and I might as well speed up the timeline."

"Didier let me know that I handled the situation poorly." Fab grimaced. "And had I just asked, you would've agreed."

"That's optimistic of him."

Creole pinched my butt.

I congratulated myself for not jumping and held out my arms to Fab. "Kiss and make up."

"Maybe later."

Didier kissed her cheek and led her to the door and out to the car.

"You can kiss me." Creole winked, showing me the car keys he pulled out of his pocket.

Wait until Fab finds out. I briefly gave thought to laughing and instead grimaced; she wasn't going to be happy when she found out I didn't have the keys. From the look on her face, she was assuming I'd grab them off the counter and hand them over for her to drive, since everyone knew she was the self-proclaimed designated driver.

As we walked out to the car, Fab sent me an expectant look. The locks flew up, and I put on a neutral face, feigning ignorance, not wanting to weigh in on the who-drives war.

Didier must have known, as he assisted Fab into the back, but not before she shot burning arrows over her shoulder at Creole.

The inside of the car was silent until Creole pulled out onto the Overseas Highway.

"Are we all agreed that we're on our best behavior tonight?" Didier asked.

"Count me in, buddy," Creole said, a smirk in his voice.

"Yeah, sure," I answered.

I didn't know what Fab's response was, if any, as I didn't hear her say anything and I wasn't turning in my seat. I did reach over and flip on the radio, set to a music station that Fab liked.

The ride to Mother's was a short one. I handed over the security gate card; Creole didn't need to know that it was counterfeit. I could get a real one but had never asked.

The four of us got out of the car, not having far to go to get to the front of the building. I punched in the code Mother had given me. Tonight was not a good time to be pulling out a lockpick. We filed into the elevator and faced forward, no one saying a word on the trip up to the third floor.

When the doors opened, I said, "We're going to have a good time." All eyes turned to me, and I added, "Just thought I'd remind everyone."

Fab rang the doorbell several times, and when the door opened, Spoon was standing in the doorway with a big grin on his face. "How did I know it would be you four?"

My mother's bad-boy husband, Jimmy Spoon—although I'd never heard anyone call him Jimmy, not even Mother—was big and burly, with a "Don't mess with me" air that he could back up. Mother had been shopping again—he had on casual dress pants and a short-sleeved shirt. She'd confided that one of the perks she enjoyed as a married woman was shopping for her husband.

Mother met us in the hallway, kissing us. "Happy you're here," she said. "Wait until you see the food; Spoon did the cooking." She beamed up at him. "He wouldn't let me help."

"Nonsense," Spoon said, putting his arm around her. "She kept me company the entire time."

"Come." Mother motioned. "I want to introduce you. If you forget their names, just smile."

That was Mother's way of warning us that there were more people than we'd originally been told about.

Spoon took drink orders, tempting the guys with some new Euro beer that neither had tried. Fab and I asked for wine.

Out of the corner of my eye, I noticed Liam had come up alongside me. He threw his arms around me. "Won't this be boring for you?" I whispered in his ear.

"There's always some excitement at a family dinner. Besides, I haven't been home in a while; it will be good to see everyone. And I needed a break. You know college—studying and partying."

Liam had been unofficially adopted into the Westin family years back. Everyone treated him like the family favorite he was.

I recognized nearly everyone in the room. Brad and his girlfriend, Phil, who, I'd heard recently was using her full name, Philipa Grey, was more distinguished now that she was a lawyer. Bordello and his date, and another couple I'd never met. Turned out to be the CFO of Bordello Inc. and his wife. I found out that Brad's new title was President. From the empty drink glasses and plates of half-eaten appetizers, the rest of the guests had been here a while.

Somehow, Phil, Fab, and I ended up standing together.

"Did you wrangle a job with the company?" Fab asked.

Phil bristled. "I'm the Chief Counsel."

"That's nice," I said in a sweet tone.

Judging by her body language, she'd had enough of the two of us, and foregoing a graceful exit, she walked off.

"Nice seeing you again," Fab called after her.

Phil had worked at Jake's while in law school, and the three of us had formed a friendship. It ended when she hooked up with my brother... actually, a little before that, but I couldn't put my finger on the exact time.

"Remember your party manners," I reminded Fab.

She ignored me and scanned the room— something she had in common with Creole— always on the lookout for wanted people. I was fairly certain that if Fab didn't have the paperwork earning her the bounty, she wouldn't bother with the person; Creole would haul 'em off to jail regardless.

"Your mother has the patio doors closed, and you know we're sitting out there." Fab nodded across the room. "She's onto one of us for always changing the seating cards."

"One thing I know about Mother—she doesn't have it figured out or she would have confronted one or both of us already. If she ever figures out that we're both guilty, we'll never hear the end of it. Well, time for us to schmooze, or we'll hear about it later."

"I'm going to go find Didier; he's better at it than me."

"That's a good idea." I nudged her in the direction of the kitchen, where I'd last seen him and Creole.

Chapter Eighteen

The dinner was over and it went well, which was code for no squabbling at the table. Brad, his business partners, and their lady friends were seated down at the other end of the table, all with funny stories to tell. Once the laughter calmed down, Mother shepherded us back inside, wanting to toast Brad's success and that of the new company location.

Mother pulled me aside and apologized. "I know I've been favoring Brad of late. I only wanted to see him settled and happy. Now, I can start meddling in your life again."

I wrapped my arms around her and squeezed. A little too hard, I realized, when she made an oof sound. "You're a great mother, and Brad and I are the lucky ones."

As I crossed the room to Creole, Phil stepped in my path.

"You got the office building," she hissed at me. "Another thing you stole from Brad."

"I didn't steal a damn thing from Brad. There was a bidding process, and the highest bid won."

"No, it did not." Phil poked her finger at me. "I know for a fact that your bid wasn't the highest, and it won anyway. More of that folksy charm of yours winning the day."

"This is a dinner party to celebrate Brad's recent success and not the time or place to air your ridiculous grievances. The last thing Brad would want is to be embarrassed by you making a scene," I hissed back, looking over her shoulder, noticing that so far we hadn't attracted any attention.

Phil leaned in. "If you don't want Brad to find out that you're the worst sister and possibly forever change his opinion of you—and who knows, he might even end your pitiful relationship—you'll owe me. When I call, you deliver."

"You're blackmailing me?" I shouted and, without thinking, pushed her back out of my face, not expecting her to land in a nearby armchair and roll off onto the floor.

A rule high on my list was to never succumb to blackmail. It was never a one-time deal.

A deafening silence descended over the room, all eyes turned on the two of us. My wall of strength appeared behind me, and I stepped back against Creole's chest.

Phil got up off the floor, straightening her clothes. Brad, who moved as quickly as Creole, put his arm around his girlfriend.

"What the hell is going on?" Brad demanded in an attempted whisper.

"She attacked me." Phil wiped her eyes. "I

asked Madison if it was true that she acquired the dock office building, and she leapt at me, screaming blackmail." She sobbed and buried her face in Brad's chest.

Good one! Even with her face averted, I'd bet she didn't have tear one in her eyes, unless she'd perfected a way to squeeze out phony ones.

"You're a bald-faced liar," I seethed. "You've got your story turned around. You were the one who said you'd ruin my relationship with Brad if I didn't come running when you called. And you might have had a chance at the property if you hadn't shown up graveside at the funeral and had the nerve to approach the grieving widow and hand out your damn business card." Out of the corner of my eye, I saw Fab lift her fists, letting me know that if I didn't want to beat the hell out of Phil, she would.

"You're the one who's a liar." Phil spit.

Good thing her aim was off. "The only one lying is you, and I can prove it."

"Madison, please stop," Brad pleaded quietly.

Fab stepped into the ring. "You all might as well know—Madison didn't buy that building, I did... for my new business."

Now all eyes turned to the Frenchwoman, who faced the room, smiling over her acquisition. Most still hadn't said a word, not even a whisper.

Mother broke the silence. "Let's get the drinks refilled." She signaled to Spoon, who was leaning against the kitchen doorjamb, arms crossed, assessing the situation.

Bordello clapped. "Congratulations on your acquisition. Both of them." He bowed slightly. "Now that coup requires a toast."

The tension lessened, but just barely.

"You okay?" Creole whispered in my ear.

I nodded.

Spoon didn't ask; he just distributed fresh drinks, taking away old glasses. He returned to Mother's side, and she pretended a big scene hadn't just taken place in middle of her living room.

Mother raised her glass. "I want to thank all of you for coming to celebrate the latest acquisitions." She then toasted Brad and Bordello and, with a smile, included Fab.

I was only half-listening. Brad and Bordello had toasts of their own, and thankfully, I remembered to tip my glass at the appropriate moments.

Fab moved to my side. "Hold onto your curls," she whispered. "I have a toast." She tipped her glass to the woman who'd been introduced as Nicole. "To Bordello's *date*. Apparently, he didn't kill her after her failed attempt on his life."

Nicole shot her a confused stare. Guess she'd forgotten her name was Jane. "Jane Jones"—the name she'd given when she checked into the hospital the night of the accident. It hadn't registered during introductions that she was the biker on the road that night, in part because the striking blonde was now brunette.

"You tried to kill Bordello?" the CFO asked Nicole in a shocked tone.

This party had already hit rock bottom and was about to descend to a new low. I caught Liam's grin from across the room.

"Who's spreading that bull—?" Bordello caught himself. "As I recall the accident..." He pointed at Fab and I. "...they're the ones that had their guns drawn. I'm certain they were following me, since I don't believe in chance."

"You were following him?" Anger radiated from Brad's body.

"Actually, we thought he was following us," I said. "Or rather she was." Brad responded with a snort. "A motorcycle blew by us, hot on the tail of a Ferrari, which turned out to belong to your sidekick." I ignored the growl that came from Bordello and didn't venture so much as a peek at Brad. "Nicole here, or Jane, as she was known that night at the hospital... but then you knew that, didn't you?" I leveled a stare at Bordello, which he returned with added menace. "Where was I? Oh, yes, the gun sticking out of the waistband of her jeans caught our attention, that and she took a nasty spill on the roadway right in front of us. We stopped to assist, as any decent citizen would."

"So, a thank you for saving your life sounds in

order," Creole spoke up, his blue eyes turned dark, boring into Bordello.

I wanted to kiss him so bad. I'd have to tell him how hot it was for your boyfriend to stick up for you in a less-than-friendly atmosphere. Later. I sighed.

"That's a highly exaggerated account of what went down that night, and had Nicole died, you two would be in jail facing manslaughter charges for your road antics," Bordello asserted.

"You're a dumbass," I snapped back. "If she'd died, you wouldn't have had to look any further than the mirror to know who was at fault. Whatever you did to her must have been a doozy for her to chase you down the highway to put a bullet in your brain. And that's what she was getting ready to do."

That brought a new round of awkward silence.

Mother to the rescue. "That calls for another toast." She looked completely flustered. "To everyone's good health."

"Love your mother," Creole laughed in my ear. "I admire her attempts to get this party back on an even keel when it's clearly sailed into the sunset."

Not willing to let it go, Brad said, "I realize that you and Fab..." He leveled an angry stare at me. "...blame Bordello for all the petty crimes in the Cove, but it has to stop. Why? Bordello is well respected, a pillar of the community. He subsidizes the library, the blood bank, and the list goes on. Stop harassing the man. Do it because he's been a great friend to me."

"Heaven help us," I said in a voice I thought was only loud enough for Creole to hear. But I was wrong; Brad heard and glared. It didn't help that I couldn't come up with even one little thing to say that would smooth the waters.

"I think it's time to break up this little party," Brad said.

"Don't stop all the fun on our account," Fab said, holding up the car keys. "We're leaving."

How did she get those?

As if reading my mind, Creole whispered, "She asked nicely, and I handed them over."

"Before we go." I pushed away from Creole, holding up my wine glass, announcing to the room, "One last toast."

"Maybe another time, Madison." Mother rolled her eyes in exasperation, an expression that she'd forbidden Brad and I from making as teenagers.

"Now's a perfect time — we're all gathered here, one big group," I practically cooed. "This is a big announcement — huge." I threw my arms wide, wine sloshing over the rim of my glass. "I love you, brother dear."

Brad groaned. "Please." He held up his hand. "Whatever it is, I don't want to hear it."

"It's a happy announcement… at least, I think so." I faux pouted.

"You're pregnant," Mother gasped.

There were more than a few smirks in the room.

Creole chuckled in my ear. "You would tell me first, wouldn't you?"

"Someone's family is expanding... or already has." I loved the confused expressions. "For those of you that didn't know, our own Philipa and Bordello... are brother and sister. Now, isn't that interesting?"

The silence didn't last long. "What is the matter with you?" Bordello demanded, not expecting or wanting an answer.

It was easy to ignore the ever-pompous Bordello and turn my attention to my brother. Brad's mouth had dropped open. After a short pause, as though he were digesting my announcement, his hand shot out, grabbing Phil by the arm, and he dragged her out to the patio without a word, Phil screeching, "Brad."

Bordello flashed me a *drop dead now* look.

I responded with a smile that conveyed, *no, you drop dead*.

"You didn't tell your best friend?" Fab said to me in a surly tone. "You better have a good explanation, but in the meantime, it's time to get out while we can."

Mother made her way across the room and hugged me. "Are you sure?" she whispered. I nodded. "Well, that's a doozy."

Just when I think I've personally set my own

mother's hair on fire, she comes through calm and collected. But hadn't she always? Even when I was a child, she was calm under stress. I'd always known her to be unwavering in the middle of chaos.

"I'll make this up to you," I whispered back.

"You sure as heck will. Lunch and a shopping day, and you will fill me in on everything else I don't know — the long version. You better go before Brad comes back inside. This has been enough excitement for tonight. If we had a larger family, we'd be the talk of the town for years." She pushed me toward the hallway, meeting up with Fab, Didier, and Creole at the door. She kissed us all.

"Drive safe." She shook her finger at Fab as the elevator doors opened.

* * *

We hustled to the car like thieves in the night. As Fab left the complex, turning out onto the road, we agreed to wait until we got home to rehash the events of the evening.

Surprisingly, Fab didn't drive like a maniac, though thanks to light traffic, we still made it home quickly.

I was happy to finally pull into the driveway. Once inside, I kicked off my shoes and headed to the refrigerator for water to dilute the wine upsetting my stomach... or, more likely, nerves from the spectacle of the evening. I grabbed enough for everyone. Creole and I settled on the daybed, Fab and Didier on the couch.

Didier spoke first. "Who's going to be the first to ask what the heck happened back there? I guess it's me."

"That's the most drama-filled dinner yet." Creole laughed. "The fallout, though..." He whooshed.

"Forget starting at the beginning," Fab said. "What the heck was that with Phil, and why didn't I know?" She practically yelled the last words.

Didier tightened his hold, kissing the top of her head.

"As you know — probably not the guys — I had a background check run on Philipa not long after she hooked up with my brother. By then, her personality had taken a one-eighty, and knowing his penchant for unstable women, I thought it was better to discover if she had a trip or two to the looney bin in her past before they got too involved. It came back squeaky clean, which might surprise all of you; it did make me happy and relieved." I took a drink of my water. "A month ago, I got an envelope in the mail, and inside was another report — updated possibly, but more likely just not scrubbed as clean as the first one."

"From whom?" Fab asked.

"No clue. Sent anonymously," I said, but since

it had been delivered with nothing but my name on the envelope, I knew it was probably from GC. "Phil and Bordello share the same father, and they found about each other back when she was still in high school. When Phil was still very young, her mother left Bordello Sr., taking her daughter and moving to another state. Not long after, she remarried and the stepfather adopted Phil."

"Bordello Sr. must have been a bastard," Creole said.

"He's got a well-known reputation as a tough-as-steel political fixer; not a single mention of him being a nice man." I tipped my head back on Creole's chest and sighed. "I suck as a friend and sister. I shouldn't have blurted it out that way."

"That latter bit is harsh," Didier said. "But yeah, knowing Brad, he would have listened if you'd told him in private, and then he could have asked his questions, if he wanted answers, without an audience. I doubt it will break them up."

"I don't like the chaos Bordello's appearance at family dinners stirs up, the choosing of sides," Creole said.

"There's more," I said.

Fab made a shocked face.

"More drama, secrets." Creole shook his head. "I want to hear the rest."

Didier chuckled. "I never thought a drama-ridden family would appeal, but now I'm always wondering what's coming next."

"You have me to thank for that, getting you all broken in; almost nothing surprises you anymore." Fab smiled up at him.

"Favorite employee Phil used Jake's from day one as a front for her information business, long before she asked me if it was okay," I continued. "Not sure why she bothered asking, unless she thought she was on the verge of being found out. It's my understanding that her clients showed up after hours. Her largest was her slimy brother. I can't play holier than thou, since we used her on many an occasion, but on our cases, no one ended up dead as a result. Not sure the same can be said for her other clients, as they largely ran illegal enterprises, according to the report. Another large client was the head of a motorcycle gang and another bestie of Bordello's."

"My character radar was way off," Fab said.

I nodded. How many times since I read the report had I thought the same thing?

"Consider yourself lucky," Creole said. "If Jake's had been linked to a crime—or worse, been the scene of a murder—it would've been shut down permanently and you'd have needed a damn good lawyer."

"You've turned Jake's into a moneymaker, and I know you have a special affinity for it, as it's one of the properties you inherited from your aunt. She'd be proud," Didier said. "I'd suggest not letting anyone run businesses of any kind out of the bar in the future."

"Madison and I trusted Phil," Fab said, not over the shock of the news. "Did Phil really try to blackmail you?"

"Sure did. I couldn't believe it myself. In exchange for her silence on the office building deal, she wanted me to jump at the snap of her fingers. To do what, I wonder? Her errands? Maybe she was looking for free investigations." I shuddered to think what kinds of jobs she might have thrown my way. "She thought I bought the office buildings; she had no clue you're the new owner. I bet whoever she paid for that information gets an irate phone call."

"You think she still uses GC?" Fab asked.

Not wanting to divulge my suspicions that the report came from GC—I mean, who else?—I didn't answer that, but dropped another interesting factoid instead. "While doing a little digging on Phil, I brought her name up to your good friend, Gunz, and he confided that they'd had some kind of falling out. From the set of his jaw and his clipped tone when he related the briefest of details, it won't be smoothed over anytime soon. The report could possibly have his fingerprints on it."

"Gunz and I have been friends a long time," Fab said. "He's a bit rough around the edges, but he's as loyal as they come. Not one of those people who says 'call me' and then doesn't give you their number."

"Since he and I called a truce, we've only hit stumbling blocks on an occasion or two, and I smoothed it right out by threatening to sic you on him."

Fab responded with a right cross in the air.

Didier caught her fist, kissing her knuckles. "Your mother took the drama well."

"And Spoon enjoyed the show." Creole chuckled. "Caught him choking back laughter a couple of times and figured out Bordello wasn't high on his admiration list. He finally caught on that he was being watched and gave me the finger."

"Now, all I need is for Brad to forgive me so we can kiss and make up. I don't want to be on the outs with my brother."

"Here's something I agree with Creole on..." Fab made a face. "...and you know how I hate to do that. This was the best Westin dinner ever."

Chapter Nineteen

I told myself to breathe and ignore the annoyance of Fab intermittently honking the horn in an unsubtle attempt to get me to move it for an unspecified job that required business dress and no flip-flops after we got to Miami Beach. Hence, my black pencil skirt and white button-down dress shirt.

I slung my new purse over my shoulder—the one Fab had insisted I purchase—shut the front door, marched to the car, slid in, and slammed the car door.

"Okay, I get it; I'm annoying. But I did it for you."

Glaring, I cocked my head, telegraphing, *Sure you did*.

"Hurrying you along means we have time to stop for lattes. My treat, of course."

Her sweet smile set off an alarm bell. What was she up to now? "In that case, I'll load up on a box of danishes. Even if I don't eat them, the guys will wolf them down." No argument. Hmm. "You're up to something; don't bother denying it. The job? Are we on our way to commit a felony?"

"I'll explain the job after we have our lattes."

I gave her the evil eye and rolled down the window, hanging my head out. Fresh salty air cured a lot of things, including Fab's antics. Another red flag on the mounting stack—Fab didn't complain and demand I power the window back up.

Fab pulled into the drive-thru and ordered our lattes, ignoring my request for a dozen cinnamon rolls and getting me an apple muffin, as they were out of my favorite kind.

"I'd rather have cookies, cheapskate." I turned away. To my surprise, she changed the order.

As soon as she handed me my cup, I snapped off the lid and inhaled, licking whipped cream off the top. Fab held out the box of cookies, which I ignored. She turned and placed them on the back seat.

Once we hit the highway and headed north, Fab said, "Mr. Coker is an old client; I did a couple of jobs for him in the past."

"Coker as in Coker Industries?" I asked. When she didn't answer, I let out a low whistle. "The names on your roster of old clients never fail to impress me. Against my better judgment, I'm going to ask, what did you do for him in the past?"

"Retrieval jobs."

"A little breaking and entering? Scaling the side of a building? Parachuting off the roof onto a patio?"

"That was in the old days." She hit the gas. The sports car in the lane next to her had apparently challenged her to a race in that subtle gunning-of-the-engine way, and she took the driver up on his invitation, pressing the pedal to the floor, eliciting a screech of tires.

I made a barfing noise that I'd perfected. It now sounded more like the real thing, as opposed to a cat coughing up a rodent.

"I'm slowing down," she grouched. "You suck the fun out of everything."

"This case is about...?"

"Mr. Coker is having neighbor issues. He owns a waterfront townhome that he bought as a party place for him and his other single male friends. Turns out the woman across the sidewalk can see into his bathroom and has taken pictures of his private parts. He claims he didn't know about the view."

"That must be some window. I'm assuming you suggested window coverings?" I said.

"That ship has sailed. She not only took pictures, she threatened to post them."

"Did the threat come with a warning to put a covering on the glass?"

She didn't answer that. "He ignored her, thinking she was mad because he wasn't interested in her, and didn't take her threat seriously until one was hung up at the mailboxes."

I had a good idea what the man wanted—a

breaking-and-entering felony—but waited for Fab to tell me.

"We're splitting up on this job. A meeting has been set up between Mr. Coker and the neighbor, Susan East, at a sidewalk café to try to come to an agreement. She refused to go to his office. He wants me to negotiate a settlement, and he'll agree to some small figure. He also wants her apartment searched for any more pictures and a virus installed on her computer."

"Hmm…" I rubbed my forehead. In response to her unspoken *What are you doing?* I said, "Seeing into the near future. I'm receiving a vision about how this will shake out. I'll be negotiating with Susan, and you'll be tossing her place."

Fab nodded.

"Twenty bucks says Didier doesn't know what you're up to today. No hot sex for you." I shook my finger. At her outraged look, I added, "Just repeating what you tell me." Another glare. "I have a few stipulations of my own before agreeing to go along with this." Waving off her complaints, I continued, "You will not go off on your criminal pursuit until we're certain this Susan person is at the café. When she leaves, I'll text you, and you won't dawdle showing back up. Got it?"

"Great minds thinking the same thing. You're going to have to smooth over the bit where Mr. Coker isn't going to be showing and keep her talking as long as you can. I don't need to tell you how do that."

"Have your phone available, in case I need a few tips. If Miss East is part-nutjob, that will make it easier for me."

"Seriously, you've come a long way under my tutelage."

I snorted. "You'd think the memories would make me all warm and fuzzy, but nope, thinking about past jobs, I do believe my hair is standing on end."

Fab handed me her phone. "Her picture is attached to the first message."

I clicked through her phone. "Ordinary looking, nothing conveying crazy, but then, it's only a picture."

"What are you doing?" Fab held out her hand and snapped her fingers.

"I'm forwarding this message to my phone, since it has the woman's information, in case, as in most of our jobs, something goes awry." I heard my phone ping and handed hers back.

Fab exited the Causeway and made her way over to a quiet side street in South Beach. She slowed and pointed out a laidback sidewalk cafe before making a U-turn, hugging the curb on the opposite side of the street. The eatery must be a local favorite, as most of the seats were filled.

"That's her." Fab pointed.

"Because it's the only woman sitting by herself?" I couldn't see around Fab, and the back window didn't offer a good view. "Drop me off farther down the block so she doesn't see me getting out and the SUV disappearing and start wondering who's behind the wheel."

I pulled my phone out of my purse, prepping a message to send to Fab. She drove to the corner, out of sight of the restaurant, and pulled over. I sent my flip-flops airborne, slipped into a pair of heels, and got out. Before I closed the door, I reminded Fab, "Let's not deviate from the plan."

As Fab pulled away, I let out calming breath, thinking that I should sign up for yoga or something. It had been a while since we'd done something that crossed that grey line. I didn't know if I was having an attack of nerves or an adrenaline rush.

Not wanting to give Ms. East an excuse to get up and leave, I hustled up the street. Entering the restaurant, I assured the hostess I was meeting someone and nodded in the direction of the outdoor patio.

I walked up to the table and smiled down at her surprised look. "Susan East?" At her nod, I pulled out a chair and, before sitting, ordered an iced tea from a passing server. "I'm here on Mr. Coker's behalf, in the hopes that we can come to a mutual agreement." I sat before she could tell me to take a hike.

A middle-aged woman with a short, curly grey wash-and-no-style hairdo, Susan was wearing a conservative polyester pantsuit with a jacket, even in this heat. "I didn't want this face-to-face meeting." She scowled. "But Coker insisted, and now I'm here and he's not. What a coward. I should've known he'd screw me." She shoved her chair back.

"Hear me out." I patted the table. "You know how men are—they hate emotional scenes of any kind. Let's get this settled today and put it all behind us." I pasted on my pretend smile.

"I'll listen," she said sullenly. "But I'm not making any promises."

"None expected. I've been apprised of the details, so we can skip the recap." Probably not all of them, and I hoped that didn't come back to bite me. "I would like to hear your side of the story. I'm certain a nice woman like you must have some justification. Then we can discuss terms."

The waiter delivered my tea and refilled hers, asking if we were ready to order.

"We're not here to eat," Susan snapped. "This will be all. Bring a check." She moved her chair within reach of her glass.

The disgust on the young man's face at learning that one of his prime tables had been taken by a pair of squatters with a five-buck tab had me wincing. I tried to smile reassuringly, but he ignored me. I'd make sure the tip more than made up for his restraint, in that he'd like to kick us to the curb and couldn't.

As soon as he was out of earshot, Susan started talking. "Mr. Coker may be some big wheel in business, but he's the worst neighbor ever." Her nose turned up. "Wild parties—and not just on the weekends—drinking, smoking, loud voices until the early hours of the morning. I finally got sick of it and called the man on it, telling him some people worked for a living and needed their sleep. He cussed me out in terms no one's ever called me before."

"I can understand how that would be upsetting. What happened next? Did he quiet down?"

"Oh, heck no, it got worse. I couldn't take another night, so I confronted him and threatened to call the police. Coker called my bluff, except I wasn't bluffing and two uniformed officers showed up at my house. They listened to my complaint and then talked to him. When they came back, they said there was nothing they could do. He called me a liar and said that none of what I told them ever happened. He also told them that the neighbors gave me a wide berth because I constantly made unfounded accusations. That's another big fat lie. I've lived in the complex for years and never had a problem with anyone... that is, until he moved in. The cops called it a 'he said, she said' situation."

"Did things calm down after that?"

"It got worse, and he started stalking me.

Somehow, he knew when I was outside and would come out and stare while I worked on my plants or read a book, minding my own damn business. I even complained to the property manager, but that man's a coward."

"So, in retaliation, you took naked pictures?"

"Noo," Susan ground out, jaw clenched. "I went to close my bedroom blinds, and there he was, standing in the bathroom window—always thought that window was to a bedroom—his, uhm… well, it was in his hand. At first, I thought he was doing his business, and then realized he was… well, other things."

My cheeks burned along with hers. It reminded me of the neighbor whose bathroom window backed up to the side of The Cottages. He liked to shoot his urine out the window and had to contort his body to accomplish the show.

"I mentioned to Coker that he could be seen urinating from the sidewalk and suggested he get window coverings, and he exploded. After that, every time I was in my bedroom, there he was in the window. He knew I was taking the pictures; he made sure I got good shots. I suppose men think one side is better than the other and not that they all look the same."

Unsure how to respond, I took a long drink of iced tea. "And you thought it was a good idea to post a couple. Why?"

"I was sick of seeing him and thought he'd stop if I made his behavior public. Boy, did that backfire, and fast." She brushed her curls away from her face in a frustrated gesture. "I came home from work one night, and he came out of nowhere and got in my face, spitting the ugliest language. He backed me up against the bumper of my car. I hit the alarm and jumped in, locking the door. By the time I stopped shaking, he'd disappeared again. I finally got the courage to get out of my car with my phone in my hand, ready to call 911 if I saw him again."

"Did you?"

"Not that night. A couple of nights later, he was standing on the landing at his front door, chatting with a neighbor, and the bastard put on a big smile and waved, saying, 'Good to see you, Susan. Hope all's going well.' The other neighbor, who I barely knew, also waved." She waved the waiter down and asked for another refill. If looks could kill, he would have ended Coker's problem right there.

She sucked down half her glass of tea and banged it down on the table. "I'm afraid to go outside, and no longer enjoy my evenings reading. I hired one of my neighbors who's retired to walk my dogs. Told her I had brought home a lot of work from the office; she knows I work from home some days. All of my blinds are closed tight. It's like I'm a prisoner."

Much as I wanted to sympathize with her, I couldn't afford to. "How do we settle this? Any deal would have to include no more pictures."

"I want him out—as in he moves. Googled his net worth; he can afford a party house somewhere else, and with property values rising, he can afford the cost of moving. I cannot. I've lived there for ten years and have friends close by, and like I said, I can't afford the expense of a move."

"Coker moves, and you hand over the pictures and any files?" I pulled my phone out of my purse.

"I'll turn them over the day the moving van arrives."

I called Fab, who answered on the second ring. "I'd like to speak to Mr. Coker. This is Gertrude; he's expecting my call." Once again, my phony name came in handy. Fab had chosen it for me. I looked up in time to catch Susan's snicker.

"I'm about ready to leave," Fab said. "You got me a deal?"

I almost laughed. "I do. Ms. East wants you to move out and will hand over all files on moving day."

"I'll call you back. I'm going to advise him to take the deal, in case she has a backup I couldn't find."

I hung up and set my phone on the table, my hand over the screen. "He'll be calling back."

"What's he up to now?" Susan demanded.

"Calm down. While we're waiting for the return call, this gives us an opportunity to talk about *your* liability issues. Posting pictures of

Coker that you took through a window of his house leaves you open to criminal charges, such as possible sex crimes, and if that led to a guilty verdict, it would require you to register as a sex offender." Fab should warn Coker that his antics could also end in him having to register for exposing himself.

"I don't believe you." Susan paled.

"Consult a criminal lawyer. I'm certain he'd recommend that the two of you reach an amicable solution. I'm not a lawyer, but a mutual resolution is in the best interests of you both. Yes, you could smear his reputation, create a PR nightmare. But he's a powerful man to make an enemy of, and guaranteed, he'd come after you. You're running the risk of your reputation also ending up in tatters. Right now, you have him spooked, but why have his legal team come after you, possibly putting you in jail? End this, and you two can pretend that you never met."

My phone rang. Susan jumped. "Yes, Mr. Coker," I answered.

"The 'For Sale' sign is going up tomorrow," Fab said when I answered.

I looked up at Susan's expectant face and asked, "Can I tell Mr. Coker that it's agreed that neither of you will speak of the incident, ever? It's not like you run in the same circles, so chances are, you won't run into one another again. And you agree to hand over all files on moving day." Again, she nodded. "She's agreed," I said to Fab.

"I'll tell him. I'll be there in ten to pick you up. Walk to the same corner and stick your thumb out. I don't usually pick up hitchhikers, but for you, I'll make an exception." Fab hung up.

"Mr. Coker is putting the place on the market immediately," I said to Susan. "Since it's a great area, I'm sure it will sell fast." I handed her one of Fab's and my old business cards—the one that had only a phone number on it and rang through to a phone that was automatically answered, with a message sent to both of us. "If there are any issues, just call this number." I picked up the check.

"How can you stand working for that man?"

"Like you, I work from home a lot." I pushed my chair back and smiled, then went to find the server, who was standing by the bus cart, laughing it up with another server. I handed him the check and enough money to make his day a good one. I'd be sure and bill Fab.

"Thank you," he sputtered.

I couldn't wait to get out of the restaurant and my shoes. By the time I circled around the hostess stand, got back out to the sidewalk, and turned, Susan had disappeared. There must have been a back entrance.

While I waited for Fab, I decided I'd stress to her that Coker honor the deal with no waffling. She might remind him that once you lose your reputation, it's impossible to buy back and suggest he throw in a few bucks, since Susan's computer was now ruined. That was doable without appearing guilty.

Chapter Twenty

Creole and I sat at the kitchen island, enjoying a last cup of coffee. I planned to take the day off and only be available in case of emergency. Creole tipped back on his stool, staring out the garden window. "The duo just returned."

I recognized the roar of the Porsche as it flew into the driveway. The extra gun of the engine let anyone listening know that Fab was behind the wheel. The two early birds generally left at the crack of dawn and went in to their office, Fab returning mid-morning and Didier in the late afternoon, depending on their appointments.

Fab and Didier strolled through the front door holding hands, the picture of casual business elegance. They always dressed to go to the office, clients or no.

"You're both here," Fab said with a smile.

"Wonder how she figured that out?" I asked Creole with a roll of my eyes. "Both of our cars are parked outside."

Creole slid off his stool and onto the one next to me. "She's up to something," he whispered.

I leaned forward and brushed his lips with

mine, then flashed a smile.

"Enough of that," Fab scolded and sat opposite us.

Didier reached into the refrigerator, grabbing cold drinks for himself and Fab. "Let's go for a run," he said to Creole. "I'll try not to leave you in the sand."

"I've almost got my game back." Creole flexed his muscles. "Then watch out, buddy."

"I've got exciting news," Fab said, and all eyes turned to her.

"I'll bet," I groaned.

"I got you your own case." She slapped a piece of paper down in front of me.

I glanced down briefly. "That's so sweet," I said sarcastically. "Can't *wait* to hear the details."

Creole and Didier laughed. From their expressions, they were hoping for our version of a girl fight — sarcasm with no bodily harm.

"You're going to love this one. Thought of you when I got the call."

"I bet. At some point, you're going to have to get to the details. Or do I have time for a swim?"

"You know how you're always saying we should take cat cases?"

At the word "cats," Jazz and Snow wandered in. Jazz let out an ear-splitting howl, translated as, "Treat time." For an old cat pushing a hundred, he could be loud. His girlfriend, half his age, waited patiently while he made a scene.

Didier stood. "I don't want to miss a word, so

give me a minute." He reached in the refrigerator, taking out a can and spooning it into their dishes.

Cats! Now that's a job I'd like. Unless there were nine hundred of them and they all needed homes.

"Where was I?" Fab smiled coyly. "Ah yes, cats or, in this case, a dog." Apparently noticing the narrowing of my eyes, she hurriedly went on. "You know my friend, the one that lives around the corner?"

"Friend?" I asked in confusion. "I thought I was your only friend. Now I have competition? Who the hell is it, and why haven't I met this person?"

Creole pulled me to his side, laughing in my ear.

"You've met him. Well, sort of," Fab insisted.

"A man?" Didier demanded. "You better have a good explanation." Despite his tone, you couldn't miss the upturned corners of his mouth.

"You're the only man I love or will ever love." Fab flashed her sexy smile.

I let out a cat-barf noise.

Creole grinned, shaking his finger at me.

"You remember Hank Roberts—he lives a block over?"

Better at names than Fab, I racked my brain. "The old man? The one you flirt with by honking at him, rolling down the car window, and yelling to get out of the street? I'm surprised you haven't scared him to an early death. That one?"

"He's a very sweet man. His Maltese, Maddie, is missing. Reminded me of your mother, and I asked if he knew her, thinking the dog might be named after her. But no."

I put my head on the counter and laughed, conjuring up the image of Mother's face as she was told there was a dog named after her. It would help that it was a cute, white, fluffy one.

Creole patted me on the back.

I straightened. "What do you want me to do? Find it? How? Door-to-door search?"

"Hank has walked his neighborhood for two days without luck. That's when he called me. I'm going to go get a picture to make flyers, and I thought you could ride along so I can introduce you."

"That's nice of you." I'd rather go buy a lookalike dog, but with my luck, the original would show up and I'd be left to explain. "How did Maddie go missing? I don't want to hear that the little dog was running the streets."

"Hank let her out in his fenced yard, as he does every morning. The phone rang, he went in to answer it, and when he came back—which he says was only a minute or two, as there was no one on the phone—the dog had vanished. He thinks someone set him up to steal it."

"Has he checked the animal shelter?" Didier asked.

"We don't have one in the Cove; he'd have to go up to Homestead," I said.

"Hank says dognapping is big business. Thought he'd get a ransom call, and when he didn't get one right away, figured whoever stole Maddie doesn't have any intention of returning her."

"Well…" I lifted my face to Creole's. "…what do you think?"

"Possibly someone stole her to keep as a pet. Or, like cars, someone is stealing to fill an order. Didn't hear anything while I was on the force about dog theft being a problem. I can make a call for you."

"What's the job pay? Enough for me to hire backup?"

"Backup." Fab snorted.

"Yes, but only because it's one of your cases, which means that if the unexpected can happen, it will."

"You need to get changed for the appointment," Fab directed.

I looked down, smoothing out my bathing suit cover-up. "You, too. Dress and heels aren't appropriate for an animal case. I'm certain you don't want to come back covered in dog hair." I reached out and tugged on Creole's hand. He stood. "You need to change, too, so you can outrun Didier's ass on the beach."

Creole grinned.

"You have a half-hour before I come kicking the door down," Fab said.

* * *

Creole and I made it back downstairs with minutes to spare. The guys promised pizza for dinner and went out the back and down to the beach.

It took less than five minutes to get to Mr. Roberts' white, cottage-style house surrounded by a white picket fence.

A grey-haired man in his seventies in khakis and a t-shirt came down the walkway, opening the gate as we parked in front. He had a big smile and a hug for Fab.

She introduced us.

"Your red hair reminds me of my Myrtle." He winked.

"Where did you last see Maddie?" I took out my phone, snapping a couple of pictures of the yard. I had no plan, not even a good idea where to start.

"Let her out the back like I always do and left her chasing after her ball when I went into the house. Came out and she was gone. Checked the gate, and it was closed; I never lock it. It happened fast."

"Anyone else around here complain about missing a dog?" I asked.

Mr. Roberts shook his head.

"Don't worry." Fab patted his arm. "We'll find Maddie."

I hoped she was right and not giving the man

false hope.

"I'm going inside to get a picture of the dog. Be right back out," Fab announced as the two walked back up the walkway.

The yard was well kept; the mostly green grass hadn't been allowed to grow into a field of weeds. I walked the perimeter, looking for holes in the fence, and found none. There was no other gate; the only other way out would be through the garage.

Going back to the front, I scanned the street. It was typical for the neighborhood—a few new houses, but most were original construction; nothing overly fancy. I walked up to the corner and back, and not only didn't spot a single person outside, but no animals either. By the time I got back, Fab and Hank were waiting.

My phone beeped, and Fab held hers up, indicating she'd sent pictures.

Before getting into the car, I turned and asked, "Have you seen any strange cars or people hanging around the neighborhood?"

Hank shook his head. "Not sure I would've noticed before, but I'm keeping my eyes open now. If I see anyone lurking about, I'll get a license number."

"You be careful," Fab lectured gently. "You are not to approach anyone. You leave that to one of us."

I couldn't hear what she said next, but whatever it was put a smile on the man's face.

Hank waved, and I waved back and jumped into the SUV. When Fab slid behind the wheel, I said, "Whoever stole his dog—and that's most likely what happened—Maddie's not coming back." It was clear she didn't like my assessment. "I've got several places to contact before calling it case closed."

"This is why you're the right woman for this job. I wouldn't know where to start."

Chapter Twenty-One

I had the house to myself. As usual, Fab and Didier had left early, with Creole not long after — he had enrolled in the necessary classes to get his licenses. I showered and dressed in a pair of Creole's sweats, rolled up to just under my knees, and a t-shirt. Setting my coffee on the island, I spread out the notes that I'd scribbled all over and then had to retrieve a pad to make another list so I could make sense of everything. Fishing my phone out of my pocket, I added it to the pile. I could have claimed an official office in Fab's building, but I preferred my kitchen. I could sit on a stool and put my feet up on another one, not to mention not having to dress up.

Scooting my notepad in front of me, I poked at it with my pen. Earlier, not sure why, I'd flipped open my laptop and typed in "stolen dogs," and to my surprise, in addition to a ton of articles to choose from, there was one result that stood out — a top-ten list of desirable breeds for resale. The Maltese had been included in that group. I'd never have guessed that that criminal enterprise could be so lucrative. Unable to find any information about missing dogs in Tarpon Cove, I called a shelter where I knew the owner. When I first identified myself, her tone was noticeably cool, but once she realized I wasn't calling for emergency rescue of a truckload of dogs and cats, as I'd done in the past, she warmed up.

Brenda confirmed what I'd researched. "There's dognapping. That's a popular scam where they steal highly sought-after breeds, generally the small ones, and then ransom them back."

"If someone stole my dog, I'd agree to their terms and then get the police involved."

"That would be a difficult crime to prove, unless you have a camera set up in your yard. Some contact the owner and demand a finder's fee; others wait for a reward poster to go up and then call, haggling on the amount offered. In those cases, when asked where they got the dog, the answer is generally the same: 'found it wandering in the street.'"

"I'll be posting reward posters today and see if that gets us a call."

"There's also dog flipping, and since we're talking a Maltese, it's highly possible that your dog could have been stolen to fill an order and re-homed. Big money in that one... to the right buyer. Another avenue for flipping is procuring and selling dogs for fighting, but yours wouldn't fit in that category."

"This has been an enlightening conversation." I'd discovered new levels to which people would sink, and it made me sad.

"There's also the chance that someone stole the dog because they wanted it for a pet and couldn't afford the fee a dog breeder would charge." Someone in the background yelled her name. "Good luck getting your Malty back," she said, her tone conveying *probably not going to happen*.

I thanked her for her time, and we hung up. Since it had been a couple of days and still no sign of Maddie, it wouldn't surprise me if the dog had already been sold to a new owner. I hoped the other party had no clue they were buying stolen property and would treat her well.

A more gruesome alternative entered my head. I called Animal Control, and to my relief, no dogs, dead or alive, had been picked up in the last week.

Next call, I hit speed dial. As soon as the call connected, I said, "I've got a freebie for you." Nervy, but then, I had plenty of audacity.

"Free doesn't pay my bills." GC's words dripped in sarcasm. "You're the only one I know who has brass enough to call with such a request."

"Consider it character building." Cutting off his response, I asked, "Know anything about stealing dogs for profit?" I went on to tell him the story of Maddie and her broken-hearted owner.

After a moment of silence, he said, "Yes," grimly. "Dirty business."

"In Tarpon?"

"Close enough."

"Why in the heck haven't you done something to stop it?"

"That's my ear you're yelling into," GC grumped. "This is not the do-gooder hotline. Besides, those people carry guns and I have other reasons, and don't ask, it's none of your business."

"Guns? That takes animal thieving to a new level." I made a note. Creole wouldn't be happy. "You'd have run these thieves to the North Pole if it were your dog."

"My cat, Catsy, never goes outside."

"You stay up all night coming up with that name?" I laughed.

"My girlfriend left it when she moved out. Said I stole its affections from her."

"Girlfriend?" Embarrassed that I sounded shocked, I added, "I'm learning more than I ever thought I would about you."

"You think I'm some nerd that lives in the basement of my parents' home?"

"Yep." After a silent moment, I checked the screen of my phone. Still connected. "Don't hang up. I need to know the address of this dog operation. I know finding Maddie's a long shot, but I can try. Either way, the least I can do is run them out of the Cove."

"They'll just go to another town."

"Too many animal lovers on social media; they can make their names and pictures go viral, and there'll be nowhere to hide."

"You need to be very careful. This is a family-run operation, and they won't take kindly to any attempt to shut them down." He paused, and beeping noises could be heard in the background. "I'll text the information, along with one of my famously drawn maps. It's a bit weedy back in there once you leave the road."

"Is this personal for you in some way?" I had an uneasy hunch that he knew more than he was sharing, which was practically nothing.

"Here's some general advice—if you do get involved, be damn careful, and take backup and firepower of your own. Criminals don't like having their illegal activities exposed."

"I'll let you know what happens."

"No need. I'll know the facts before you even think about calling."

Those are impressive resources. "Say hi to Catsy for me."

He hung up with a snort.

The front door opened and closed. Fab walked in, a couple of shopping bags lining her arm, and kicked off her shoes.

"Great timing. This dog case just got more complicated," I announced.

Fab eyed the countertop of the island. "You could have office space—I'll even decorate—and you wouldn't have to clutter up the kitchen." She crossed the room, took a stack of Maddie flyers out of one of the bags, and dropped them in front of me.

For now, I was ignoring the discussion about joining her and Didier at the office. For one, I didn't need a bunch of space, and truth be told, I'd rather hang out with Creole. I held up one of the flyers. "Cute picture." I caught her up on my phone calls and the information I'd uncovered, pushing my notepad under her nose. She stared at it and then pushed it back with a shake of her head, leaving unsaid, *I can't read your scribble.*

"As much as I would enjoy going in guns blazing, I'm open to your idea of a replacement lookalike dog." Fab grinned. "But not until after we give these a couple of days to work." She tapped the stack of flyers.

"You're fine with an illegal dog operation in our town?" I tried not to snap at her, knowing she'd help if I asked.

"I knew you wouldn't be satisfied with a simple swap, but it was worth a try." She backed up and reached into the refrigerator, pulling out a pitcher of cold water that was jammed with freshly sliced fruit, courtesy of Didier. "Maybe Creole can talk some sense into you. I'm certain he's going to hate the idea of you riding in to save the animals. I'm also happy that, for once, I'm not the one with the half-baked idea." She got two glasses from the cupboard, filled them, and pushed one at me.

"If it were Jazz or Snow?" I asked.

"Simple. I'd shoot the thief and drag them outside for the crows to eat."

I wrinkled my nose. "That would be messy."

Chapter Twenty-Two

My phone rang, interrupting the intense conversation between Creole and Didier as they decided where they would be running the next day. Sweaty from their morning workout and still in running clothes, they downed bottles of water.

Fab reached across the counter to grab it and realized it wasn't in its usual place at the same time I slid it out from under a pile of paperwork.

"I wouldn't have to hide it from you if you'd let me answer my own phone," I said in response to her glare.

"At least, put it on speakerphone," she demanded.

I glanced at the screen, seeing Brad's face. "Not this time." I answered and in a soft voice said, "Hey there."

Conversation ceased, and all eyes were now zeroed in on me. Creole sent me a questioning glance that I answered with a wink.

"We need to talk," Brad said.

"That depends. Do you still love me?"

"Of course." He snorted.

"Me, too." I giggled, turned away from my

rapt audience, and walked out to the patio, and stood just outside the doors, one eye on Fab to make sure she didn't sneak up on me.

"As I remember, when you start with the mushy stuff, it's because you're about to include me in some scheme that only I get in trouble for. Is that happening now?" Brad asked in amusement.

"Not this time, and I'm holding up my right hand."

"Meet for coffee tomorrow. I'll buy the pecan rolls."

"My favorite. How are you doing?" I hesitated to ask, but at least I'd have some idea of his state of mind.

"Dinner at Mother's…" He paused. "…was eye-opening. Not sure why we can't have these confrontations in a civilized manner and without an audience. At least we weren't in a restaurant." He half-laughed. "It's been a little weird with Bordello, but we're both pretending it's all good."

"I apologize. I'm not going to make excuses for not controlling myself, and if I had a do-over, I'd have chosen a better time." I sighed. "I truly wish I could blame drinking, but liquor wasn't a factor and is also a poor excuse."

"If it were happening to someone else, I might have found it mildly amusing. After you left, Mother said, 'Take a seat, we're having dessert,' and followed it up with a look that defied anyone to argue with her." He laughed heartily. "On the way out, I scooped her up into a hug and whispered, 'Next dinner, Westins only. That way, we can let the situation descend into a good brawl.' That left us both laughing."

"Ohhh…"

"Enough of that," Brad said gruffly. "Don't get all emotional; you know I hate that. I can never figure out anything to say that sounds appropriate."

"You think you're the worst comforter and you're not." I wished he was standing in front of me so I could throw my arms around him. "Tomorrow… I'm thinking, instead of meeting at The Bakery Café, you should come here. We can sit by the pool; there's plenty of privacy. How long has it been since you've run with the guys?" Without waiting for an answer, I lowered the phone and yelled inside, "What time are you running in the morning?"

Creole held up six fingers.

"Be here before six. When you get back, we can coffee it up. Then you can shower and change into your designer duds."

"Don't you think Creole and Didier should get a heads up? Their answer might be, 'Oh, hell no.'"

"Hey, hot-looking guys in the kitchen," I yelled again. This time, I heard Brad chuckle. "You got room for another runner tomorrow?" I jogged in place as though I meant me.

Their mouths didn't quite drop open, but close.

Creole recovered first. "Sure, hon," he said with an amused smile.

Didier rolled his eyes.

"I saw that." I pointed at him and turned away. "It's a date."

"Five bucks says they think you're the plus one to the group."

"They'll be so relieved when they find out it's actually someone who can keep up with them; they'll be fine."

We both laughed.

"You little troublemaker. I'll see you in the morning." We hung up.

"Who was that?" Fab asked when I walked into the kitchen and slid onto a stool.

The guys were also interested in the answer, but didn't say anything.

"Big surprise," I said with a hand flourish.

Fab groaned. "Not a single one of us likes surprises."

I ignored her and changed the subject. "Since we're all together, the dog case got more problematic than I expected. I had hoped to get a quick response to one of the flyers I posted, but instead, not a single phone call." I directed most of what I had to say to Creole, so he wouldn't think I withheld on purpose. "Surely, if someone in the neighborhood had snatched Maddie up, some nosey neighbor would be calling for the reward money. And I think we can rule out the idea that she could have trotted out of the neighborhood by herself."

"I'm the one who got the picture from Hank and had the flyers made up," Fab boasted.

"You know what else she did?" I narrowed my eyes at her.

"I want to hear." Creole waved his hand.

"Me, too." Didier smiled at Fab.

"She helped me hang flyers. That might be an exaggeration. More like supervised, pointing out which ones were straighter than the others... helpful little things like that."

Creole and Didier laughed. Didier had moved to her side and hooked his arm around her. Fab glared at me.

I stuck out my lower lip. "The timing was perfect; quite a few of the neighbors were porch-sitting. Stopped to talk to one neighbor. It went well. Our friend here was well-behaved, no inappropriate noise-making, not a single slug to my back or kick—the usual signs meant to convey 'move along.'"

"You're being overly dramatic," Fab said. "As usual, I might add. In this case, it's your rendition that is extremely over-exaggerated."

"Really?" I waited for the foot stomp to go along with her disgruntled look and was disappointed. "Where was I...? At the second house, I paused momentarily, interrupting the man doing yard work. He took a flyer and said he'd keep an eye out. Pleasant fellow, wouldn't you agree?" I arched my eyebrow. "But you wouldn't know. I turned around and poof." I threw my hands over my head. "Gone. No good-bye, see you, nothing."

Didier enveloped Fab in a hug. "Too boring."

Fab straightened with a huff. "I told you," she growled. "My phone rang."

"That's right—the business call." Did I detect a slight squirm? "I did get some useful information. The man told me about a shelter that I didn't know about. I called them and found out they had a Maltese. Not the one we're looking for. This one had been abandoned by its previous owner when they moved—left behind with no food or water. I don't understand people."

Creole hugged me. "I'm surprised we don't have a dog running around."

I smiled up at him. "I called Hank and told him about the dog, and he threw a hissy fit over the phone. Demanded to know if I was giving up the search after only a couple of days. I reassured him I wasn't, but didn't go so far as to admit there wasn't much else I could do and the only reason I mentioned the dog was because it needed a home." I turned to Fab. "When it comes time to tell him about Maddie—good or bad—you're going to be the one to handle that visit."

Fab nodded, not liking the idea.

"Why do I think there's more?" Creole asked.

"Because you know me so well." I winked and gave him a slow smile, wrapping my arms around his chest for a quick hug. At the sound of Fab clearing her throat, I filled the guys in on my conversation with GC.

"Damn," Creole said. "Had a murder case a couple of years ago, and it turned out that in addition to drug-running, they also had dog-fighting operation. Thought when we wound up that case that was the end of it."

"Don't tell us that you two plan to go to wherever and check this property out." Didier narrowed his eyes, getting more intense as they turned in Fab's direction.

Creole slapped the top of the island. "Of course, they are. You think they're going pass on an opportunity to show up at the property looking for that perpetually missing cat? Or some other story—I know, how about a dog this time? Provoke a shooting? Because you can be damn sure whoever answers the door will do so with a gun."

"Calm down. I've come up with a plan." My smile of satisfaction never faltered as the guys groaned. "We're going to drive out to the property, check it out, and not set one foot over the property line."

"You think you're going to find Maddie?" Creole asked, his tone conveying *fat chance*. "Odds are that dog has been delivered to the highest bidder."

"This isn't just about Maddie any longer," I said. "Pretty much figured out from the beginning, when she wasn't found wandering the neighborhood that it would be a long shot." Mimicking Creole, I slapped my hand on the counter, which earned me a grin. "This operation needs to be shut down, and I'm going to do whatever it takes to see that happen."

"Promise, now, that neither of you will set foot on the property in question. Don't come back with an 'I forgot' excuse." Didier stuck out his pinkie finger.

This is a first! I chuckled and leaned across the counter, hooking fingers. To my surprise, Fab hooked hers with a kiss.

"Let's coordinate this for another day. The four of us can go on a road trip," Creole said.

Fab was indignant at the suggestion that we couldn't handle this case ourselves.

"Come over here." I jerked on Creole's arm. "If looks could kill, when Fab turns on you, you'll be dead. If you're sitting next to me, she probably won't make a second attempt on your life. She won't hurt me; she needs backup." I sent her a cheesy smile.

Creole and Fab engaged in a "who's going to blink first" contest, and it turned out a... tie.

"It's not the worst idea, as long as you're not getting out of the car." Creole didn't sound convinced. "I'm telling you now, this is a case for law enforcement. You gather the facts, and I've got a contact or two on the force — animal lovers, by the way — who would enjoy shutting the operation down. You need to have some patience, though; it's not going to happen overnight."

"What happens to the animals?" Didier asked.

"I started a list of shelters, rescues, etc… which is on one of these papers someone organized for me," I said, glancing up at Fab. "I'll have it ready for law enforcement, so Animal Control isn't their only option."

"Such a mess," Fab grumbled. "This is why you need to start coming to the office. You can have a big desk and spread paper everywhere."

Creole cupped my chin and turned my face toward him. "Where's my promise that you won't trespass or do a single thing that might get you shot?"

I pushed forward, my lips to his. "Promise."

"There's no need to worry… this time. Here's the proof." Fab raised her shapely leg, pointing to her shoe — a black heel. "This pair is one of my favorites, and I do not go *running* in them."

* * *

Fab blew down the highway after making a stop for cold drinks. She'd ordered some exotic tea combination, and I barely restrained myself from turning up my nose when she asked, "You want me to order two?"

"No, thanks. Lemonade," I'd replied in a sad tone and thought about adding sound effects, then decided they needed to be saved for special moments.

I thumbed through my notes, finding the map GC had texted over. "I'd say there's nothing out here, but we're used to these kinds of areas. They always hide a secret or two." Thus far, it appeared to be the perfect place to run something illegal and not attract any attention. I twisted in my seat, scanning both sides of the road. Since leaving the Overseas, there'd been nothing but trees, overgrown grass, and the occasional cow. It surprised me that farming was legal, even out here.

"No surprise, based on the directions." Fab snapped her fingers at me. "Keep an eye out for mailboxes, addresses painted on rocks... something to give us a clue."

"Or none of the above." I turned my head. "The properties out here mostly have wood fencing. We've passed several rock driveways. No welcome signs. This one is interesting." I pointed as we drove past. "That property is not only surrounded by chain-link, but has an overly large lock on it. It's the first one so far, which moves it to the top of the list."

"Why no mailboxes?"

"There are some areas that the post office doesn't deliver to—they require you to get a box in town."

Fab hung a U-turn and slowed. "We'll make one more trip, and this time, we'll check out the properties on both sides of the only one that shows any promise."

"I'm telling you now, not getting out of the car and trudging up a gravel road for something that could turn out to be a big nothing, even if I hadn't promised Creole. It's creepy out here." I adjusted the side mirror and rolled down the window before sticking my head out, then told her, "Slow down so the bicyclist can go by us and don't do anything to scare the rider."

"What are you up to now?" Fab asked in exasperation.

Reaching down, I hurriedly pulled my wallet out of my purse. "Need a good dog name. Spot?"

Fab snorted.

"You have a dog picture on your phone? Besides Maddie's?" Knowing that was probably a no, I didn't wait for a response. Instead, I waved to the rider and pasted a smile on my face. "Have you seen a... dog running around?" That was lame; hopefully, he wouldn't notice. "I'm from the next neighborhood over. I know it's a long shot, but had to look everywhere, no matter how remote."

The rider—a teenager, maybe fifteen—dragged his foot along the road, coming to a stop. "Lost dog?"

I nodded. "Reward, if you've got any information."

"Never seen a stray animal around here. Cats would probably get eaten."

I flinched, not wanting to ask by what.

"There's a dog breeding farm up the road." He pointed. "Big 'no trespassing' sign. I wouldn't ignore it and go up to the door. Can't anyway, unless you climb the fence." He laughed. "About a year ago, my dad and I heard gunshots coming from that direction, and now I'm not allowed to go any farther east than our house."

I handed money out the window. He waved it off. I pushed it towards him again. "You could've jerked us around with some made-up nonsense and you didn't. Now we know to try another street."

He took the cash. "Thanks. This will buy me a new bike tire."

"One more question." I handed another bill out the window. He looked at me expectantly. "The dog farm—" I inclined my head. "—is it a legal operation?"

That question made him nervous. He looked up and down the road, which was still empty, as it had been the whole time we'd been here. "Don't want to get in any trouble. Dad's always saying that minding one's own business is the best route."

That was probably good advice... except to a person who didn't know how to do it. "No trouble, I swear. Another thing I can swear to— you'll never see us again. At least, out here."

"The folks around here get together for barbecues on occasion. Lots of chatter about that property. People think they're doing something illegal; most believe they're growing weed. No one knows for sure—no one's ever been invited on the property. Old Cassie—one of our neighbors—baked up a batch of cookies and took them over shortly after they moved in. She drove up and didn't get her car door open before a woman about her age leveled a shotgun at her and told her to turn around. Cassie thought pushing the cookies would get an invite inside; instead, the woman told her 'Sugar's bad for you, now git.' She didn't need to be told twice. Me, I'd have been long gone at the first sight of the gun. Truth, I wouldn't have gone in the first place."

"How old are you?" I asked, impressed by him.

"Birthday's coming up soon; I'll be sixteen. Mom says I'm thirty. I think it's a good thing."

"Nice meeting you. We won't exchange names, in the spirit of anonymity."

"That's cool. You two be careful. Good luck finding your dog." He rode off with a wave.

"Like that kid," Fab said. It surprised me when she turned around and headed back to civilization.

"Lots of maybes here. Maybe we found the property, maybe not. Maybe they're doing something illegal—dogs, weed. We're not making any headway finding Maddie."

"It's not even enough to get the cops involved." Fab continued to check out both sides of the road.

"We'll run it by Creole."

Chapter Twenty-Three

Sitting on the patio under a big umbrella, I heard footsteps coming up the side path from the beach and knew the guys were back. I had set out an ice-filled enamel bucket with bottled water. They each took a couple and, instead of collapsing into the chairs, headed upstairs.

Brad went to my bedroom, where I'd hung his clothes. He was the last to come back downstairs, in a pair of linen shorts and a short-sleeved shirt. I always liked the more casual look on him better than the suit. Walking out on the patio, he grabbed a mug from the counter and filled it with coffee I'd made from one of Didier's blends, then grabbed a cinnamon roll, stuffing it in his mouth. Creole had already told me that he and Didier were taking off, wanting to give me and Brad time alone.

"You can bring the pot over here." I pointed to the empty chairs around the dining table. Another favorite place for me to spread out my paperwork.

"Where's your shadow?" Brad asked, pulling out a chair across from me and sitting down.

"Fab keeps the worst office hours — dawn until mid-morning." I wrinkled my nose. "She reminds me she's busy building her clientele and they're early risers; she won't be caught sleeping in. She thrives on a couple of hours' sleep, and me, I whine and complain and look for an excuse to sneak off and take a nap."

"I don't know anything about her business, but I know she's taken some dicey jobs and I'm hoping you say no to accompanying her on anything that could get you hurt." Brad grimaced. "And with those hours, I hope I never have to hire her. What about you, everything going good?"

"For you lazy execs who don't get to the office until nine, you'd be her last client of the day." I wanted to ruffle his slicked-back do, like an annoying sister would, but didn't want to spoil our time together. "Working with Fab is fun most of the time. Every once in a while, a case comes up that doesn't go according to plan." More often than not, but I wasn't going to admit that to my brother.

"You two involved with the Sacks murder?"

The question surprised me, and I couldn't read his face to know where he was going. "Yes, but not exactly." I almost laughed at how dodgy my response sounded. "How did you know Fab had any involvement at all? As for me, I ride along and take notes on what to follow up on later." I tapped the notepad in front of me that

I'd filled up, starring the ones that needed to be done ASAP.

"You think I can't decipher your responses? Translation: Fab is up to her eyelashes and you're *note-taking*." He rolled his eyes. "You probably know that Bordello was at Sacks' funeral and wasn't too happy to see Fab there, cozying up to Alta. Apparently, he was friends with Marshall and Alta—couldn't get out of him if it was purely business or an actual friendship. People toss the word 'friend' around fairly easily these days, and heck, in some cases, they barely know one another."

"Bordello got any ideas who might want Sacks dead?"

"Here's some gossip that's been pretty well substantiated. Probably shouldn't be telling you, so don't pass along where you heard it—to anyone. Sacks was a popular guy—life of the party—except with his wife. They didn't get along all that well, and it's well known that they both had lovers.

"Wonder if Alta would pay to have his boat explode? I can't imagine she had the skills to do it herself. If there was trouble in the marriage, laying claim to his estate and not having to share might be a motivator."

Brad half-laughed. "Bordello doesn't think Alta had anything to do with her husband's demise. But if that was her plan, she's screwed; they had the reading of the will and everything goes to the ex-wife. Marshall didn't bother to have his will updated and never removed her name as beneficiary. Another shocker—turns out Sacks' net worth was millions short of the estimate."

Wow! "So much for wives two and three. Bet Alta wasn't happy after finding out that all she gets is what she came into the marriage with."

"Heard she threw a gigantic fit in the lawyer's office. The lawyer calmed her, telling her that under Florida law, it's not legal to disinherit a spouse—she's entitled to a percentage of the value of the estate. Which is something, but not the one-hundred percent she was expecting." Brad stood and returned his coffee mug to the sink. He grabbed two waters from the refrigerator, holding one up. I nodded.

Brad sat back down. "Another thorn in Alta's side is the house. The title is also in the ex's name, and it's not clear what the courts will decide about who ultimately gets it. Alta has the right to live there in the meantime, but it's unlikely a judge will decide that she gets to inherit more than a half-interest." He downed his water, tossing the bottle in the direction of the trashcan. "The lawyer gave her that news in private, which might have been the reason for the scream that was heard shortly after they went into the conference room."

"This is some good info." I patted his hand. "Bordello, I assume, must be good friends to get invited to the reading of the will. I thought it was beneficiaries only."

"Bordello got it secondhand. I happened to be there when the call came in; he put it on speaker. We both heard the screech loud and clear, and whoever was on the other end of the line had to hang up when Alta screamed. It's unnerving at times how much information the man is privy to; there's nothing he doesn't know, at least, nothing I've discovered so far."

"More water?" I pointed to the bottle in his hand, now empty as well.

"I'll hold off until I leave and load up before going out the door." He laughed. "If I were at Mother's, she'd be filling a large bag with leftovers for me to take home."

"They don't stick around long here." I laughed with him, and it felt good. "You and Phil still...?" I scissored my fingers.

Brad rolled his eyes. "Yes, we're still doing it," he said in exasperation. "Happy?"

Not really, but I thought better of voicing that opinion. "Again, I'm sorry about outing Phil's secret; she had every right to do it in her own way. I'm sure she had a good reason."

"Phil told me that she'd kept the secret about Bordello being her brother for so long that she didn't think about it. When it all started, she didn't want her mother and stepfather to find out that she'd tracked him down and stayed in touch, especially since they didn't want her to know about that side of the family."

"Upfront disclaimer: I know this is none of my business —"

"But?" Brad arched a brow.

"When did Phil plan to tell you?"

"Since she's a lawyer, I expected a better explanation than that it didn't occur to her, especially since she'd kept the secret from me for so long. I must've let on that I didn't believe that one. Next excuse was she didn't think it was that big a deal once Bordello and I became friends. The longer I stayed silent, the longer her list of explanations grew, ending with that she'd have told me after we got married and if that happened, she knew I'd understand."

"Would you understand?" In fairness to her, she'd probably been worried about the outcome, but I wasn't in the mood to defend her even a little.

"Not really." He paused, lost in thought for a moment. "I told her I forgave the deceit, but I haven't really, although I want to. The thought of marrying someone with secrets and not finding out until after the I dos makes me shudder." He scowled. "Are you done with the questions? You know I'm going to have to answer the same ones again when I get up the courage to face Mother."

"Do you want to me fill her in and then suggest she not bring it up? Point out to her that it would make the next meeting a lot less awkward? You know she'd do anything for her favorite son."

"Can you guarantee no hurt feelings?"

I nodded.

"You've got the job. And we won't talk about it either. Send me a thumbs up on my phone, and I'll know it's all good."

"I won't even bill you." I gave him a cheeky grin. "You can be one of my freebie clients."

Brad groaned. "Any more questions?"

"A couple." Before he could change his mind, I asked, "How's your relationship with Bordello?"

"Awkward at times. We ignore it and concentrate on the business at hand. He said he honored his sister's request to keep quiet and asked if I wouldn't do the same for you. And the answer is yes."

"If Phil's brother is half the man you are, then she's a lucky woman."

"I started this partnership thinking it would be one that would last for years. Now I'm not so sure. But we got a great deal on the apartment complex in the upscale area of Brickell. Needs renovation, and there's plenty of room in the budget to do it right and make a good profit. It won't take long to know if we work well together or not."

"I'm happy for your new deal and that you're happy. New projects are exciting. I want you to know that I had nothing to do with the initial decisions on the dock deal."

He brushed his hand, as if to say, *no big deal*. "Bordello is a Type A personality to the extreme. He's not used to losing, and when he does, he's a sulker. Told him that the stress of the chase was going to kill him before any of his women. He's a guy with particular needs when it comes to the opposite sex. Don't ask because I'm not discussing it with my sister."

"What's up with the woman who showed up at Mother's with him? Are they in a relationship?" Noticing his frown, I continued, "I know, more gossip, but that was a weird night on the road, and Fab and I really thought she was going to shoot him." I told him what really happened that night and emphasized that we weren't stalking the man. "I'm not going to tell anyone anything you share with me — maybe Creole, but he's tight-lipped."

Brad laughed. "None of you mind your own business. The guys already grilled me about Nicole. You know, I figured I'd been written off as a crappy friend since I got all wrapped up in myself and my petty problems and stopped coming by to run my ass off. Totally wrong. They still have my back, like always, and they rubbed it in, reminding me."

"That makes me very happy. A good friend can blow up the problem, shoot it, whatever it takes as long it goes away."

"I can see our other sister is a bad influence on you," he said, amusement in his eyes. "What made you think Nicole planned to hurt him?"

"In our spirit of honesty, it was only nosiness that kept us following the two of them after we figured out that we weren't the target. I spotted the Smith & Wesson in her waistband—thanks to your tutelage, I know my handguns." I smiled at him.

"Remember when Mother found out I was taking you to the gun range? My ears are still ringing. I'm surprised to this day that she bought my lame excuse—'well, I couldn't leave her home by herself.' You were a teenager at the time and could entertain yourself, but thankfully, that wasn't questioned. The reason I'm sitting here instead of having met an early demise is that Mother never found out I started teaching you to shoot back then, and I convinced her later on that I didn't start the lessons until we were adults. You know her—the next thing you know, she enrolled in a gun class."

"Coolest mother ever. Until we did something stupid, which was way too often." I laughed along with Brad.

Brad turned serious. "Nicole and Bordello were in a relationship, and it didn't end well. I'm not judging, since I've only had one relationship that didn't crash and burn. When he mentioned that he's currently 'smoothing the waters' with Nicole, I kept back an eye roll and warned him to watch his back. The whole gun thing creeped me out and brought back shades of Patty."

Mental-case Patty. Brad had been lucky to get out of that relationship alive, and now she was once again locked up in the looney bin. I hoped they kept her this time.

Enough of Patty and the haunted look in my brother's eyes. I changed the subject. "When are you relocating to Miami?"

"Just closed on a condo. Got a great deal, which makes it a good investment. I'm not cut out for a daily commute. Liam can use my condo here when he doesn't want to stay at Mother's."

"She'll flip when she finds that out. And when she does, I know nothing."

"Did I hear my name?" Liam said from the doorway, a soda and plate of food in his hand.

Chapter Twenty-Four

Brad waved him to a seat next to him. "Updating Madison on the housing situation. And reminding you again that Mother better not find out about our arrangement."

"Mother needs a hobby. She'd like grandchildren to spoil, and I nominate you," I said to Brad.

"Noo," Liam said between bits of food. "I like being the spoiled, can-do-no-wrong chosen one."

Brad and I laughed. Liam took Mother's hovering better than we did.

"What brings you here in the middle of the week? When I went to college back in the old days, we had classes every day."

"Afternoon off. My roommate's friend comes from down here and needed a ride to the dentist; his face is swollen." He puffed out his cheeks. "He's going to call after he gets the bad news and needs a ride back to school."

"Good to see you," I said.

"You, too. Good news—I got a job. You gotta swear not to tell Grandmother."

"Why?" I asked suspiciously.

Brad sat back and crossed his arms. "Can't wait to hear this. Just know, if you're doing something crazy, I'll get you fired."

"That's cold. It's not like I applied for that stripper job." Liam grinned.

I laughed until Brad glared at me. "They probably wanted women."

"Nope." Liam shook his head. "Men."

"What is the damn job?" Brad demanded.

"Keep an open mind until you hear all the details."

I laughed again. *Oh, this was going to be bad.*

"Great pay, flexible hours. I've gone in twice already, and they liked me so much, I got another call yesterday, and that job paid double." Liam broke the stare-down first. "Professional funeral mourner."

Brad's mouth dropped open.

"Oh, no." The air sucked out of my lungs. "I'm going to get the blame for this one."

It took Brad a minute to recover. "There's no such job. What kind of job did you really get?"

"Shows what you know. At Grandmother's dinner, I overheard—well, eavesdropped on— Creole and Didier laughing with Spoon when they told him about Madison speaking at a funeral for pay. Spoon had heard the story somewhere else and didn't believe it. And who better to ask about such a job than Dickie and Raul? They told me what was expected and set me up with an interview at a cemetery that

'Meets your loved ones' needs'," he said in a solemn voice.

Brad looked at me for confirmation. I nodded and said, "In my defense, I was tricked into speaking for the deceased man, Mr. Basket." The details weren't any of their business. "And neither Fab nor I accepted money for filling seats."

"You've lost your mind," Brad told Liam, then said to me, "I can just imagine how you got roped in."

"It's not a career move," Liam said. "The pay is better than any on- or off-campus job I could get, and the last four of those I applied for had over a hundred applicants. Factor in the perks— better pay than any of the campus jobs; it only takes three hours max of my time, and that includes travel; and the big one, it helps me polish my public speaking. There aren't many of those opportunities on campus. Yesterday I spoke, which pays more, and several people came up to me afterwards, telling me what a good job I did." He sighed. "A couple of the seat-fillers weren't happy, jealous that I'd moved up so fast. I wanted to suggest that they lose the Dockers; I'd shown up in a suit that Didier helped me pick out."

"What are you going to do about this?" Brad barked at me. "This is your fault. All the crazy stuff you do, it's wearing off on him."

"If I had known ahead of time—" I turned a

stern eye on Liam. "—I would've done my best to talk him out of it. I could've talked up the perks of being a PI, which might get him shot. At least, in this job, it's the other people who are dead."

"Now that would cool."

I glared at Liam. "If Mother asks, I know *nothing*. If you rat me out, I'll get even."

Liam laughed as if he thought my threat sounded fun.

"This is the damnedest family," Brad said. "I'm also pleading ignorance. I'm doubling her threat and making her carry it out."

"I suggest you tell Mother in confidence," I said to Liam. "Break it to her over lunch; she'll love that—food and confession. It works for me and Brad. You get hired to go to a splashy, celebutante send-off, invite her; she'll want to come."

Brad's phone buzzed. He picked it up and glanced at the screen. "Got a meeting." He jumped to his feet, looking relieved to have a good reason to bail. "Give me a hug." He wrapped his arms around me, lifting me off my feet.

"You, Brad Westin, are going to a meeting in shorts?" I clutched my heart.

"Rebelliousness. I keep a couple of suits at the office for meetings that require one. Rubbed off on Bordello—he showed up in jeans the other day—and I ribbed him about it. Told him the relaxed look made him seem friendlier, more approachable. He must have listened, because he's loosening up the wardrobe."

I shuddered to think of Bordello as friendly—I'd sooner cozy up to a shark—but knew better than to say anything. "I'm so happy that we got together—feels like we're back on track." I hugged him again. "I know we can't do this all the time, but we should make an effort. I expect to see you every time you come to town."

He turned to Liam, and they engaged in a convoluted man handshake. "You get tired of hanging with dead people, give me a call and I'll hook you up with a real job."

"Probably can't match the pay," Liam teased. "Not with anything legal, anyway."

Brad ruffled Liam's hair. "I've got a standing workout invitation from the guys, so you'll be seeing me around. You should join us when you come to town."

"We'll book in advance so that we're all available." Liam jogged in place and feigned being out of breath.

"Both of you behave." Brad shook his finger at us.

"I can be a good influence," I said.

Brad laughed his way through the house.

Chapter Twenty-Five

Mother had been excited when I called and set up an all-girl lunch. My treat, her choice of restaurant. She immediately chose a hotel in South Beach she liked that had good food, a sidewalk café, and a view of the Atlantic Ocean.

She informed me that it was perfect timing because she had received a postcard informing her that she'd won a thousand-dollar shopping spree and her time to redeem it was running out.

Judging by the address she'd given me — which, thanks to my phone, I found located in an industrial zone — I chalked it up to some sort of come on. Spend even more money and then you get your reward, or everything was marked up a thousand percent. Or it was one of those warehouse places that she and her friend Jean liked to frequent that, in my opinion, sold suspicious goods. Which was probably why she'd issued the warning not to tell Spoon.

Fab pulled into Mother's complex, and I sent her upstairs to hustle Mother back down; she had a way of getting people to hurry up. I used the time to re-settle into the back seat and barely got the door closed when a fist banged on the window. Squelching a scream, I sat up and pressed my face to the glass. Spoon. I made a face, and since I wasn't sure if he could get the full effect through tinted windows, I opened the door and got out.

"You break the glass or make even so much as a crack with that mammoth fist of yours, and you'll pay up, buddy." I straightened and looked him in the eye.

"Try and make me." He smirked.

"You forget, I have Mother as my trump card. I'll whine long and hard until she pays to shut me up, and the whole time, you'll have to listen to her grumbling." I thrust my chin out, mimicking him. "You must want something?"

"Oh, I do." He narrowed his eyes. "The three of you running loose without a chaperone gives me the chills, especially since I know my wife is hiding something."

"It's shopping and lunch. Besides, it's not my fault you can't control your woman."

He growled. "You keep Madeline out of trouble."

"Or what?" I loved that he was so protective of Mother, and it was fun to tease him, since our outing was a legitimate lunch.

"Or... I'll kick your boyfriend's ass."

I laughed, and his brow shot up. "You lay one finger on Creole, and I'll shoot you." I flashed a toothy grin. "I promise we're not going to drive around looking for trouble."

Fab and Mother came through the glass doors.

"I thought you'd left." Mother hugged Spoon.

"Saw Madison loitering in the parking lot and stopped to say hello." He opened the car door and helped her into the passenger seat. He kissed her and, before closing the door, said, "Text me on your way home." He turned to me. "Would you really shoot me?"

"Yes. Just like Mother would shoot Creole if the tables were turned."

"Yeah, I suppose." He helped me in.

Mother rolled down the window and waved as we drove away.

"Where to first?" Fab asked as she pulled out onto the highway.

"Let's go claim my prize. I'll share it with you two." Mother pulled the postcard from her purse.

"Hand me that so I can read it." I scooted up and put my head between the seats. "I already got the directions, so I can yell them out to Fab while she drives. She loves when I do that. Why weren't you upfront with Spoon about our plans for the day?"

"I showed him the card when it came in the mail, and he pronounced it a scam. So I tossed it in the trash, and when he turned his back, I retrieved it. Even if I didn't really win anything, it will be a fun adventure, and we haven't had one of those in a while. Besides, I get lunch with my two favorite girls."

"I recommend we do this more often, especially with Madison paying," Fab said.

She and Mother exchanged a look and laughed.

"I've got some news," I announced, taking a deep breath. "Before sharing, I'll need a promise from each of you that you'll never mention this to anyone, and if you get wind of it in some other way, you know nothing. The only exception is husband/boyfriend. I want to hear your oaths loud and clear."

"A little overdramatic," Fab said.

"So, you know, I had to make the same promise that I'm asking you to make, and before you ask, I have permission to relay this news to you."

They both promised.

"Brad stayed for coffee the other morning after running with the guys." I planned to leave out the part about Liam's impromptu visit and new career choice. "Here goes." I relayed what Brad had told me about Phil and Bordello. "He doesn't want to be further embarrassed by this situation, and you can hardly blame him."

The silence continued for a few miles up the road. "I'm happy to know and to sweep it under the carpet," Mother said. "Good thing, too. I have no clue what I'd say. I like Phil, but I also don't think she's the one for him. That's the last thing he wants to hear from his Mother. What is it you told me, Madison? He'll come to his own conclusions on his own timetable?"

"You do listen to me!" I beamed at Mother. "The only thing we can do is be there for him in silent support, and that will make it easier for him to turn to one or both of us."

"Knowing how you enjoy the art of the fix-up," Fab said to Mother, "you'll have to find a sweet and kinky woman. You know, just in case they do break up."

I rolled my eyes and smacked her on the back of the head.

"Ignore her." Mother patted Fab's arm. "I know what you mean. Madison's the prune in the family."

"It's prude, and I am not." I waved my hand in front of Fab. "Turn at the next signal."

"See what I have to put up with?" Fab appealed to Mother.

"Children, really." Mother smiled at our antics.

I clipped Fab's head again, not as hard this time. "Turn at the next corner."

"Left or right?" she asked in exasperation.

"You'll figure it out. According to the map, there's only one way to turn." I slid back in my seat, a contented smile on my face. "Mother, you need to be on the lookout for the address."

In response to Mother's insistent pointing, Fab pulled into the driveway of an industrial strip mall. "This isn't quite what I expected." Mother's tone conveyed disappointment.

Fab parked in front of the single door, the outside of which appeared to be covered with purple silk material bunched together with a tassel. The glass behind had a layer of blackout on it.

Mother leaned forward, checking out the building. "Doesn't matter if everything inside is junky; I'm just happy we did it and can laugh about it over lunch. Or it'll be a happy surprise, and we'll get something good."

I voted for the laughing part. I scoped out the area, which was row after row of small matched warehouse buildings.

As we got out, Fab shepherd us into a group. "If shots ring out, I get to return fire first."

"I get to go second," Mother blurted.

"Neither of you are the least bit funny." I ran my hand up Mother's back. "Where did you holster your firearm?

"My thigh." As though the answer was a no-brainer. "Otherwise, Spoon would've felt it when he hugged me. Then I'd never have gotten out of the house."

"If he finds out, you're going to be in big trouble." Fab wagged her finger. "Men don't like being played."

"I know." Mother beamed.

I ignored them both. "Come on." I motioned toward the door. "Let's get us some loot so we can go have lunch and a couple of drinks."

Fab led the way. She tugged on the door, and

it was locked. She knocked on the glass.

"Try the doorbell—once." I was too late; her finger jabbed at it several times.

A man unlocked the door, sticking his head out. "Which one of you got the card?" The man's hardened eyes roved over the three of us.

I answered, "We're all together."

The man glared, apparently taking exception to my tone. Too bad. But he held the door open when Mother showed him the card. Mother went first, and then Fab and I squeezed by the man, who attempted to block our way.

I followed Fab's eyes as the man who let us in stayed outside. I listened for the turn of the lock, and it didn't happen. Or did it? Fab patted the small of her back, a signal that something was off to her. I shook my head slightly, telegraphing for her not to pull out her gun unless there was no other way out.

Inside the yellowed space, there was a layer of grime on the walls and floors, and a handful of mammoth cockroaches, toes up, dotted the side walls. The company was utilizing a small portion of the entry space, with garment racks rolled out to block the view of the rest of the room with curtain panels.

An eight-foot wood desk was the focal point, holding a laptop and a stack of papers flipped over in front of a man with a welcoming smile. "Please, take a seat." He waved to a line of uncomfortable plastic chairs that had been set up along the far wall. A woman occupied one, looking bored; she didn't make eye contact.

The three of us stepped back but didn't sit. For once, I ignored the table with the bagged snacks, and none of us were interested in one of the cold drinks that were spilling out of the old galvanized tub I'd bet came out of someone's yard.

A boom box filled the room with annoying music I couldn't identify and hoped I never heard again.

I want to leave now, but Mother wouldn't take kindly to being dragged out of here and that's what it would take.

Another man walked through a gap in the panels and introduced himself to Mother. They shook hands, and he escorted her to the desk and planted himself next to her.

The man behind the desk asked Mother, "ID?"

Fab nudged my arm. "They're videotaping this," she whispered and nodded to lenses that were sticking out of the far sides of both curtains.

The man checked Mother's ID and spoke something unintelligible into his earpiece.

"Taping?" I mouthed to Fab and got a nod in return.

The front door opened again. Two uniformed officers entered and another came from behind the curtain. They surrounded Mother, one producing a badge.

"You're under arrest for writing bad checks

and credit card fraud."

My mouth fell open, but before I could take more than a step, the woman half-asleep in the chair came to life, stepping in front of Fab and I and holding up her badge. "Sit," she ordered. "Follow directions, or you'll be the next to be arrested."

Mother had been handcuffed and searched for weapons, the Glock in her thigh holster located, removed, and laid on the desk. The officer then recited the Miranda warning, advising her of her rights, which included an attorney.

"Madeline, don't say one word without legal counsel present," Fab said loudly, returning the glare of one of the officers.

One officer took Mother's arm and led her towards the curtain.

"Wait," I shouted. "My mother has never committed a crime in her life. She doesn't even jaywalk. You've got the wrong woman."

Fab tugged on my arm when I stepped forward.

The two officers left at the desk approached Fab and I. One said, "I'll need to see some identification."

"If she's under arrest, I'll need to contact our lawyer, Cruz Campion," I said as I handed him my ID and permit to carry. I noticed that Fab had done the same thing with the other officer.

He snorted at the mention of Cruz's name, as if to say, *Sure he's your lawyer.* "Don't be a smartass unless you'd prefer to do this at headquarters. Hands over your head and turn around," he ordered. Fab and I were handcuffed with the same speed as Mother. "Where's your gun?"

"My thigh," I answered.

Fab spoke up: "Mine's holstered at my back."

The officer relieved us both of our guns and ushered us to the chairs, which were even more uncomfortable than they looked.

"I'll run these two." Fab's officer disappeared behind the sheet.

"If it comes back that neither of you having outstanding warrants, you'll be free to go." The officer went back to his desk, sat down, and proceeded to ignore us, fumbling through the stack of paperwork.

"How long is this going to take?" I whispered, discreetly tilting my head towards the officer, making sure he heard. I got a speedy answer.

"We're under no time constraints," the officer answered. "Get comfortable, and you'll be out of here in no time. Or after you're booked, you'll be packed into the van out back for a ride to the Miami police department."

I scooted back in my chair, leaning my head against the wall, and stared up at the ceiling. A spider weaving a web in the corner caught my eye.

I had no idea how much time passed before Mother reappeared from the other side of the curtain. Uncuffed, which was a good sign.

"Sorry for the inconvenience. Thank you for your understanding," the officer at the desk told Mother.

"What about my daughters?" she asked.

"As long as they have no outstanding warrants, they'll be released. In the meantime, you can wait outside." The female plainclothes officer escorted her to the door and unlocked it, held it open for her, and locked it up again.

"What's going on?" Fab asked. "Rounding up criminals with the free gift ruse?"

That would be the last "free" gift anyone in the Westin family would claim. "How did my mother get on your list?"

"Not sure. But she checked out." Not the chatty sort, she went back to ignoring us.

"You two also got the all-clear. You're free to go," the officer who'd released Mother said. He nodded to the female officer, and she unlocked the cuffs with speedy efficiency.

"Do we at least get an explanation as to what's going on here?" I asked.

His mutinous glare motivated Fab and I to collect our guns and hustle out the door.

Mother, who'd been leaning against the bumper, rushed over and group-hugged us. "I knew you'd be out sooner or later, but I worried all the same." She kissed our cheeks. "Did you know these kinds of stings are common? They tempt criminals who commit minor crimes with the offer of a great prize."

"How did they get your name?" I snapped. Feeling bad at her frown, I drew her into another hug and squeezed hard.

Mother pushed back. "Really, Madison." She smoothed her hair.

Fab laughed.

"There's a criminal Madeline Westin," Mother announced with a certain smugness.

I groaned. "How many of you are there?"

"That's not funny." She slid into the passenger seat.

Fab closed the door and went around to the driver's side. "This calls for a liquid lunch."

I barely refrained from telling Fab to step on it.

"If Spoon finds out, I'll be in so much trouble," Mother moaned.

Fab reached over and patted Mother's hand. "I've got a couple of sure-fire tricks that will have Spoon forgetting why he was mad in the first place. I'll share when you-know-who can't hear." She cast a glance at the back seat.

Chapter Twenty-Six

Thankfully, Fab had just as much to drink as Mother and I and wasn't awake at the crack of dawn, insisting we leave the house before it got light outside.

Fab had flipped a coin to decide who would get the three of us a ride home, and I lost. I knew the toss was rigged, but she'd pocketed the coin before I could contest.

"We need a ride," I groaned into the phone when Creole answered.

"You okay?"

"Yeppers. I'm pitchy," I giggled.

"I think you mean peachy. Where are you?" he asked, the concern in his voice ratcheting up.

"Where are we?" I whispered.

"The Crab Sack," Mother yelled. Once the police had determined we were "free to go," we'd taken a vote, and it was three-zip to head back to the Cove.

Over the phone, I heard the start of the truck's engine; it had an unmistakable badass sound. "Is this a special occasion or just a 'let's get drunk'?" Creole asked.

"We're not drunk," I said. Fab and Mother laughed. "Just a drink or two. We're celebrating... stuff." I tried to cover the phone before he could hear the shushes.

Creole showed up with Didier, who took Fab home in the SUV, and when we dropped off Mother, Spoon was waiting outside. I'd heard later he wasn't happy about his wife coming home drunk and singing at the top of her lungs. He scooped her off her feet and hustled her inside, since a couple of the neighbors were peering over their railings from the next floor up. I got the same treatment when we got back to my house. Neither Creole nor Didier asked any questions, and I considered that a coup. The only one, given even really tying one on last night didn't get me out of today's meeting.

"I left out a couple of details." Fab gripped the steering wheel, maneuvering around slow traffic and not honking her displeasure.

To my immense relief, she wasn't in race car-driving mode. My stomach had calmed considerably after I'd foregone my usual coffee and ordered weak tea and a bagel, and Fab, who initially sniffed at my order, ordered the same thing.

"That's a shock." I shifted in the passenger seat, straightening my skirt.

"Let's not ruin a perfectly nice day."

"You sound just like Mother. I suppose that comes from spending way too much time whispering back and forth." I was happy that, despite how yesterday turned out, we were able to laugh and ended up having fun. "Tell me already. What am I going to do? Ditch you here on the interstate, head back home? Not likely."

"As you know, I have a meeting with Brick. The part I left out was that he requested that I come alone."

"Ohh. That's so sad." I fake-cried.

"Stop that noise; it's dreadful."

Too loud maybe. "I'll stay in the car—feet on the dashboard, since you won't be here to tell me to take them off—and play on my phone."

Fab shook her head.

"I hope the reason for his excluding me is our mutual dislike, and it has nothing to do with him trying to talk you into doing something dangerous. What's the magic number of houses and offices a person can break into before getting caught? It will happen sooner or later, as evidenced by all those that end up behind bars." I clapped my hand over my mouth. "Oh, that's right—you *have* been caught. Several times. And we're here to laugh about it because it's sooo funny." I squinted at her.

"If you get a call from me, don't bother answering; just come upstairs with one of those hokey excuses of yours."

I shot her a thumbs up. "I think I'll be particularly annoying and make it about my cats."

She laughed, much to her own disgust, I was certain.

Fab pulled into Famosa Motors and claimed the parking space in front of the roll-up doors.

"No one here but him; his car is parked in its usual spot." She turned in her seat, scanning the parking lot. "It's the perfect time. His bodyguard/receptionist hasn't arrived yet, so I don't have to come up with something nice to say." She jumped out of the car and reached in the back for her briefcase, which held the reports he'd requested on the players in the Sacks murder case.

I couldn't put my finger on what was bothering me about Brick asking for all those reports. Why not use his own man? Whoever that was, since he'd never shared that information. I'd mentioned it to Fab, and she shrugged it off as business as usual. Except that it wasn't.

"Don't hesitate to call; I don't mind making an ass of myself."

"I'm going to hug you later."

"Sure you will."

She slammed the door and crossed to the entrance. I watched as she paused briefly to check out the reception desk and then disappeared from view a few strides later as she walked behind the elevator, where the stairs were located. Brick's office was on the second floor, with a view of the entire property.

I checked the time, trying to remember how long previous meetings had gone. Generally no longer than fifteen minutes, as he always professed to have something pressing that needed his attention. I reminded myself not to worry, as Fab had me on speed dial, and if anything got out of hand, she'd be hitting the button.

How many times had Brick Famosa been named businessperson of the year? I'd lost track. And he won in spite of the fact that he owned cash businesses, which were always a red flag for the authorities, and a strip club out in Alligator Alley. Who'd have thought you could do a robust business out there? He boasted it was a packed house every night except Monday.

For as long as I'd known Brick, he'd sent us out on one dangerous job after another, and what had soured my opinion of the man was figuring out he didn't have a care about our safety. I'd always understood that, in his mind, I was expendable, but Fab… she'd always been loyal to the man, and it seemed to me that that mattered little to him.

I adjusted the seat and lay back, opening my phone to check out what was happening in the world — or South Florida, anyway.

A half-hour later, the door opened, and Fab handed me a small manila envelope. "Our payment. He says he doubled it to cover expenses."

I undid the clasped and peeked inside, and there was the stack of hundreds, which was how we'd always been paid. I used to wonder if he printed them himself, as they were always crisp and new, but none had ever been rejected at the bank.

"How did the meeting go? Was he happy with the reports?" I asked.

"He skimmed them and seemed pleased. Brick's hard to read unless he's yelling."

"I guess you're going to make me ask." I paused, waiting for her to continue, and when it didn't happen quickly enough for me, I asked, "What did he want? If it was just the reports, they could've been messengered yesterday. At his cost, of course."

"Alta Sacks was arrested," she blurted. "First-degree murder. Wonder what evidence was uncovered."

"Double wow. I admit she didn't make a very good first impression, but a murderer? She came off as more disinterested. The cops need to be looking for an accomplice because she didn't blow up that boat by herself. Nothing in her background report showed that she had any kind of explosives knowledge."

"That's why you're the perfect partner; you read all those reports. I skimmed them, and nothing stood out."

"I also made a copy… just in case."

Fab continued to drive the speed limit, staring intently at the road. It should have brought me a certain level of relief that I didn't have to clutch the door handle; instead, it made my neck hair stand on end.

"So… job over? One other thing, why are we headed east when we live south?"

"Brick wanted to thank me in person for the files and smooth over our relationship, reassure himself that I'd still do jobs for him."

Fab had ignored both of my questions, as though I wouldn't notice. "You might want to pull off the road so I can throw water on your dress before it's engulfed in flames."

Fab looked down. "What are you talking about now?"

"Liar liar, pants on fire. In this case, your dress. I can break it down even more for you," I said with a wave of my hand. "You're lying. You will tell me the truth now, or I'll use threats. Your choice."

"Brick wants me to go search the Sacks mansion and remove any incriminating evidence."

"Absolutely not," I came close to shrieking. "In case you've forgotten in the last minute or two, this is a murder case. The removal of evidence is a felony. Another reminder: that means jail time, ugly orange clothes, and hideous food."

"I've got the picture," Fab snapped.

"Do you really? Didn't you have a hundred questions after his request? I certainly do. My first being why would Brick, who was also friends with Marshall, want to protect Alta if she is, indeed, his murderer? Did it escape both of your minds that the cops have probably been to the property an untold number of times, and

DEBORAH BROWN

they don't leave evidence behind? Another thing you've forgotten—the butler and the rest of the staff."

"The executor of the estate gave them a severance package. And as a PI, I can legally enter the property."

"I suppose Brick gave you that reassurance. You weren't hired by Alta or one of her lawyers, and you think Brick will step up for you if you get caught and risk his big ass going to jail? And to make this job appear even more legit, you're using your lock pick to get inside? That's called breaking and entering. You seem hell-bent on getting yourself arrested," I said in exasperation. "You won't get away with ransacking a mansion out on Fisher Island that's surrounded with security cameras."

"No worries. Brick visited Alta yesterday, and she gave permission for me to check out her property."

"That's reassuring." I sniffed. "This case is high profile; I'm certain the police detectives sent to investigate weren't newbies. In addition to the inside of the house, they'd go over every square inch of the grounds with a forensics team. I'm telling you now that your chances of finding anything are nil."

"You're being so damn mean today." Fab pouted.

"That's what friends are for." I pouted back. "One of us goes all crazy Nancy Drew, the other reels her back from the clanging of a cell door." A quiet Fab was problematic. "If you've got questions about how the boat blew, read a copy of GC's report; it's detailed, complete with pictures."

"We're going home."

"So you can sneak back by yourself? I don't think so. We'll go now." I turned my head and sulked out the window, mulling another option. "You could tell Brick you rifled the place and came up with nothing. Unless... Brick wants something specific, or perhaps presented you with a laundry list?"

Fab zipped across the lanes and hung a left. "Get the change out for the toll."

Chapter Twenty-Seven

Fab was uncharacteristically quiet on the ferry ride across Biscayne Bay. It was the first time without prodding that she wanted to get out of the SUV and sit on one of the benches. I hopped at any opportunity to soak up the sunshine and ocean air. Dark glasses covered our faces, the wind whipped through our hair, and for the first few minutes, we watched the water ripple out from under the boat.

Fab scooted closer to me.

"Would you like to sit on my lap?" I laid my head on her shoulder. "Close enough?"

"When I first got to Brick's office, he was on the phone. He had his back to the door, so I listened in. I couldn't make out every word, but what I did overhear had to do with Marshall Sacks. Suddenly, Brick spun around in his chair. His first reaction when he saw me standing there was anger, and in a way I'd never seen before. I'm certain it was lucky for me I'd prepared for getting caught by having my hand raised as though I was about to knock. He ended the call abruptly and waved me into a chair. I passed it off as good timing, which calmed him down...

somewhat." She shivered, even though it was warm on the water.

"If he's so involved to the point of covering up evidence, I don't understand why he's not out here doing this job himself."

Fab laughed. "Brick delegates. I can't remember the last time he was hands-on on a case unless it involved him."

"Nothing the man does surprises me. There's a lot about this case that doesn't make sense. Here we are in the middle of it all, not knowing a lot." I stared out at the water. "Whatever you do, don't let Brick catch you snooping, listening in... You need to be careful. I hate to think what he might do if he thought you'd overheard something he didn't want anyone to know."

The ferry captain honked the horn; it was time to get back in the car and get ready to disembark. The workers frowned on any delay that held up the other cars.

Fab drove off and circled the island, pulling up to the gates of the Sacks mansion and inserting a gate card. Nothing. She huffed in annoyance and took another card from the ashtray, one that opened any gate in town. A gift from a friend of hers. She stuck it in the security panel. Nothing.

"What...?" she said in frustration. "Maybe the electricity is off." She backed out, circled around to a condo complex, and pulled into visitor parking. "When there's no on-street parking, this is the next best option."

From what I remembered from our previous trip, we could cut diagonally through the park that had been built around the circle, ending up a couple of houses away. I got up on my knees and reached over the seat, grabbing Fab's gym bag, unzipped it, and handed over her tennis shoes. Tossing it back on the floor, I did the same with mine. Before getting out of the SUV, Fab pocketed her lock pick and grabbed some latex gloves.

"How are you getting over the security gate?"

"As we drove past the house, I noticed that there's a door just after the start of the wooden part of the fence."

"How are you getting into the house?"

"Brick gave me the security code." Fab held up her phone before shoving it in her pocket.

"Let's hope it works better than the gate card." I wanted to slap the shrug off her shoulders. "If Alta and her lawyer didn't give their permission to be on the property, your backside is hanging way out on a limb." When she didn't answer, I added, "If the code doesn't work, I suggest that we return to Brick's office and you get one that does work."

We covered the distance to the Sacks' gates in silence. Fab picked the lock on the service entrance—I knew what it was because of the sign someone had hung up. She produced two pairs of latex gloves from her back pocket, tossed a pair at me, and led the way along a path and around the side of the house to the massive backyard, pool area, and boat dock. Whipping out her phone, she snapped pictures as she headed to the dock first, pausing in front of a storage box, lifting the lid, and dropping it immediately.

Trying to make myself useful, I scanned the backyard and made my way to the kitchen area, opening and closing the cupboard doors in the outdoor kitchen. They were all empty. Perhaps, someone had cleaned them out, or maybe they didn't entertain outside.

Fab waved for me to follow as she veered off in the opposite direction from which we came and ended up in front of the side entrance to the four-car garage, to which she picked the lock.

I guarded the door—one eye on the outside, the other in—as Fab made her way around the interior. If the cops had tossed the place, they'd been respectful; nothing looked out of place. It had me wondering once again what evidence the police had to arrest Alta.

Fab closed the last of the cabinet doors. "This is a garage that no one uses. A few household supplies but nothing else, not even a toolbox."

"They probably hire people who bring their equipment with them. I'm surprised they have two empty parking spaces. Doesn't seem like two cars is enough for two people, even if they are a Lexus and a Mercedes."

Fab laughed. "I'm going inside through this door." Once again, she whipped out her lockpick.

I grabbed her arm. "No key? Surely Brick had one."

She shrugged out of my grasp. "He must have forgot."

"I'm sure he didn't; the reason he didn't give you one is that he didn't have one," I crabbed. "Since you're now crossing the line into illegal, do you want me staking out the front gate? I could wedge myself between a couple of palm trees, or there's bushes out there. I have experience crawling around in those. Hopefully this time, an animal won't come along that wants to pee on me."

"Didn't I somehow get the blame for that one?" Fab cocked her head. "This time... mingle amongst the trees; no one will be able to see you from the road. If anyone stops out front, call me. Or if a car pulls up to the gate. Stay out of sight. I'm not expecting the cops. If they were coming, they'd have been here already."

"If they do show up and your story needs corroboration, is Brick available to back you up? Cruz, perhaps? Anyone that will keep us from going to jail?"

How did I go from trying to keep Fab out of trouble to being a co-conspirator? Creole was going to kill me, and I didn't really blame him.

Her lack of response spoke volumes.

"Be careful and make it snappy," I said as the door closed. Locking the door, I retraced my steps, peering in all the windows. The living room was as I remembered it—pristine, stark, nothing out of place. The kitchen door tempted me to turn the knob, and to my surprise, it was unlocked. Pushing it open, I stuck my head in and yelled, "Back door is unlocked. What do you want me to do?"

Fab squealed. "You know how to scare a girl. Lock it," she yelled back.

I continued my trek to the front and stepped in between a couple of palm trees. They weren't much for cover, but it did give me an unobstructed view of the street. The downside was the limited view of comings and goings from only one direction. Fisher was exactly what it advertised—a quiet place to live. Low crime rate, though there'd been a murder or two in the past few years over business deals gone wrong. Cars were frowned upon, the use of golf carts encouraged. The only excitement so far was two women joggers running by, engrossed in conversation.

My heel-cooling time was longer than I expected. I was about to text Fab when the woman in question rounded the corner, a file folder in her hand.

"And that is?" I asked.

"Some notes I made—it was the only thing I could find to write on. I discovered a fire-and-flood-proof security box full of files; it was tedious taking all those pictures. It also held a fair amount of cash and a handgun that I left untouched when I put everything back in its cubbyhole."

"I take it the box was the only interesting find." I breathed a huge sigh of relief. We'd dipped into the illegal by breaking into the place, but, at least, we hadn't sunk to the point of committing a felony.

"It surprised me to find anything, since I knew the place had been thoroughly searched." She pulled the car keys out of her pocket and handed them to me. "I'm going to take some outside shots while you go get the car and come pick me up."

"I get practice driving? Wouldn't want to forget how." I shot her a lame smile, opened the small gate in the wall and stuck my head out, looked both ways, and made my getaway. I jogged through the park—once again, not a single person in sight. Good thing, since there weren't any benches or tables, and if you wanted to sit down, the only option would be the grass. The idyllic setting must be for looks only.

It was a short drive back to the Sacks' manse. I drove under the twenty-mile-an-hour speed limit so I could check out the street and make sure no one was likely to appear suddenly. When I got there, I'd barely braked before the door flew open and Fab hopped inside; I was halfway down the street before she got it closed. Once again, there was no waiting for the ferry. Must be a record. Once onboard, I'd swap seats—so much easier on my nerves if I didn't have to listen to her complain about my driving.

Once back on the mainland, flying down the Causeway, I flipped off the radio, thinking it considerate of me to have given her brain a rest from plotting and planning. "We're not going to be able to keep this from the guys. Besides, if this is an aboveboard job, then there shouldn't be a problem." Ignoring her hands stiffening around the steering wheel, I went on. "They're psychic when it comes to the two of us."

"Let's wait to update the guys until I've reviewed all the pictures."

Why isn't this "case over"? We haven't uncovered a scintilla of evidence to prove innocence or guilt. Instead, I asked, "If Didier finds out you're withholding information again, how long will you be deprived of the chandelier... hmm... since we don't have one, ceiling fan sex?"

She shot me an icy glare, which she accentuated with a honk at some poor driver.

"One last thing."

Fab groaned.

"If at any time the fan plummets to the floor, you're paying to replace it. And not with some cheapie one. Just so you know." I flashed her a cheesy smile, which she saw but ignored.

Chapter Twenty-Eight

"What the hell?" Creole boomed. The bed dipped as he rolled over.

I opened one eye and noticed it was still dark outside. A large hand reached over my head, grabbing my phone off the bedside table. I wasn't sure which was louder, the shrill ringing or Creole.

I whined at the loss of his warmth and because I didn't want to be woken up.

He continued to grumble as he answered the phone and barked, "This better be good."

This was a first—Creole answering my phone. The late-night calls irked him. I'd tried placating him by telling him they were the downside of doing business and that problems happened.

"Go back to your house and stay inside until we get there." His tone softened. "Do not put yourself in danger in any way. Or you'll answer to me," he added gruffly before hanging up.

I sighed. Must be Mac. That tough talk would turn her on, and she'd be all giddy when she saw him.

He stood up and pulled on a pair of jeans. "You stay in bed; I'll take care of this one."

"I'm guessing a Cottages problem. I'm telling you now—you leave without me, I'll follow you, even if I have to walk in the dark," I threatened, sitting up and throwing my legs over the side of the bed. "I want to know what's going on and what you plan to do about it."

He assessed my mulish glare and held out his hand, pulling me up to stand in front of him. "There's some kind of mini-riot going on, if I deciphered Mac's ramblings correctly. It's calm for the moment, and she doesn't want law enforcement involved." He grabbed up the sundress I'd had on earlier, which I'd draped over a chair, and tossed it at me. "You got a shotgun? I'm thinking buck shot would have them hitting the road sooner rather than later."

"Thank goodness, I have neither," I said as I slipped my feet into a pair of flip-flops.

He grabbed my hand and pulled me down the hall. "You're going to let me handle this. With luck, I'll have the miscreants under control in no time." He flexed his muscles. "I'm forbidding you to get hurt—not so much as a scratch."

I saluted with my free hand.

At the top of the stairs, he turned and bent down for me to climb on his back and piggybacked me to his truck.

"This is fun." I nipped at his neck.

"Behave." He laughed.

"Are you going to fill me in?" I asked after he deposited me on the front seat and slid behind the wheel. "What time is it, anyway?" I checked his dash clock and groaned. One in the morning.

"What I want to know is why, when a *riot* happens..." His eyebrows shot up. "...Mac calls you and not Kevin? It was important that I inform you the RV is back; what does that mean? Code for wackos gone wild?"

I tried not to laugh at Creole's frustration, but it was hard. I'd had plenty of experience dealing with the drama that The Cottages could produce and managed to take most of it in stride. So far, I hadn't heard a word about shots being fired and was happy about that. "According to Mac, the Denvers—'a lovely couple'... on the phone, anyway—made a reservation for two, but when the motor home doors opened, a line of people filed out. I'm still uncertain of the exact number. Once they unloaded from the RV, the first thing they did was refuse to move it. I hadn't heard any complaints of late and assumed they were back on the road, off to their next adventure."

"Sounded to me like Mac didn't have an accurate head count," he said in disgust. "She did mention liquor, weed, and oh, yes, a couple of dogs."

I covered my face with my hands and struggled not to laugh. "Sorry," I said through my fingers. "It's just that I'm used to bad behavior but not usually by the tourists. Maybe you should let me handle this."

He let out a laugh, but he wasn't amused.

"These RV guests of yours, do you want them to stay or go? I vote for hit the road."

"That makes two of us."

He careened around the corner. Finding the driveway blocked by the RV and a couple of cars parked behind it, he backed into a space at Mac's house across the street.

"It looks like the cops aren't here yet," I said.

"I'm here. You even think about doing something crazy, and I'll arrest you."

"Yes, sir." I giggled. "That sounds fun." Fab was rubbing off on me after all.

He flipped up the top of the console, unlocked the compartment underneath, and took out his old badge, which he pocketed, and a Glock that he tucked into the back of his pants. He barely got the truck door closed before Mac ran across the street in Princess shortie pajamas and matching fluffy slippers. Whatever she was about to say got cut off by the sound of shouting, screams, and dogs barking. It sounded like it was coming from the pool area.

Mac handed Creole a megaphone. "You're going to need this to be heard over the noise."

"You two wait here," Creole ordered and took off down the driveway.

"No chance of that," I said to his retreating back, but not loud enough for him to hear. I grabbed Mac's arm—she'd been staring at Creole as he disappeared around the corner—and we ran to catch up to him. "You better stop fawning over my boyfriend like you do Didier. Fab's not here to restrain me from shooting you, and she might not save you anyway."

"You shoot me and I'll quit."

"Then a little nick will have to do," I said as we came to an abrupt halt at the pool gate, which had been propped open with a chair.

The pool area had always been my favorite—the most tranquil spot on the property, especially in the mornings. Tonight, it was teaming with an assortment of adults from twenty to eighty and five children—maybe six. All were strangers to me. I was certain I hadn't laid eyes on a one of them before. Several of the adults stood on chairs and chaises that they'd pitched into the water. The kids splashed water everywhere, screaming across the pool to one another. There were three big dogs in total, of the German Shepherd variety. Two jumped in the deep end, swimming the length of the pool, climbing up the steps, and running around to do it again. Totally cute if it weren't my pool. The third one had snagged a floating ring and was sacked out across the center of it. It surprised me he didn't have a beer in the cup holder.

Two middle-age men teetered close to the side of the pool, fighting like sumo wrestlers, arms around each other, gyrating in a circle, head butting and landing a few stray punches. One had already lost his trunks.

I noticed Crum and Joseph huddled together,

sitting in the corner on the far side of the tiki bar with their feet on a chair. Crum tipped his beer in acknowledgment of our arrival. Joseph waved. About to yell at the two for not stopping the melee, I paused; the last thing I wanted was for either of them to get hurt.

The bar held an assortment of liquor bottles, most notably bottles of Tequila. Some were enjoying beer, judging by the number of cans on the ground. A card table had been set up, and more adults crowded around it in various stages of undress, enjoying a spirited game of strip poker. It was clear who had already lost—the two who were completely naked, white butts glowing under the lights.

Creole clicked on the megaphone and bellowed, "Knock it off. Turn off the music." He gestured to the man closest to the boom box.

"Who's going to make me?" A topless woman with an enormous pair of breasts climbed out of the pool. Biggest pair I'd ever seen.

"You think they're real?" Mac whispered.

I shushed her.

"You're no fun," she whispered back.

The woman planted herself in front of Creole, hands on her hips. "You? Don't think so." She eyed him from head to toe. "You are kinda cute," she hooted. "Now be a good boy and get lost; these festivities are invitation only."

He flipped out his badge and shoved it under her nose. "You sit down and behave. If not, I can arrange a ride to the local precinct. I'm here to expedite the end to these *festivities* in an orderly fashion and without jailtime being imposed."

"Hey, everyone," she yelled, which she didn't have to do, since everyone had quieted down. Even the dogs were no longer barking; lapping up pool water instead. "The Man is here. Or so he says. I'm thinking the badge was part of his Halloween costume."

Several laughs earned a glare from Creole.

A slamming noise echoed into the area. "Shut up or I'll come out and shut you up." A disheveled woman, hair on end, shoved her head out of the bathroom window of a cottage fifty feet away. She continued to yell, but as she'd worked herself up, it was hard to make out everything she said, although the few curse words came through loud and clear.

"Come and make me, you old bag." The half-naked woman stepped away from Creole. "If you got laid once in a while by that wimpy husband of yours, you wouldn't be so bitchy."

"Last chance before I get my Glock and shut your mouth for you," the woman across the walk shouted.

Mac nudged me. "Check out Studly No-shirt."

I followed her finger and watched as barely legal Studly picked up a rock and hurled it at the bathroom window. Thankfully, it bounced off the frame.

"I'm calling the cops," the woman shouted

and slammed the window shut.

I gave Mac a slight shove. "Go work your charm and make sure she doesn't call. Reassure her that this situation is being taken care of. Hurry." *Creole's got this under control.*

Mac hustled out the gate.

Creole dragged a chair across the concrete and pointed to the over-endowed woman. "Sit." Back on the megaphone, he told the rest of those gathered around to do the same thing. "All of you who want to go to jail tonight, raise your hand." No one liked his idea, as not a single hand shot up to take him up on his offer. "In case you think I'm kidding, there's plenty of charges to go around that could result in your incarceration for a few days at least. Assault, drunkenness, nudity, gambling, and violating noise ordinances for the humans, plus separate charges for those dogs of yours." He held up a finger as he ticked off each charge.

"You see here—" The topless woman shoved her chair back and stood.

"Virginny, you sit your ass back down," one of the naked poker players bellowed. "Now. And not another word."

The woman took the chastisement well. She appeared embarrassed and sat back down.

"I'm here, as a favor to the owner, to disperse all of you in an orderly manner," Creole said. "If you don't want to play ball, I can have a few squad cars here with a phone call." He pulled his phone out of his pocket and held it up. "Anyone change their mind?" He made eye contact with the group. "Just so you can make an informed decision, if you're hauled off to jail—and that would include the dogs—you'll all have to make bail, which won't happen until after you've seen a judge. The judge has the discretion to set a high bail, lengthen your stay, or release you on your promise to return for trial, which he'd be reticent to do, since you're from out of the area."

"What do you want?" the naked player asked, apparently the head of the group.

"One-time deal—you haul yourselves out of the pool area and go back inside your cottage, where you'll stay quietly until morning. Then you'll pack up and leave the property," Creole said. "We'll forget this happened. You also agree not to come back."

"I got one better for you," their spokesperson said. "We're leaving tonight." He leaned over and said a few words to his fellow poker players.

They stood and branched out, giving instructions to the others. Everyone picked up something, including the kids, who were now laughing at one another. The dogs jumped in the pool again, and a woman yelled at them to get out, which they did after they finished their lap.

Studly checked out the bottles on the bar and grabbed one, leading the parade out the gate. He marched across the driveway, unlocked the door of the RV, slamming it against the side, and flung the stairs into a down position. The people filed inside.

It seemed a never-ending line. Where would they all sit? I'd missed two teenage girls in the original head count. The dogs were the last to board, unleashing one last shake, sending water and fur flying.

The leader of the unruly pack thrust his head out the driver's side window. "We'll be back tomorrow to clear out our stuff. Don't expect no recommendation." The engine of the RV roared, and Studly, who hadn't boarded, guided the motor home as it backed out onto the street.

I looked around and double-checked the pool area. What a mess. "Where did Crum and Joseph go?"

"They mingled with the other folks exiting and beat it over to Crum's cottage." Mac who'd come back, stood by my side. "They'll be back out when the coast is clear, which means when you two are gone."

Creole turned to Mac. "I have so much respect for what you put up with and do it everyday."

Mac giggled. "It makes it easier, knowing that if I call one or both of you, you'll show up."

Chapter Twenty-Nine

I was awake earlier than usual. Creole had already left, dropping a kiss on my lips and saying he'd see me later. The phone rang right after, Mac calling to tell me that the Denver family had returned at dawn, packed, and left. Kevin had come out of his cottage in sweat pants, his holster around his waist. Mac sighed, saying he resembled Wyatt Earp. The movie version, I assumed. He told Mac to pass along a message to me: "About damn time."

It was easy to tell, when padding down the hall, that there was no one else at home... except the cats, and they were asleep. I paused at the top of the steps and sat down, mulling over my plans for the day, which had changed to include a trip to Fab's office. She'd been secretive of late, and maybe I could get answers by tossing her office files. I needed practice, as Fab had complained after my last run-through that I took too long and she needed to follow me to make sure everything got put back in its place.

I headed back to my bedroom, laughing at the thought of what Fab's response would be if I showed up in a bathrobe and bedroom slippers.

She'd flip out; more so if I didn't have a regular outfit on underneath.

* * *

The security gates rolled back at "the offices." Fab had made the executive decision that there'd be no sign. I'd arrived in record time, even after stopping for coffee and following the speed limit, which I reminded myself to gloat to Fab about later. The property consisted of two warehouse buildings, almost identical in construction. Fab had chosen the building on the right side for its view of the inlet below. The other building had been used as a residence, and thus far, she'd ignored it.

It surprised me to see an old, red beater truck parked in the front. A client? It resembled the white one I owned and was in the same run-down condition. You couldn't judge a car by the exterior; mine ran like a charm. To keep it ready for use as our undercover vehicle, when not in use, it stayed parked on the bottom level of the warehouse, which was used as parking space.

Mulling my options, I skipped the elevator and instead made the hike up the thirty-two stairs to the second floor. To my surprise, the door was unlocked. It had been a while since I'd graced Fab with a visit, and it took a minute to register all the renovations that had been made, starting with ripping out all the walls that separated the rooms and making it one large space, which she and Didier split. Her side was all white and chrome; Didier had followed suit with the chrome but infused his side with color.

At my entrance, Fab looked up, startled. So much for tossing her files.

Another surprise, more like shock, was the reed-thin man sitting in one of the chairs placed before Fab's desk. He grinned at me, his one tooth front and center; instead of wobbling back and forth like the last time I saw him, it was now gold. He'd clearly had it fixed… because one tooth was better than none?

"Madison," he hollered, jumping out of his seat, hand extended. "Remember me… Toady?" He dropped his hand and rubbed it on his pants. "Sorry, forgot."

It took a lot to shock me into speechlessness, but this was one of those rare moments. I was surprised, but happy that he remembered about my no-handshaking policy. He'd cleaned up somewhat. Instead of being covered in fifteen layers of dirt, he'd managed to get it down to three. But he still had the skin of a reptile.

"I could never forget you." I smiled lamely. "And here you are. Everything okay?" I flashed Fab a confused look, and she leaned back in her chair, a huge grin on her face, enjoying the endless, awkward moment. "Problems in Alligator Alley?"

Toady's lot in the middle of nowhere backed

up to my brother's, and when Brad wasn't around, which I suspected was pretty much always these days, Toady patrolled the property with a shotgun, discouraging two-legged intruders. The four-legged, or sometimes more, didn't bother him.

"No, no." He shook his head. "Me and Frenchie here are doing a little business. She broke my heart." He clutched at his t-shirt. "I'm hoping she comes to her senses and dumps that other guy."

Didier being described as the *other guy* almost had me laughing. I crossed the wide-open space, dumped my purse in what was now *my* chair, and propped myself against the corner of Fab's desk. I contemplated branding the chair with a black marker, writing my name in all caps, but knew that at the first opportunity, Fab would trash it or give it to Crum. "Business, huh? What kind?" I knew I sounded suspicious but didn't give a damn.

"We got us a confidentiality agreement." Toady wagged his finger between himself and Fab.

"Ohh," I cooed. "Fab must have forgotten to tell you that I'm her partner, sidekick, backup, and we don't keep secrets." I turned to her, a silent dare for her to refute that. "Do we?"

"He's an independent contractor," Fab said after a long pause.

"Are we going to play one hundred

questions?" I demanded.

"Toady is one of my investigators, and he's done excellent work." Fab pushed a file across her desk.

Barely giving it a glance, I turned to Toady and asked. "Are you licensed?"

"Got me a PI license and one to carry this." He pulled open his polyester jacket, exposing a Sig Sauer and a well-defined bicep.

I took stock of his work outfit—wife beater tucked into cotton pants, belted, the end hanging down. The man's bony build was deceptive; underestimate at your own peril.

"Is this your first rodeo with Frenchie?" I tapped the file.

"There was that car retrieval fiasco out in my neck of the woods—had to bring in the law," Toady said, not surprised he was the one to enlighten me. "Got me some great connections—boys in blue that I've known since military days. They know I'm a straight arrow."

"If you'd stop with the questions and open the file, you'll be pleased," Fab grouched, her stiletto making contact with the glass-top desk.

I stood up, dumping my purse on the floor, and settled in my chair. Why would I want my own office? Intruding on her space suited me just fine. I propped my feet on her desk, happy my jean skirt kept me covered.

"You know that's not allowed," Fab growled.

Toady hacked a laugh and rubbed his

stomach. "I need a cigarette."

I missed whatever look Fab sent his way.

"I know, no smoking in here," he said mournfully. "Not even on the property. Thought she was joking, but no, serious as a bedbug."

Ick!

"Toady doesn't have all day." Fab flicked her hand. "Hurry up and read, and he can answer your questions."

One thing I could say for the man after flipping open the file, he put together a professional-looking report. Noting the address with an audible gasp, I pulled out the photos first.

The first one showed a large fenced-in area with dog runs housing more than two dozen large dogs that I recognized as breeds used for fighting. One photo after another showed every section of the property. Toady had captured a half-dozen more photos of dogs that had been crated and loaded into the back of a moving van. A nice close-up of the license plate. Additional pictures of the parties involved, including the shotgun-toting female property owner.

"You got so close," I said in awe. "You didn't get hurt? Guess not. You wouldn't be here to tell about it if Grandma had shot you."

"No one's shooting Toady and living to boast about it. Besides, the bullets would bounce off my rubbery skin." He puffed out his chest. "Did a little recon, crawled along the property line, and after getting a few shots, got lucky with the pooch transfer. Radioed my partner, who had street stakeout; he followed the truck while I hiked back to the road. Picked me up later at a gas station that was closed for the night. Old Toads knows how to lurk in the shadows and not attract attention."

"I'm afraid to ask where the dogs ended up," I said.

"Good and bad. Good because it gives you the proof you need to have it investigated as a dog-selling operation. Bad: the dogs were delivered to a start-up group of dog fighters. Did some checking the next day. The neighbors were close-mouthed, telling me not to come back asking questions about 'those people' again."

"Tell her the rest," Fab said, a note of smug satisfaction in her tone.

"That night, just happened that I was able to get the dogs back. They've got better digs now, where they don't have to fight to the death—a pit bull rescue farm up north."

"How long ago did this go down?" I asked.

"Two nights ago. Dozed off in the weeds. This time, I wore long sleeves—still scratching when the medicine wears off." He patted one of his arms. "The sound of a truck roaring up the gravel caught my attention real quick as it jerked to a stop and four men piled out and began yelling that the old broad stole back the dogs they'd paid for. They came prepared for an armed confrontation, and as soon as the shouting calmed down, both sides were pointing guns at one another. The front door flew open and the house emptied out with more men and guns. Finally, the dog fighters backed off, as they were outnumbered, and piled back in the truck with shouts to watch their backs." Toady's eyes glowed with excitement.

"You went back out there on a hunch?" I asked.

"Frenchie agreed with my plan and okayed the extra pay. Doesn't take no rocket person to figure out that once the dogs disappeared, they'd be back. Who else? Had to be the people they did business with." He pointed to my lap. "At the bottom of the stack are the photos I got that second night."

I wanted to let out a big sigh of relief that Fab and I hadn't been the ones out hunkering down in the weeds. Not with the way Toady had begun to itch. "Is there enough to connect the dots?"

Fab nodded.

"Frenchie told me the plan is to turn it over to one of your law enforcement friends, and once they get a gander at the report, they'll know you're not jerking a knot in their tail."

"It's unclear how many animals are involved, and they're going to need a place to go. As you know," Fab said to me, "the local pound is always full. Your job is to find them accommodations."

"We're not getting these people closed down only to have the animals killed. Not happening. I'll find them placement, even if it's temporary until they can get a forever home."

"Frenchie said you were one of those altruist people, and... well... I laughed, but now I believe her."

"Isn't that sweet." I narrowed my eyes at Fab, which earned me another smirk.

Chapter Thirty

Toady's departure took a turn toward the amusing when he stood and sidled over to Fab with the intention of laying a big kiss on her. As he bent down, she planted her hand in the middle of his chest, putting an end to one of his fantasies.

"I want to apologize for interrupting any interlude you might have enjoyed with the backup boyfriend," I said to Fab after the door closed.

Fab made a gagging noise. "I'm hungry."

"You're grouchy. Your stomach will have to wait." I pulled my phone out of my pocket.

"You in trouble?" an irritated male voice answered.

"Not exactly—I need a favor, preferably sooner, as in today, unless you're chasing felons."

"Who is that?" Fab demanded in a voice that could have been heard downstairs if the door were open.

"Help," I mouthed.

He groaned into the phone. "It's my day off,

and I don't do favors. This is an emergency-only line."

Fab jabbed her finger at the phone, impatient sign language for *put the call on speaker*.

"Free lunch." Men always liked food.

"Beer?"

Fab shot me a thumbs up.

"None of the cheap stuff, either. On my way." In Help style, he hung up without a good-bye.

I texted him the address; otherwise, he'd show up at my house and be even more annoyed when no one answered the door. My next call was to Jake's. I got Doodad and placed an order, asking for a step-on-it delivery.

Help claimed his name was Stephan, which neither Fab nor I believed, so we'd given him a cool moniker. He and Creole had partnered on many an undercover assignment, which was how we met. More than once, Help had answered a distress call from Fab and I with a rapid response of muscle and firepower.

"You're turning the dog file over to Help? Why not ask Creole?" Fab shot her foot out, kicking my feet off the desk.

"This little twelve-inch space over here is my desk." My finger drew the space for her, and I rested one foot on the corner, out of her reach unless she stood up. I could move to the twelve-foot-long conference table that ran the length of Didier's side, but I was certain Fab would like that even less. "Creole would do it, but he's not on the force any longer and I don't want him getting into trouble."

"You're irritating," Fab fumed.

"I think you've told me that before." I rubbed my chin.

"How did one little missing ankle-biter turn into going after a dog-stealing operation? You're more confident about placing the dogs than I am. I'll drive you around; that will be my contribution."

"I just sent a text to Mother, letting her know I'd be surprising her with a visit later. There's nothing she can't organize." My phone beeped— Mother texting back to say she'd be at home the rest of the day.

The gate buzzer rang. Fab looked at the video monitor. "Food and Help are here. Wonder if Help got his car at the wrecking yard. It's an old-time gas pig; no A/C, I assume, since the windows are down. Guess he doesn't worry about getting shot."

"Try to get along." I got up and opened the door. "Up here," I called down. To my surprise, the delivery guy was already back in his car, waiting for the gates to open.

"Wouldn't have figured that out, since the only door is up there," Help said, taking the steps two at a time, the shopping bag with Jake's logo in his hand.

"Did you at least tip the guy?" I asked, taking the bag and walking over to a small round table in front of the kitchenette area that seated six.

"You calling me cheap?" He bristled, his eyes narrowing.

"Let's not get sidetracked." I set out the containers and pulled out paper plates and utensils. Thank goodness I'd remembered to ask for them to be included.

The first purchase for the kitchen had been stainless steel appliances, followed by a fancy coffee maker and the eight glass espresso mugs in the cupboards. End of the dishware. At least, they bought silverware.

Help opened the refrigerator and bent down, checking out the selection of beer and finally choosing one. "Great choices — the guys make a list, you fetch?"

"You're making it hard for me to remember that I need a favor and, therefore, have to refrain from dumping food on your head." I flashed him a flinty smile.

He chuckled — not a happy sound, more disgruntled. "On the way over, it occurred to me that I failed to ask where the hell Creole is on this favor business. Called the man himself, and the bastard laughed when I told him about your call. Demanded details, and his response was he didn't want to spoil the surprise. Told him he was a bastard and hung up."

"Is that the way you guys bond?" Fab asked. "Trading insults?"

Help grinned around a mouthful of food,

eating like a man who hadn't had a meal in a long while. Fab and I traded raised eyebrows and let the man eat.

Noticing he'd finished his beer, I got him a second one and picked the report up off the desk. "I'm sure you're wondering why I called you here. So, without further suspense…" I hit the bullet points of the dog case, pushing the file across the table. "Hence, the call to you. I'm hoping you can expedite this to the right person who won't drag their feet and will put these people out of business pronto."

Help flipped through the pictures. "Nice work," he complimented Fab.

She accepted the praise with a sneaky smile. It wasn't pertinent to the case for Help to know who did what.

"Got a couple of friends on the local force — both dog owners; one owns a damn rooster, too. They'll investigate this report, and if it checks out, these folks will end up behind bars. Need to warn you, though, don't expect them to stay locked up long. They will get bail."

"Another thing, we'll help with dog placement," I said. "Fab's got a friend of a friend with a pit bull sanctuary, and my plan is to call in favors, looking for friends to shelter them until permanent homes can be found."

"We don't want them killed," Fab said, emphasizing it with a glare.

"Is that it?" Help stood and started to gather his trash.

I waved his hand away. "I got that. You have any objection to taking leftovers? They'll go to waste here." So it was a big lie; he didn't need to know that.

"Heck, yeah. If you're sure."

Fab stood and snapped lids on containers, piling them back into the bag they came in.

I grabbed the handles, handing it to Help. "We have a cop discount at Jake's, in your case, Mr. Undercover, tell the bartender you've got the Madison discount. Eat it there or to-go, doesn't matter."

"You'll get a call once the bust goes down," Help said. "Text me the number of the rescue place and we can expedite the transfers through them." He was at the door, hand on the knob. "Don't be telling anyone…"

"That you did something nice?" I laughed.

"No worries," Fab answered.

The door opened and closed.

"That went well," I said.

Chapter Thirty-One

On the way to Mother's, I mulled over my various projects. This case had turned out to be more than I'd planned. My idea was to interest Mother in helping with the shelter proposal.

Fab and I had talked about it briefly as we walked downstairs to our respective cars, me to go see Mother, Fab to meet Didier.

"Let's go get that Maltese dog from the shelter. We won't actually say that it's not his dog; just shove it in his arms and maybe he won't notice," Fab said.

"That's shameful." Not to mention impossible. It was clear Fab had never been a dog owner if she thought that would work.

"You got a better idea?" Fab asked in a huff.

"Give a girl time to think. I'll call and find out what it takes to adopt the dog. Then we tell Hank that we couldn't replace his Maddie but hoped that having another dog would soften the blow a bit."

"Don't forget, if it works out and Hank is happy, this was my idea."

Once I cleared the security gates to Mother's condo complex, I messaged her, letting her know that I was on my way up. Lucky me, I scored the only visitor space at the front of the building.

Getting off the elevator, I was surprised to see that Mother's door stood open. I called out, closing it behind me.

Mother poked her head out of the kitchen and waved.

I did a double take, thinking I'd seen a frown on her face, but she'd disappeared. I dropped my purse into the nearest chair and crossed the room in search of her. I found her sitting on a stool, nursing a glass of iced tea.

The flinty stare she leveled at me had me standing a little straighter and wondering what I'd done. Arms out, I started to give her a hug, but she stepped back and pointed to the only other stool.

"Sit." She grabbed a glass, tossed in an orange slice and filled it with ice and tea, then set it down in front of me with a thud. "Now, tell me why you encouraged Liam into the funeral business."

If she weren't so annoyed, I might have laughed, but that would be a bad idea. "I didn't—"

"Let me guess, you talked up how much fun it was to speak at the funeral of a stranger? Don't you think it's rude to pass yourself off as a friend of the dearly departed?" She tried to hide a laugh by looking down.

So, she isn't that mad.

"What if Liam changes his major to funeral arts?"

"He could intern with Dickie and would probably be really good at it."

Mother banged her head on the counter. "Ouch." She rubbed her forehead.

"Just how did you come by this information? Not to mention, it's only half-accurate." I slid off my stool and walked around the counter to where Mother stood, dragging a stool with me. "Now it's your turn to sit. Before you do, here's the hug you blew off when I got here." I put my arms around her and squeezed until she grumbled at me to let go.

"I need to know what my children are doing. So, I have to snoop around a little; it's a mother's prerogative."

"Are you paying a squealer?"

Mother thought for a minute, a devilish smile on her lips. "That's a good idea. Wonder who I could buy off? The only obstacle I foresee is that you *do* engender loyalty."

And hopefully she wouldn't be *able* to buy anyone off. Not that this family had many secrets, as they tended to leak out, or be shouted out, at family get-togethers.

The front door slammed. "Honey, I'm home," the deeply masculine voice of Spoon yelled.

I stuck my head around the corner and waved. "Hi yourself." I reclaimed my stool.

Spoon went to Mother, kissing her cheek. "Have you upset my wife?" he growled.

Mother smirked.

"If she'd let me get a word in, she'd know I'm an innocent party."

"This ought to be good." He laughed. "Innocent party, huh? Let me grab a beer." He grabbed a bottle from the refrigerator and joined us. "Is this about Liam? Brad? Something you've done? Apparently, you don't need bail money since you're sitting here."

Mother socked his arm.

It was too late to cover my eyes to keep from witnessing the flirty smiles they exchanged.

"I'm assuming this is about the funeral gig, and although my wife isn't that upset, I'd like one good reason you'd help Liam get such a crap job."

"I knew it. You're not as mad as you let on." I mimicked one of her stares, which always left me and Brad squirming. "Listen up, you two, it's my turn to defend myself." I traded glares with Spoon, his far more ferocious and scary than mine. The only reason I wasn't running for the door was I'd also caught a glimpse of amusement and knew the man wouldn't hurt me. "Liam hasn't made a career choice — he's in college, it's a side job, and it pays good. If you want to blame someone..." I pointed at Spoon. "He heard about my experience right here in this living room from the big man himself, laughing as he heard the story of how I got roped into that job. Next in line for finger-pointing are Dickie and Raul."

"Those two weirdos." Spoon snorted.

"They're family friends," I said, as though he needed reminding.

"Not really," Mother said, a squeamish look on her face.

"Yes, really," I said. "It's not like I volunteered. Fab orchestrated the event without my knowledge." She wasn't there, so I could throw her under the bus. I told them that after overhearing that little bit of gossip, Liam had sought out the funeral guys, and they were the suppliers of the information he'd needed to kickstart him getting a job.

"It's just so…" Mother stuttered. "You can talk him out of it."

"Before or after you attend a funeral with him?"

Mother's face burned.

Caught again.

Spoon put a finger under her chin, turning her face to his. "Really?"

Mother nodded. "He eagerly accepted my offer."

He hugged her to his side. "You should get a cool-grandmother award. Mine was four feet of scary."

"You know how kids are," I said to Mother. "You had two, probably felt like six at times. Pressure him and he'll dig his heels in."

"I suppose you're right."

"Could you repeat that?"

Spoon laughed.

"I really should listen to my husband; he said pretty much the same thing." Mother gave him a lovestruck smile.

"Okay, you two. No PDAs. Too much for my tender eyes."

"You staying for dinner?" Spoon asked.

"Does the invitation include Creole?" I asked.

"Of course it does," Mother said. "I'll call and invite him; that way, he won't say no."

"That's so manipulative." I laughed. "He loves you and would never say no. Besides, you always have the best food and plenty of it."

"Then we can talk about what you wanted." Mother winked.

More manipulation! "Or we could talk now, and I could hustle home with a box of donuts."

Spoon shook his head and picked up Mother's phone off the counter. "I'll call him." He went out to the patio.

"You don't have him trained very well, going out on the patio where we can't eavesdrop."

"He's better at other things."

I stuck my fingers in my ears.

* * *

Creole picked up his beer bottle. "I propose a toast—to the hostess. Thank you for inviting us to dinner."

"What about me?" Spoon thumped his chest. "I grilled this gourmet feast."

"Good job, dude."

Mother and I laughed.

We were seated around the table on the patio, eating hamburgers and skewered vegetables.

"Madeline says that the reason you called is that you've gotten yourself into some kind of trouble." Spoon gave me a penetrating stare. "You need her brains and our brawn." He toasted Creole.

"You're not funny," I shot back.

Spoon clasped his chest, and when he was finished with his histrionics, I told them about the dog case from the beginning, finishing with today's events. I reassured Mother that law enforcement was now involved and Fab and I wouldn't be having anything to do with the arrests.

Creole leaned over and kissed my cheek. "I'm proud of you."

"Tarpon doesn't have an animal shelter, and I was thinking it would be a great service that would benefit our city and the surrounding ones," I said. "I realize it won't happen overnight, though. What's needed is money to get this project off the ground; I'm thinking a fundraiser and using Jake's." I looked at Mother. "I need help, and who better than you to organize such an event and shake money out of people's pockets?"

"I think it would be fun," Mother said, appearing to have already come up with an idea or two. "Spoon and I were just talking about me needing something to do that didn't involve illegal gambling. This sounds like a project I'd enjoy taking on."

"I may know someone — have you met Blanche Bijou?" Spoon asked Mother. "She's an older woman who lives on the outskirts of town — used to run a rescue called Sanctuary Woods that took in big dogs. She hit hard times and had to stop fostering animals."

"If she's still got the licensing and is interested, it would be easy to re-open, and if not, hopefully her license could be renewed easily enough," Creole said.

"This could turn out well for both Blanche and the dogs," Spoon said. "As I recall, in addition to a large, rundown house, there's also a good-size barn. Throw in a renovation of the entire property to sweeten the pot. It would be a lot easier to fix up than start from the ground up. I've got plenty of guys that would volunteer time."

"Do you think she'd be interested?" Mother asked.

"Broke her heart to stop taking in the animals," Spoon said. "Seems like she'd jump at the chance to start up again."

"I nominate all the members of the family to join our informal group," Mother said. "It's a good reason for a family dinner; we can use the time to throw out ideas."

"Thank you." I leaned sideways and hugged her.

Chapter Thirty-Two

My phone pinged with a message from Doodad not long after Creole returned from running himself into a sweat ball, showered, and left for the day. "You coming in today?"

I answered back, "Be there before we open."

When I pulled into the parking lot at Jake's, I breathed a sigh of relief at seeing that the property was still standing. Last night had been theme night, and I'd forgotten. When Creole remembered, he'd be happy that neither of us had gone.

Gunz apparently kept early business hours—he finished locking up the lighthouse, waved, hauled his considerable bulk onto his Harley, and roared out into traffic. He'd assured me his business was legal, and I didn't question him beyond that, hoping it didn't come back to bite me.

I drove around to the back entrance of Jake's and parked, going in through the kitchen and waving to Cook as I headed down the hall.

Doodad straightened from stocking underneath the bar.

I waved to him. "Early morning summons,

must be good news."

"Everything is good news; just depends on how you choose to look at things."

"I'll have a double orange juice," I said and slid onto a stool. "Then you can spin your happy story."

Doodad poured my juice and set it in front of me. "Hula night was a success."

I mimicked a hula dancer. "And Jake's is still standing. You're right; it is good news."

He refilled my orange juice. "I could put a little tequila in here."

"Tequila in the morning?" I turned up my nose. "Just blurt out what you're struggling to say."

"I should've called… it was after midnight…" He ran his hand through his hair. "…no one got hurt or arrested."

The front door flew open, and Kelpie blew in like a wild wind in what I'd guess to be a bathing suit tucked into poured-on jeans over an ample backside, her bountiful cleavage on display. Doodad had had the say on her hire, and as it turned out, the regulars loved her. I'd seen her in action. She entertained her fans with an outrageous sense of humor; men filled the stools at the bar, and she even had a few women vying for the seats. She boosted the bottom line on the shifts she worked, so that made me happy.

Kelpie waved. "The bar fight was my fault. Don't you take any blame," she said to Doodad, dropping a large bag on the pool table. "No one was maimed," she yelled over her shoulder as she crossed the threshold out onto the patio, turning on the fans and lights.

Not again.

Kelpie came back inside and began flipping over chairs, setting them on the floor. She whirled around the space until she had everything ready for business, finally joining us. "I'll take a soda, Bossaroo." She slammed her hand on the bar top. "I tried to get here earlier, knowing the fight would be the topic of the day, but couldn't get my ass in gear." She scooped her multi-colored hair — brown and blond, with a shock of purple in the front — into a messy knot, producing a clip from somewhere and affixing it to the top of her head. "If you didn't know, bar fights fill the house for days to come."

"I'm the one who told her about fights being good for the bottom line," Doodad said sheepishly.

I knew all about the benefits of bar fights. Couldn't wait to hear the rest.

"Coming up with the idea was the easy part, but I didn't factor in that some nit would call the police." Kelpie sighed.

I barely restrained myself from covering my face with my hands. "Did you start the fight?"

"Sort of… I paid for it."

"You what?" I screeched.

"Damn, girl." Kelpie rubbed her ears. "That

noise could make a person go deaf." She mimicked the noise I'd made, then laughed. "I paid for a little well-orchestrated bout of fisticuffs."

I narrowed my eyes.

She threw her hands in the air. "Ask anyone. A good time was had—laughing, joking, downing the beers... That is, until the police cruised through the door. Next showtime..." She picked at one of her nails. "I'll check and make sure Deputy Kevin has the night off. We aren't simpatico."

I hoped that it didn't have anything to do with the two of them getting horizontal. "You haven't met my boyfriend, Creole, yet, but just so you know, he has zero appreciation for any bar fights and less for ones that are orchestrated. When he finds out, he'll flip," I said. "Frankly, I'd like to skip the lecture."

"Easy fix. We don't tell him." Kelpie wiggled her chest. "Creole—sounds hunky and just my type. You introduce us; I can persuade him." She winked.

Doodad smirked and looked down, busying himself moving things around.

"Creole is *my* boyfriend. I'm well aware I can't beat you up, but a well-placed bullet would be a good reminder that he's mine."

"It's like that, huh? Gotcha. Plenty of man hunk in this town. No need to fight over 'em, especially not with my boss. And did I tell you how much I like the job?" Not satisfied with a mere shake this time, Kelpie rearranged her girls, licked her finger, and ran it across her cleavage.

I laughed, thinking if Mac Lane had a sister, it would be Kelpie Reese. Whatever reservations I'd initially had about her were gone—well, almost.

"What if your paid fighters sue me?"

"No chance." She snorted. "They're professionals… up and coming, anyway. It was staged to look like a raucous chick fight, one where no one gets hurt. Bruise or two, probably. As a favor to me, they did it on the cheap with the promise of a free meal."

"I'd like to say I was completely innocent, but I knew in advance," Doodad said. "I had faith that Kelpie could make it happen, but like her, didn't plan on someone ratting us out."

"There was one fatality," Kelpie said.

My mouth dropped open. "Someone died? And you two didn't think that deserved a middle-of-the-night phone call, or, at the very least, think to open this little sit-down with that headline?"

"Calm yourself. Just kidding." Kelpie patted my hand. "No one croaked. Jimbo's ex showed up at the end of the night—skinny little thing, no bigger around than my finger." She held up her pinkie. "All coked up, gyrating around, hands flying everywhere, demanding a reconciliation. And when he tried to push a stool between them to get some room, she kicked it, vaulted herself onto the big man, and proceeded to claw his eyes out."

"Jimbo go to the hospital?" He was our designated driver for weekends and theme nights. He'd been hired at Christmastime and stuck around. Turns out drunks are good tippers.

"Before I could get around the bar..." Kelpie twirled on her stool, hands swinging over her head in what I assumed was an imitation of Jimbo's ex. "...a couple of regulars each grabbed an arm and a leg and hauled her outside. She got up and hopped off like some jackrabbit."

"Jimbo's fine," Doodad said. "There was a school nurse here last night, and she fixed him right up using the first-aid kit. Did mention that we ought to upgrade our kit." At my frown, he added, "I'll pick one up today."

"You said Kevin showed up; how did that go?" I'd often wondered how he seemed to always draw the short straw on these emergency calls. "I'm thinking no one went to jail or you'd have mentioned that by now?" As an afterthought, I asked, "You would, wouldn't you?"

"Old Kev, uptight as usual, had a few questions," Kelpie said. "One of our thick-and-thin regulars who never bolts for the door told him that most of the customers beat it out the back. His response: 'Don't they always?' A couple of guys I assumed to be friends gave him a shout, he joined their table, they had a few laughs, and he left."

"He was long gone before the Jimbo thing," Doodad said. "So see, all kinds of happy news."

"Next theme night?" I asked.

"Two weeks. Wet t-shirt night."

"Isn't that kind of sexist when you know the girls will win all the prizes?" My next thought was it sounded better than fighting.

"The men... we're going to soak in a different area," Kelpie said.

My cheeks felt like they'd caught fire. "No, no, we're not doing that. Besides, we don't have a faucet inside."

"We have one and a hose on the deck," Kelpie said, her tone clearly telegraphing the unspoken question, *Did you forget?* "That's why we're setting up out there, and then they can come inside and parade around."

"We'll do two prizes—free drink to the winner," Doodad said.

Two regulars came through the door, ready to drink a late breakfast. They shouted hellos to Kelpie and Doodad and claimed stools at the other end of the bar.

Kelpie came around the bar and stored her bag in a cupboard. She went down to the men, slapping down napkins. "What will it be, gentlemen?"

Chapter Thirty-Three

Dropping my briefcase on the bench in the entry, I snapped my fingers at Fab, who was sitting at the island, chin on her hands. "Okay, backup, let's get going."

"My feet are tired," she whined, holding one up before setting it on the stool next to her.

"Feet off the furniture. This isn't a barn."

The barn comment didn't sit well with the sophisticated woman, but she kept whatever sat on the tip of her tongue to herself.

"We all have to do things we don't want to. And if you don't come with me, I'm going to tell on you." I started sobbing, congratulating myself on improving my noisemaking.

Fab stuck her fingers in her ears. "I'm tired of your blackmail. One of these days, it isn't going to work." She stood up.

"When that day comes, I'll think of something else. We're going to the docks, so go shoe-appropriate." I gathered my briefcase and purse and headed out the door. Not hearing Fab behind me and not about to turn around, I yelled. "Hurry up or I'm driving." I smiled as the door slammed shut.

"What's so important?" Fab asked, getting behind the wheel of the SUV. "I've already had a long morning."

"I wonder if I can get a violin app on my phone." I checked the time on the dashboard. "I'm meeting Quattro in ten minutes, and he's usually early. If he complains to Didier, I'm pointing the finger at you."

Quattro claimed to have been a friend of my aunt, but I'd never heard her speak of him. We'd met at her funeral, and since that day, I'd run into him a couple of times around town. Recently, he'd been promoted inside the Code Department and had once told me, "You need anything, shout." Today was that day.

Fab hit the gas and squealed the tires, sending us shooting down the road. "We'll be there in five."

I grabbed the armrest. I should've known she'd take it as a challenge.

A few alley shortcuts later, we arrived in one piece and pulled up right behind Quattro's pickup truck, which had just arrived.

"Be nice," I said, getting out and shutting the door on any response.

Quattro gave me his signature two-handed wave, showing that he was missing a middle finger on one hand and a thumb on the other. I'd heard that Quattro was a nickname, but he'd liked it so much, he had his name legally changed. In his sixties, with slicked-back grey hair, his beer gut diminished since the last time I'd seen him. He looked professional in his pressed tan slacks and white shirt with pocket protector.

"Thank you for calling." I smiled at him. "Not sure how our original appointment got missed. The guys appreciate your rescheduling." And without a lot of hassle, I thought, but didn't say. I took the building key out of my pocket—all the locks had been rekeyed after the fire; one key made access to the various buildings much easier.

"You were always nice to me back in the old days, when most people thought I was an old weirdo. Now that I'm cleaned up, those same folks barely recognize me." Quattro barked a laugh.

"People. Ignore them. I know for a fact that you're an easy man to get along with, so that makes it their problem." I handed over the key. "What do you need me to do?"

"Not a thing. I'll be going through each building, checking to make sure the work was completed to code, and then I can sign off on this first part and you can move the project along."

"We'll wait out here."

He nodded. "You'll be seeing a lot of me; I asked to be assigned to this project. Old Corndog still has a trick or two up his sleeve, and this is a doozy of a renovation."

"Have you heard if the cops have any leads on

the fire? I'd hoped to hear about an arson arrest by this time."

"At first, it was all the talk at the office, but I haven't heard any rumors lately. Guess the cops are being tight-lipped. Probably, cause everyone's interested. This is the first case of arson I remember in Tarpon Cove since I went to work for the city." He reached in the window of his truck and grabbed a clipboard. "This shouldn't take long."

I watched as he walked down the block to the first building and went inside.

Fab came up, phone in hand. "Just talked to Didier. Told him we were here and that I insisted on driving. Didn't want you coming by yourself, since it's creepy when there's no one around."

"You should send a p.s. that I was humbled by your generous offer."

"That's a good one, but I'll rephrase it so it doesn't sound so snotty. What does a backup do on this particular job?"

"You make sure that nothing *creepy* comes out of one of these shells of a building and snatches us up." I looked up and down the street; Fab was right about the eerie vibe.

"I've got my Walther, and it's fully loaded." She patted the small of her back.

I glanced at her silk pants and sleeveless top, and then down to her tennis shoes. "You need to apologize to the rest of your amazing outfit for the shoes."

"This isn't the area for a cute pair—too hard to run in."

"I'm changing your title on this job to official photographer. The restoration needs to be recorded in pictures—it would make a great book."

"I've got a file on my computer with pictures from the first time this project got mentioned and add more on every trip we make down here."

The roar of an engine would have had me turning, but Fab grabbed my arm.

"Trouble just turned onto the street. I may get to use my weapon, after all. You think for a few extra bucks, Quattro would help us dispose of a body?"

"Who is it?" I jerked my arm from her grasp and turned.

"Bordello, and he just parked behind the Hummer."

"Not today," I groaned. "Let's ignore him and go catch up with Quattro."

Fab stepped away from my grasping hand. "He has no right to be down here. We do. I, for one, want to know what he wants. You know it's something or he wouldn't be slumming it."

"Judging from his smarmy smile, it's something we're not going to like." I watched as Bordello closed the distance between us. Surprised me that he'd loosened his tie and left his jacket in the car.

"Hello, you two," Bordello said as he

approached, perusing us from head to toe. We clearly came up a wardrobe disaster. "Imagine seeing you down here." His tone conveyed that he wasn't happy, and he looked like he'd bit on something sour.

Exchanging a quick look with Fab, I telegraphed, *You first.*

No, her militant response came back.

You're the trespasser didn't sound friendly and neither did *you don't have business interests down here and we do, so why the heck are you here?* Instead, I asked, "How's my brother?" That seemed like a safe subject. Fab moved closer, which I appreciated.

"Didn't you just have lunch with him?" He quirked a brow.

"You'd think I'd remember that, but sadly, I don't." Was he fishing? For what? I needed to calm down and stop suspecting every word out of his mouth. Try for amiable and maybe he'd go away.

"I wanted to purchase this area." He waved his hand around. "But then, you two are well aware of that. It wouldn't surprise me if you persuaded that old man to take on a project he's not capable of handling, even with that new partner of his. A model," he sneered.

I felt Fab stiffening and reached behind me, tugging on her pant leg, a gentle reminder that we didn't have enough to justify self-defense.

"The deal. You lost. Want to know why?" I

ignored the tightening of his facial features. "You. You're the reason. Besides being short on personality — " Okay, that was mean. " — those so-called accidents that happened to the man, oh so coincidently, which I don't believe in and I'm sure you don't either... Where was I...?"

"Coincidences," Fab whispered loudly.

Bordello's face now radiated anger.

"Ah, yes. Every single time Corndog turned down one of your offers, he ended up in a doctor's office or a hospital. Just because you and your lackeys aren't in jail doesn't mean that you're not guilty. There are some that give you the benefit of the doubt, but only because they want to believe in you." He and I both knew I was talking about my brother, though that all-encompassing support seemed to be waning. "Not to mention, you've never once denied any involvement."

"That's me — the big bad wolf."

"It's been swell running into you." I checked my watch. "My attention is needed elsewhere."

"We're not done here," he said in a threatening tone, stopping us both in our tracks. "Don't you want to know why I came down here today? I wanted to see how the area's recovered from yet another fire. Sad to see the only moneymaker, the docks, reduced to rubble. And not the first fire. Be interesting to see if it's the last. If only you — " He stared me down. " — had minded your own business."

"Grow up, stop your whining, and get over it. Don't you have a new project to keep you entertained?"

The anger radiated off him in waves. "And you," he sneered, turning to Fab. "Who would sell *you* an office building?" He laughed, if it could be called that, a frightening sound that was meant to raise our neck hair and succeeded.

Fab unleashed "creepy girl" on him. "You have your *sister* to thank for that—showing up at the funeral, handing out her business card."

Mentioning his secret sister elicited a snarl. "I heard how close you two came to ending up in handcuffs over on the Venetian Islands. Damn sad you aren't locked up and rotting away. There's always next time. Who knew you'd take that ex-cop with you? I'll have to plan for that contingency next time."

That rattled me. "You set us up?" I asked.

He threw his wrists out in front of him. "Arrest me. That's right—no proof and there never will be. Go ahead, tell anyone you want, just the rantings of lunatic bitches."

"Don't you think it's about time to call a truce?" My first option would be to see him tossed in the Gulf, never to resurface. "You're in a partnership with my brother, and should we see one another again, we can agree to be cordial." I planned to tell Mother I'd never attend another dinner that he'd been invited to.

"I'm a magnanimous fellow. No hard feelings.

Just know that if we ever go head-to head on another deal, You. Will. Not. Win."

"We'll be on our way," I said.

"There's one more thing. I don't like having a gun pointed in my face; make damn sure it never happens again, or you'll wish you heeded my advice."

"Enough with the threats," Fab snapped. "Truce or not?"

He nodded. Fab jerked my arm, and we walked toward the building Quattro had just entered. "Don't say anything until Bordello's back in his car," I whispered.

We heard the car door slam shut. Several minutes went by before he fired up the engine.

"We have a powerful enemy," Fab said.

"Look at me. I'm going to fix this." I looked her in the eye. "Promise. Pinkie swear. That bastard will never bother us again. I give you my word." Damn, if only one of us had thought to push the record button on our phone.

"You're not going to take one of those fishermen you know up on their beer-and-cash deal to make him disappear, are you?"

I laughed, releasing some of the tension in my body. "That's a tempting idea."

"I really want a drink. I'm thinking double vodka and mini-tacos. How long before Quattro is done?"

"Yum." I licked my lips. "Don't go bothering Quattro or he'll never get done; he'll be too busy ogling you and trying to figure a way to get you to dump Didier. He wouldn't be the first man to concoct that loser plan." I was pleased I'd made her laugh. "One other thing, we're not going to mention running into Bordello until I enact my plan. Then we'll line up the Euro beers and tell all. They won't like it, but I don't want them going half-cocked and hunting Bordello's behind down. You know they would, and Bordello would end up black and blue and have two more grudges to hold."

"You better know what you're doing."

"I'll take the blame."

"We'll go halfsies." She jumped back. "No hug."

Chapter Thirty-Four

Fab and I were sitting out on the patio, drinking our morning coffee and commenting on what a quiet couple of days it had been. We'd both had plenty of work to do, just no emergencies.

My phone rang, and I picked it up off the chaise. I glanced down at the screen and, seeing GC's name, wondered if he had the information I'd recently requested.

Once connected, he didn't wait for even a casual hello before launching into what he wanted. "I need your help and I need it now."

"What's going on?" Normally, I asked before putting him on speaker, but the urgency in his voice told me it would be okay.

Fab raised her eyebrows and moved closer until she was sharing my chaise.

"The dog raid went down. The cops rounded everyone up, and they're in jail—the Boyer family and some of their associates."

"That's good news," I said.

"Cara's missing, and you need to find her." GC sounded frantic. "I'd do it, but you're closer."

"Who?" Fab mouthed.

I shook my head. "How can we help?"

"I need you to get out to that property and find Cara before the cops do. Keep her safe and away from law enforcement. She's not on their radar, according to the police report; her grandmother didn't mention her existence to the cops. Probably on purpose."

Judging by the noise in the background, something had been thrown and smashed to bits. He continued, "The cops swarmed the place in the early hours, and Cara, who's fourteen, somehow managed to stay out of sight and slip off the property. The report says that they searched the property and all the outbuildings and there's no mention of her."

GC calmed somewhat. "Cara thinks she's thirty and can take care of herself, but that's not going to happen. I need you to find her and take her to her other grandparents, who she knows and will be happy to see. They're expecting her. I gave them my word to send the best, and you better not let me down."

"Is this illegal, as in kidnapping or something?" I asked.

"Hell no," he growled. "The story will be that she spent the night with her other grandparents. While Mabel is behind bars, I'll get this to court and get Mabel's rights terminated. In case you're feeling any sympathy, Mabel's the one who guards the place with a shotgun."

"Text me Cara's picture. Any clue where she might go? Friends?"

"Mabel never allowed her to have friends. In fact, she took her out of school to homeschool her, and she's not allowed to leave the property. Check out the surrounding properties; she could be hiding out anywhere... including back at home. She's smart enough to go back to the property once the cops clear out."

"Give Fab and I two minutes and we'll be out the door," I said.

GC grunted. "Good job, by the way, making it easy for the cops to relocate all those dogs. Heard it went orderly. They're thankful, too, knowing that these animals will be taken care of—food and a safe place. Don't know anyone in law enforcement that doesn't have a pet."

"There are lots of people to thank for making that go smoothly. No one turned us down or asked a lot of questions we couldn't answer in advance. They'll know now," I said.

"Call me if you need anything."

"We'll stay in touch." We hung up.

"Pants." Fab motioned to our bare legs. "We don't need to get eaten by bugs."

The two of us ran upstairs to change into jeans and long-sleeved t-shirts, and made it back downstairs and out to the car in under five minutes.

Fab headed south out of the Cove, and I didn't offer directions. Once Fab had been to a place, she didn't need to be told a second time.

"I think that GC wanted a way to shut down

that dog operation without leaving his prints on it, and it was his lucky day when you called." Fab gripped the steering wheel tighter. "When you asked about the dogs and he had a quick response, I wondered if he had some connection. Do you suppose he's related to Mabel?"

"If he is, he doesn't like her. It wouldn't surprise me if the connection is to Cara or her grandparents. What surprises me is that, with his attention to detail, he didn't factor in Cara going missing."

"If the cops had found her, she'd be in child protective custody right now, and how soon they'd let her go live with a different family member, I'm not sure," Fab said.

My phone alerted several times. The first message was Cara's picture. "According to the second message, Cara is 5' 2" and 90 pounds—skinny little thing. Hope she's naturally thin and not starved. Brown shoulder-length hair and brown eyes. She's smiling and has a cute dimple."

"How are we going to convince Cara to get in our car and not come off as kidnappers?"

"We both have kid rapport," I reminded her. "Look at Liam—he loves us. We'll talk to her like she's the thirty-year-old GC said and not a kid."

"You want to make a wager?" Fab asked. Without waiting for a response, she said, "I'm betting that if we have any problems and get GC on the phone, he can make it happen."

"Not taking that bet. That's a great back-up plan. GC also included the grandparents' number, which could be plan C. I'd like to test out B. We know nothing about the man, and this would give us somewhere to start. He'll flip, but he can't stay hidden forever, no matter what he thinks."

"We run the risk of him dumping us as clients. He gives us good, thorough dirt."

"Thought of something else. Remember the kid on the bicycle? I remember which driveway he turned into; maybe he's got some helpful information."

"Except that if I was his mom, you showing up out of the blue would be a huge red flag and I'd shoot you. Most people aren't as high-strung as me, but they'd at least call the cops."

"High-strung? That's a good one."

* * *

Fab turned off, driving slowly, each of us scanning our side of the road.

I pressed my face against the passenger window. "Do you suppose that's the same cow as before?" The animal appeared content, munching on the grass.

I didn't get a response and peeked over my shoulder.

"Were you expecting an answer? I'm certain this is your way of telling me that you don't know what we're doing next."

"We continue down this street to the end, on the lookout for any human being, and if we get lucky, we pull over and ask if they've seen Cara. That might raise an eyebrow, especially since no one's probably seen her around before. Now there's a sad thought. She should be focused on school, friends, and a boy or two. I would like to know how she ended up out here with crazy Mabel."

The road appeared to go farther than it did, and we came to the end without having spotted anything unusual.

"I noticed, as we drove past the property, that the gate was left standing open," Fab said. "Lucky us. It's not trespassing to drive up to someone's house."

"What if someone's there? It's unnerving out here, a little too isolated for me."

"We'll pass ourselves off as friends of Mabel."

"Hmm... I bet if they know her, they won't believe us. Let's just hope that if there's anyone around, they don't come out the door, gun in hand."

We'd only seen pictures of the house. In person, it was a worn-down piece of property. Several of the repairs to the wood-frame house had been done by someone who took no pride in their work.

"Have your Glock ready," Fab said. "For once, I'm thinking going into the house for a sneak around might be a bad idea." She shuddered. "If the door's unlocked, we call inside to Cara, which would probably scare her. Be sure you mention the other grandparents up front."

I opened the last message on my phone. "Wright is their name."

"We're not splitting up. After the house, we'll look in the outbuildings. She's been living with criminals for who knows how long; she's probably learned a few survival skills."

"The Wrights better be decent people, or I don't know what we're going to do."

"At fourteen, Cara will know whether or not she wants to live with the people," Fab said, parking across from the front door.

"You do realize that no one knows we're out here except GC, and the guys aren't going to like it?"

"Send a message before we get out of the car." Fab handed me my phone.

"I can guarantee the phone will ring two seconds after Creole reads the message."

Fab got out and surveyed the property.

I came up behind her. "Remember, we stick together."

Fab kicked the steps to determine if they were safe to walk up. "Give it your best knock," she said, standing at the front door.

"That would scare Cara." I knocked and got no response, which didn't surprise either of us. I pulled out the end of my t-shirt, wrapping it around my hand, and turned the knob. I exchanged a glance with Fab and shoved it open. The smell of mold was overwhelming.

"Cara," I called. "I'm here with a message from the Wrights."

The house remained eerily quiet.

Fab scooted past me and into the house. "Guard the door." She drew her Walther.

"What about that 'not going in' speech?" I asked.

"Changed my mind." She looked into the kitchen and disappeared down the hall. "Cara, we're here to give you a ride to the Wrights if you want one." Fab banged a door closed, making me jump. "If not, I'll take you anywhere you want to go," she said, followed by another bang. Fab made her presence known by opening and closing doors as she made her way through the house. Finally, she reappeared. "If Cara's in here, she's got a good hiding place."

"Let's get out of here."

The next stop was the first barn-like structure, where dog runs had been constructed, opening on one side to a fenced yard. There wasn't anywhere for anyone to hide without being noticed. It was weird to know that only a few days ago, this building had been full of endangered dogs.

The only other building was an actual barn, with four enclosed stalls and an empty tack room. Only one stall appeared to have been recently occupied. The other three were clean.

"Cara, I'm Fab, and my friend Madison is with me." She made her way quietly over to the far corner, where there was a ladder to a small loft overhead. She motioned for me to talk, then reholstered her weapon and climbed up.

"This is Madison. We're here to give you a ride to your grandparents—the Wrights. If you don't want to go, fine, but just know that we'll help in any way we can."

No answer.

Fab now stood at the top of the ladder. "Cara, I know you're up here," she said in a soft voice. "Where else? It's a great hiding place. You want to know how I figured out your hiding place? You moved and that caused an ever-so-slight creaking noise. Most people wouldn't notice, but I've got great hearing, to the annoyance of most of my acquaintances." Fab waved down to me and twisted her fingers in front of her lips for me to be quiet. "You thinking it over?"

"You can go. Don't try anything—I'm armed," came a small female voice.

"Armed?" Cara had Fab's full attention. "If you're talking about a gun, don't fire it; it will ruin your life. I know about jail, and it's a sucky place. Of course, I was innocent."

That elicited a giggle.

I ignored Fab's "be quiet" edict. "Cara, Madison again. The reason we're here is that a cranky know-it-all called and is worried about you. I'd give you his name, but he's a secretive fellow. I'm thinking you might know who I'm talking about. I can toss up my phone, and you can talk to him."

"Why don't you know... his name?" Cara asked.

"I don't know. He just never gave it to us, instead, told us to call him GC, as in Gunz's Connection, for the man who made the introduction. We assumed he's a nerdy geek and loves the drama," Fab told her.

"Theodore?" It was clear that she liked Theodore Gunzelman, aka Gunz, aka badass biker.

"He's a friend of mine. Madison... not as much as me, but they're working on it. No fistfights so far."

Cara laughed.

"Forget Madison's phone; mine is way cooler. I'm sliding it across the floor. You can call either man and check us out."

"I don't know their numbers. I'm not allowed to have a phone." Cara sniffed now, sounding distraught.

"You might as well come out from behind the hay. Doesn't it smell?" Fab asked. "Stick out your hand. My phone will have GC's name on the screen; all you have to do is push call."

"I'm not sure I can trust you; you're a stranger." Cara now sounded younger than her fourteen years.

"If we had plans to kidnap you or whatever, it would be over and we'd already be down the road," Fab said. "Here's a tip for you: if you ever have to hide in the future, and I hope you don't, always leave yourself an exit. Got it?"

"I didn't think about that. I was surprised that anyone would come out here. Thought it might be a customer and they'd be mad that I couldn't help them."

"I'm going to leave my phone here and go back down to the ground." Fab laid it down.

From my vantage point, I could see that Cara had already crawled out of her cubbyhole. She picked the phone up and peeked over the edge. "This is cool."

"Trust me," I said as she lifted the phone to her ear. "Fab likes her toys, and they're always good ones."

"No yelling," she yelled, jerking the phone away from her ear. "No wonder the woman said you were grouchy. It's Cara. Heard you got a new name… You know I won't do that."

Now I know how Fab feels when she can't listen in – terribly frustrated. "Did you push the record button, by chance?" I whispered to Fab, who stood next to me. She shook her head.

Up in the loft, Cara said, "Can I trust these two? They want to take me to Grandma and Grandpa's house. I do love them, but I'd rather come live with you."

There was a long silence as she listened.

"Okay," she said, disappointed. "When do I get to see you?" His answer had her smiling. "I'll tell them." She laughed and hung up, climbing down the stairs. She looked exactly like the photo GC had sent over... a little older maybe. Her clothes were worn, her tennis shoes barely hanging together.

She checked us both out, handing Fab her phone. It was evident in her eyes that she'd seen too much of the seedy side of life in her short time on earth.

"He said to tell you to give him a call when you clear this 'hellhole.'" Cara laughed.

"Anything you want to take?" I asked.

"I'll get my clothes." She ran into the house.

My phone beeped, and I read the message. "GC wants us to wait with her at the Bakery Café until the Wrights show up. I don't like that idea. We don't know anything about them."

"Cara knows them and is fine with it," Fab reminded me. "I'll get their license plate number—you'll have to find someone else to run it—and then we'll at least know where they live and can check it out."

In less than five minutes, Cara reappeared, slamming the door behind her, two plastic grocery bags in her hands.

"That's it?" Fab asked while Cara was still out of earshot.

I knew why, and it made me angry. Not wanting to embarrass Cara, I shushed Fab. When

Cara reached us, I handed her my phone. "When we're on the road, call Grouchy back." I frowned at Fab.

Fab got behind the wheel, turned to Cara, and said, "Do these relatives of yours live close by?"

"I'm not really sure."

"Find out from your friend—" She pointed to the phone. "—how long we're going to have to wait. Tell him we could be doing something a lot more fun than sitting there."

Cara called GC, then tapped Fab on the shoulder. "An hour, depending on traffic."

Fab nodded.

When Cara hung up, I handed her two business cards, mine and Fab's. "You ever need anything—anytime, night or day—call one or both of us, and we'll help you out. And when you get a phone, you call, and I'll add you to my contact list."

"Fab's a PI, how cool is that?" She stared at my card. "This one just has your name on it." She looked at me skeptically.

"I'm an entrepreneur. Means I own a couple of businesses. Don't judge by my boring card; I can make things happen." I fished my phone out of my pocket and hit a number. "Mr. Gunzelman. Yes, before you ask, I want something."

"What now?" he barked.

"Cara needs a phone. I know you can make that happen. You'll need to get delivery instructions from your friend GC."

"Cara?"

"Want to talk to her?" I didn't wait for an answer and handed her the phone.

"Hiiii," she screeched into the phone. "I've… I can't… I'm not alone."

The rest of the conversation was full of "yes" and "no" and a couple of squeals. She ended the conversation with, "See you soon," and handed my phone back, saying, "Thanks for that."

Chapter Thirty-Five

If that piece of... Bordello thought he was going to ruin my and Fab's lives, he'd better think again. I wasn't a "get even" kind of girl, but I refused to live in fear. After our run-in at the docks, I had no doubt that he knew where to find the two us and that we hadn't heard the last of him.

"Does that phone call you're making have anything to do with this plan of yours that you're keeping to yourself?" Fab huffed. "If so, hang up and run it by me first."

"Have some faith."

"You again?" GC answered the phone, but then, he already knew that, as he'd given us our own phone number to call.

I suspected each of his customers got their own number; that way, if something went south, it was easy to end the relationship. He'd never disclosed an address, only set up drop-off points, and his favorite with us was the lighthouse, which worked since he and Gunz were longtime friends.

Since the day we rescued Cara, I'd talked to him once; he didn't mention her name and neither did I. Cara did call Fab and I and gave us her phone number, and we both extracted promises that she'd call if she needed anything. I know that Fab had called her again, checking in.

"Yes, your favorite client." I hit the speaker button and set the phone in the center of the kitchen island.

Fab rested her elbows on the countertop, leaning forward.

"You know I hate being on speakerphone," GC grouched.

"It's just my partner. I made a promise that I'd never allow anyone to be privy to our conversations or phone calls except her, and I'm a woman of my word."

"What do you want?"

"Coffee's good for surliness." I frowned at Fab, who was laughing. "I need a message sent."

GC cut in. "I'm not a damn messenger. Call Speedy Service in town."

"Calm down. Hear me out and then interrupt."

"Hurry it up."

"I need someone to deliver a face-to-face 'no contact' order. I'd like the man scared for his life should he violate said order, and the man in question is a tough bastard. I want all of it conveyed without leaving so much as a scratch."

"So, you want a fear-induced colon cleanse?"

"Eww." Fab grabbed her throat, mimicking sickness.

"Who is this person? Anyone I know?"

"Bordello," I said evenly.

GC laughed and continued to laugh. After a minute, he got himself together. "I'm honored you thought of me." He laughed again. "I've got just the guy. Burly fellow, square head, reminds me of that actor with the green face, used to be on television."

Fab and I exchanged a look, shaking our heads; we had no clue.

"A little too much starch in his shorts, but if he can't do the job, no one can."

"I'll want a report," I said.

"No problem. I'll set up a face-to-face at that hole you own—you know, the bar—and you can get a firsthand account and pay him directly. All cash, in an envelope. And be discreet."

"This won't be my first cash payment. I know how it works."

"My messenger won't drag his size fifteens. You'll get a text." He hung up.

I hit redial.

"What?" he answered.

"Does this guy have a name?" I asked.

"Snug. Anything else?"

I looked at the screen and saw he'd hung up once again.

"Not much on phone manners," Fab said.

"Good-bye is apparently overrated."

"Not to rain on your idea, but do you think it's going to work?"

"It has to. My only regret is that we didn't tape the confrontation on the docks. But then what? Involve the police? It gets dragged out forever, and in the meantime, Bordello will come up with some way to get revenge on us."

* * *

It wasn't just lip service when GC said it would be fast—he texted me a couple of days later to meet Snug at "the hole" at noon. "Can't miss him; he's the tall guy."

GC timed it right, as Fab and I had been about to hit up our favorite roach coach with mini-tacos on the mind. Instead of turning into the parking lot, Fab u-turned and headed to Jake's.

"Tall." Fab snorted. "That fits half the men in the Keys."

"I have a lump in my stomach." I rubbed circles in my tummy. "Hope my bright idea doesn't backfire."

"Calm down. Here's why this will work—has GC ever let us down? No. He always over-performs. Besides, I think if he thought it was a totally sucky idea, he would have told you that it was better to leave town."

"If this works, I'm going to get Snug's card and put it with the rest of my *special* contacts."

Fab laughed. "Ass-kickers don't have business cards. You're the one who's going to need a new business card; you're becoming quite the information-getter yourself."

"That reminds me, there's resistance on the city council over the dock project. I heard gossip about it and then bribed an assistant to get an expedited copy of the meeting minutes. One man proclaimed it would only attract filth. So he's a maybe, and another man also a maybe. Rumor has it—"

"More information you paid for?" Fab interrupted.

"I did offer that same clerk a bonus if she had any additional information to add and said that it could be unofficial. She told me that the second man votes the way his wife tells him to. Before you ask, she's not on the board." I looked briefly out the window as a car laid on the horn, surprised it wasn't at Fab but instead a pedestrian, who flipped the driver off.

"What are you going to do, bribe them with a plate of enchiladas?"

"Why can't it just be a friendly conversation over food? After all, we're all on the same side— what's best for Tarpon Cove."

Fab snorted. "You prettied that right up." She signaled and pulled into the parking lot of Jake's, slowing to check out what the rest of the businesses were doing. True to form, they were closed.

A family of four were hanging out in front of the lighthouse, snapping pictures of each other, the kids jumping on one of the benches and pausing to pose. Before Gunz moved into his new office space, he had the interior cleaned and a few pieces of furniture moved in. Fab's old stuff, he'd paid Junker to cart off. He made it clear he didn't care about the outside, that the chairs, benches, and potted flowers weren't a problem. Why drag them out for usage just on the weekends? I'm certain he noticed that the furniture had been chained to spikes in the ground, which happened after my metal rocker from the forties went missing.

Fab scored a spot a few spaces over from the entrance, and we entered through the front door for a change.

Doodad waved from behind the bar.

"I'll order the beverages," Fab said. "You go get rid of any poachers trespassing at our table."

"Yes, ma'am." I saluted. "This is a cherry day." The shake of her head was confirmation she'd heard. "And a couple oranges," I yelled.

A couple of regulars at the bar turned, and I waved and headed out to the deck. I tossed the "reserved" sign on a chair and took my usual seat. It pleased me that Doodad never forgot to turn on the ceiling fan and the lights strung around the ceiling and banister. It was another warm day and the fans made the air feel slightly cooler. I'd suggested a mister fan, but Doodad thought it would be "annoying as hell, water shooting everywhere."

Fab came back, tray in hand, and curtsied.

"Ma'am," she said, setting down a coaster, a drink with more fruit than liquid, and a full glass of whatever it was next to it. She repeated the process with her lime and soda, then shoved the tray under her arm. "Anything else I can get you?"

After making a slurpy sound through the straw, I said, "No, miss."

"Good, because I'm bored with this already." Fab dropped the tray on a cart on the opposite wall and took a seat. "I told Doodad to direct all tall guys out here, and he laughed. Some dude named Snug, I told him. That surprised him—his brows shot up—but he didn't say anything. I didn't ask. Why not be surprised? Besides, we're armed."

"I suggest that if things go awry, you lay on that irresistible man-charm."

Fab snorted and tipped her glass against mine, which turned out to be 7-Up. She stared into the bar. "Tall… I'd say giant, a few inches short of seven feet. Not to mention he's packing several hundred pounds." She sized up the man approaching the table.

I'd have recognized him from GC's description by the square head alone. The butch cut accentuated the flatness.

"You pretend to be me," I whispered.

"If I didn't know better, I'd think you were drunk, but I know what's in your glass." Fab patted my hand. "Don't worry. Backup's here."

The behemoth in monochromatic beige — shorts, shirt, and cotton suit jacket — didn't even stop at the bar; he headed straight to the deck. "Hello, ladies. You're Madison." His eyes crinkled at the corners. "I recognize you from GC's description." GC sounded more like Geez.

"Have a seat." I nodded to an empty chair. It shouldn't have surprised me that GC knew about our reserved table, but it did, because as far as I knew, he'd never set foot in the bar. But then, how would I know? I hadn't met him. I reached down, grabbed the non-descript white envelope from the side pocket of my purse, and pushed it across the table.

Doodad appeared in the doorway, eyed the envelope, and asked Snug, "Get you a drink?"

"Brought my own." He pulled a bottle of water from inside his jacket.

Doodad nodded and left.

Snug scanned the deck area, craning his head over the railing and scoping out the inlet of water that ran along the back side. He nodded in approval. "This Mr. Bordello, he didn't hurt you, did he? That's something I won't tolerate, hurting a woman, and I'd have to make a return visit."

"Nothing like that, threats only." *Of sorts, but I didn't feel the need to give the man a complete run-down.* I introduced him to Fab, even though I felt certain he already knew who she was.

"I've done a couple of these kind of jobs in the

past—usually includes broken bones." Snug cracked his knuckles, loud enough that both Fab and I jumped. "At your request, though, I used my special powers of persuasion, and I'm certain you'll never have any future contact with Mr. Bordello." Under his bushy brows, large brown eyes bored into us. "You so much as see him in town, looking your way, give me a call."

"You have a card?" I asked.

Fab kicked me under the table.

Snug let out a strangled sound I assumed was a laugh. "I ought to have me one of them. What kind of title could I come up with?"

"Odd jobs?" I suggested lamely.

Another kick under the table. This time, I tried to kick back, and Fab moved her legs.

Snug harrumphed. "You're a funny one."

"Not to question the quality of your work, but why are you so convinced Bordello is a bad memory?" Fab asked. "He doesn't seem like the type to scare easily."

"Don't know a man who doesn't become quite cooperative when confronted with the loss of his nuts." He downed half his water. "Caught up with the pecker-bastard coming out of one of those fancy coffee places. Suggested we talk, and that teed him off. Told him to calm down with the language. Stuck my revolver in his ribs and told him to take a seat at one of the outdoor tables."

I realized I'd been holding my breath and

released it slowly, downing the rest of my soda.

"Did he scream? Something?" Fab asked.

I'd bet Fab was disappointed that it hadn't been her holding the gun.

"He's wound pretty tightly. The last thing he wanted was any attention that might bring the cops. I'm also certain he had his revenge planned before he sat down." His chilly smile deepened the lines in his forehead. "He started in again, cursing my ancestors, but shut right up when that gun I'd been pointing at his chest was now aimed at his balls."

I winced.

Fab smiled.

"One thing I can say for the man; he can follow orders. Told him to keep his mouth shut until I was done speaking, and then it would be his turn. I told him why I was there, and he laughed at the mention of your names, but a glare put an end to that. I laid it out plain and simple, just as you requested."

Clearly skeptical, Fab didn't say anything.

"His response?" I asked.

"Bordello's exact words were: 'Why would I agree to that?' And then he went on about putting me in jail." Snug reached in his pocket and pulled out a shiny stainless steel tool.

Fab hissed.

"I'm showing you this, just like I did Bordello. I set this baby down in front of him. The color drained from his face when he recognized them as ball crushers. Leads me to believe he might have ordered it done sometime; he wouldn't get his hands dirty. The majority of folks wouldn't have a clue what these are for and the excruciating pain they can deliver."

A chill ran up my spine. I was unable to imagine what had gone through Bordello's mind. Men are so fond of their little friends.

"I take it he accepted the terms?" Fab asked in smug satisfaction.

"Not at first. He tossed out a few more threats. I took a short solid wood rod out of my pocket." He opened his jacket, withdrawing one, and held it up for inspection. "Had a handful made for difficult people that need a demonstration." He pulled open the handles of the gleaming tool, inserted the rod, and with notable strength, snapped it closed. The rod splintered.

I restrained myself from covering my eyes, certain it would be a long time before I forgot this presentation. I expected Fab to high five him or something from the admiration on her face.

"This is what will happen to you, I told him. If you or any henchman of yours ever bothers Ms. Westin or Ms. Merceau again—and that includes family members—I'll ferret you out from whatever rock you crawled under. I ended it with, 'Hire ten bodyguards and I'll still get you.'"

"He agreed?" I asked breathlessly.

"Rules don't apply to him, and he figured neither did my threats. I had a couple pictures to show him of the aftereffects of… I'm not going to go into graphic detail, since you're both ladies."

Fab's look of disappointment quickly switched to annoyance.

"I knew I finally got to him when he paled considerably, shifting slightly in his seat. Had to remind myself of my client's wishes several times, though, because Bordello is a man who deserves an ass-kicking that would take months to get up from."

"There's something we agree on," Fab said.

"You won't be hearing from Bordello again unless he's a stupid f— Sorry. But that's not his reputation," Snug said, a sneer in his voice. "Any work I do comes with customer satisfaction for life. No worries for now. Before heading over here, I checked with an associate that I had watching Bordello's every move. Told him to make his presence known with the wave of a nutcracker. Not long after, Bordello's Ferrari was headed north."

"I'm happy that he won't be popping up anytime soon," I said. "I appreciate your talent for scaring the heck out of him without breaking bones."

"If only I could've made him pee himself…" At my shocked expression, he said, "Got to get my fun somewhere."

This time, when I reached into my purse, I pulled out my business card holder and took out two and a pen. I handed everything to Snug.

"Write your contact information on the back of one and keep the other."

I pocketed the card he'd scribbled on.

"Got any odd jobs, give me a call." He laughed and pushed his chair back, pocketing his crushers, then exited through the bar.

We sat in silence for a few minutes.

"That low-modulated hard voice of his is enough to raise your neck hair, but the tool…" Fab said with amusement. "As controlled as Bordello is, I bet the display put him off his game. I know you're wondering—Gunz has a pair and couldn't wait to show them off."

"Something tells me Snug is besties with Gunz and GC," I said.

"What is it they say about the friends you hang out with?"

"And people think *we're* scary… Well, you anyway," I added in response to her raised brow. "We pale in comparison, and I'm happy about that. Do we tell the guys everything?"

"We have two choices: now or when they find out on their own and there's a long-winded lecture to listen to." She smiled innocently. "Besides, we didn't do anything wrong. Not me, anyway. I came along as backup and to keep you out of trouble." She held up her finger, then pointed to herself. "I get to be the one to describe the tool."

Chapter Thirty-Six

After dinner, Creole pushed aside the chaise lounges and dragged four chairs over, and we sat by the pool, guys on one side, us girls staring them down from the other side.

"I don't like this seating arrangement." I flung out my leg, kicking Creole in the shin, frowning at him. "What happened to sharing the same chair?"

"Didier and I agreed that you two are not going to distract us from wringing every last bit of information out of you. We know something's up—you've been too secretive lately." Creole wagged his finger at Fab and me. "No tricks. We're ready for you."

Fab ground her teeth together.

Didier grinned.

"Fine." I stood and dragged my chair closer to Fab's, the scraping sound garnering a couple of raised eyebrows. I leaned over and whispered in a voice I was certain they could hear, "I vote that we double-talk them so bad they get a headache."

Fab pushed me back, looked me in the face, and laughed, which had me laughing. She whispered, "That's a terrible idea. They're officially annoyed, so mission accomplished."

"That's enough, you two," Didier admonished with an upturn to the sides of his mouth. "You need to move your chairs apart."

I scrunched my nose and pulled my legs up under my chin, ignoring him.

Creole's expression was neutral, but he failed to hide the amusement in his eyes.

I held my closed hand under Fab's nose. "Shall we flip to see who goes first?"

"Not necessary. You go, and I'll be by your side for the show-and-tell part." Fab jumped up. "Wait. I left my props in the garage." In a flash, she raced through the patio doors.

Didier scooted back his chair. "Where is she going?"

"Hold your shorts, Frenchie. She's not about to miss this conversation."

Creole laughed at Didier's reaction.

Fab raced back out of the house, a small drawstring bag in her hand.

"Would you like a table to spread your tools out on?" I asked with enough sweetness to turn the attention to me.

The guys exchanged a "What tools?" look.

I pointed to Didier. "The small end table will work."

Shooting me a disgruntled look, he got up and moved the table over in front of Fab.

Fab flung out her hand in a flourish.

"One rule," I said. "I'd appreciate if you'd both stay seated and let me tell you the whole story before reacting."

Both men groaned.

"The day Fab and I went to the docks to meet Quattro, we had another visitor — Bordello. The man can carry a grudge." I went on to relay the conversation, Fab interrupting twice to remind me of details I missed.

"That whole boat stakeout was a setup to put you in jail?" Didier growled like an angry bear. "What the heck's the matter with him, did he forget you thought you were saving his life?"

Creole's hands tightened around the chair arms. "Is there more? Like threats?" he gritted out.

"That part was coming next."

He kicked his chair back, standing.

"You promised to stay seated."

"Neither of us actually promised."

"It was implied. Now, please." I pointed to the chair. "I'm telling you both what I tell Fab — you abuse the furniture, you buy new." That brought a smile, which eased the tension.

Didier appeared confused.

"Ceiling fan," Fab whispered, then giggled.

"Bordello did threaten us. It was the last straw for me, finding out what lengths he would go to. Fab and I weren't going to go about our lives with one eye over our shoulder, scared that the next job we went on, one or both of us would end up in jail. No! Not happening."

"Why the hell didn't you say one word about this?" Creole roared.

"So you and Didier wouldn't go off half-cocked and end up in jail," I told him. "I wasn't about to let that happen, either. I can promise you, we won't be hearing from him again."

"How?" Creole snorted.

"I called in a neutral third party to scare the holy cheese-whiz out of him. Comes with a lifetime guarantee. If there should be contact of any kind, he knows he'll disappear without a trace."

"That's some guarantee," Didier mused.

"This is where the lovely Fab can talk about our new friend Snug and present his most persuasive technique."

Fab sat forward, emptying her bag. "Snug—think basketball-player height, square head, and an extra hundred pounds." She filled them in from when he walked through the door. "These aren't exactly what Snug had—his were way cooler." She displayed an old-fashioned nutcracker, crazy-girl smile on her face. "I think I'm improvising pretty well."

Didier cleared his throat, staring at her. "I'm not certain where this is going, but whatever it is, you don't need to own the real thing."

"You either," Creole said to me.

"You take the nutcracker and one of these." She picked up a thick rod. "Visualize this as a pair of men's... goods." She inserted it into the nutcracker. "If you had the real device, you'd stick the private parts in the middle; mine only works on the side." Her disappointment was showing. She squeezed the handles together. "Snap!" she yelled.

The guys flinched.

"Get it?" Fab asked in excitement. "Bordello got the message and moved to his condo in Miami the next day."

"Damn, she got the fun part of the story." I flashed her a pouty smile. "We were honest with you, so don't go repaying us by beating the snuff out of him." I gave them Mother's best stern stare.

"Snug, huh?" Creole said. "Wonder if Help knows him. Sounds like someone he'd share a beer and war stories with. And I'd like to meet this GC character."

"Good luck, we don't know his name, have never met him, and if he has his way, never will. In the spirit of being upfront, we did a job for GC himself." I gave the briefest of details, making it sound like Cara was waiting on our arrival. Left out all mention of Gunz, who they both thought was a criminal, having blown off Fab's mention that he didn't have a record. "If you want to know how Cara is doing, just ask Fab. She stays in touch. You're going to make a great mother."

Fab's cheeks burned red.

Didier smiled at her.

"Any other updates?"

"There is one thing. This is good news. Maddie's been found," Fab announced.

"You reunited the family without involving me? I missed the happy ending," I sighed, certain that when I heard the details, I'd be thankful.

"As it turns out, I missed it, too, and I'm fine with that. Apparently, it was a neighbor lady around the corner who had the dog. I'm happy not to have had to threaten a woman old enough to be my grandmother."

"Good to know you have some limits," Creole said.

"Hank happened to be walking his new dog–"

"New dog?" I cut in. "When did that happen?"

"He adopted the dog from the shelter. Can I finish now?" Fab didn't wait for an answer. "Having gotten out of the yard, Maddie took one look at Hank and came running, Connie, the neighbor, hot on her heels."

"Connie in jail?" Creole asked.

"Think romance," Fab told Creole in disgust. "Connie collapsed in a sobbing mess after confessing her felonious deed and telling Hank all she wanted was companionship. Being a gentleman, he took her home, and now they're tangoing."

The guys laughed.

I snorted. "She steals from him and now they're doing it?" I couldn't decide if I believed her or not. "He better lock up the silver."

"True love," Fab sighed.

I made a barfing noise.

Fab's hand aimed for the side of my head, and I ducked.

Creole got up and took two steps. Standing in front me, he bent down and scooped me into his arms. "No more news for tonight." He walked over to the pool and jumped in.

"So mean of you," I said when we resurfaced.

"I'll make it up to you." He drew me into a kiss.

Chapter Thirty-Seven

Mac's face lit up my phone screen. As soon as I connected, she said, in a frenzied voice, "Get over here now. And don't bring your cohort."

I glanced up at the woman in question, who was walking out of the Bakery Café with a pink box in hand, cookies for the guys.

It took a second for her to notice I was on the phone. "Who?" she mouthed.

"Mac," I mouthed back.

Fab signaled for me to put it on speakerphone as she approached the table, to which I shook my head. Telling her she couldn't listen in was like waving a red flag at a bull. She jerked her chair out with a bounce, scraping it across the cement. I flinched, and she growled at me.

"What's going on?" I asked Mac.

"You're wasting time." She hung up.

I double-checked my screen to make sure. "Who's the boss around here?" I asked, hitting redial. It went straight to voicemail.

"Me," Fab said with a smirk, coming around to stand next to me and bumping my shoulder in case I hadn't noticed.

My phone rang again. It was Mac, and this time, I hit speakerphone. Otherwise, Fab would have hung over my shoulder. "Sorry," she said. "I had my phone between my boobs, and it sometimes shuts off the phone."

Fab rolled her eyes.

Without taking a breath, Mac asked, "Have you left yet? I've got to go." She whispered the last part and hung up.

"Mac's not known for hysterics; we should get going." Looking impatient, Fab used the remote to unlock the SUV.

We'd lucked out when we arrived to sip lattes at our favorite sidewalk table, getting the best view of the rest of the tables and also getting a parking space right in front.

"She explicitly told me to leave my 'cohort' at home," I said as she handed me my purse.

"Tough tooties." From her smile, she clearly liked her new phrase.

"Did you learn that from the same kid who taught you 'totems'?"

"Made it up myself," she said proudly.

"Well, aren't you cleaver." I cut in front of her with a hip bump and ran to the car.

"You're a grown adult."

"Good thing you told me. Next race, winner gets to drive."

Fab's expression—*not happening*—was easy to read.

I'd mostly stopped complaining about not

being the designated driver. I got practice driving when I went down to Creole's house to fool around.

Fab took all the shortcuts, which included a dirt lot and an alley, and we made it to The Cottages in one piece. She didn't bother parking in the driveway, but instead backed into Mac's driveway.

We barely had time to get out and close the car doors before Mac rounded the corner from one of the cottages, spotted us, hiked up her skirt, and ran to meet us.

"Crum's in trouble," she whispered. "I'm worried about him and decided that calling you was better than the police, as you know how to handle these sensitive situations."

Instant stomachache. I really didn't want to ask what the man had gotten himself into.

"Crum wouldn't want anyone to know, and we don't need the bad press, since we just got the place classed-up."

Fab coughed.

"I know you don't like Crum, but just for today you could try." Mac glared at her. "The woman is threatening to kill him."

"Kill him?" It was all I could do to keep from yelling, *Get to the point.* "Start talking. If this situation is as bad as you're suggesting, I'll call 911." I pulled my phone out of my pocket.

Mac pushed my hand down. "Remember Mango? She's in Crum's cottage, threatening to shoot off his... you know. I was walking by and heard screaming, so I jimmied open the bathroom window and stuck my head in and heard him trying to talk Mango down."

"She's the one that bit Gunz's nose off, or part of it anyway, and it had to be surgically reattached?" At Mac's nod, I said, "Unstable doesn't cover it when talking about that woman. What is it with men searching out hardcore crazy?"

"The sex," Fab said matter-of-factly. "Why not kick the door in?" she asked Mac. "You've got a gun, and I know it's holstered on you somewhere." She gave Mac's ankle-length skirt and blouse with bell sleeves a once-over.

Mac's cheeks pinked. "I didn't bang on the door because I didn't want to interrupt anything personal, and all things considered, if I'd done that, she might have gotten an itchy trigger finger."

"Enough with the guns," I said. "You're sure Mango's got one?"

"From the way she talked—yes. I could hear the conversation but couldn't see a damn thing. From what I did hear, she convinced me she'll shoot Crum once she finishes tormenting him with her threats."

"The key." I held my hand out, and Mac handed it over. "You're backup." I nodded at Fab. "I'm going in without a gun, thinking two might provoke her to shoot. You'll be right behind me, gun drawn. Try not to kill anyone. Less paperwork."

We were already at the door, and I could hear an angry female voice but couldn't make out her words.

"You take cover," I said to Mac. "Wait until I signal you or call before you come back."

Without a word, she took off for the little seating area at the front of the property. Best spot to watch all the action in the driveway.

"Ready?" I knew the answer. Fab had unholstered her Walther.

On the off chance it might work, I tried the knob but found it locked. I slid the key into the lock as quietly as possible and opened the door. The loving couple wasn't in the living room, so that left the bedroom, which in this unit was the door to the right.

I crept over to the open door and peered in. Six-foot Mango stood an arm's length away with her back to me, naked except for a G-string, her gun at her side. Crum had been tied, naked and spread-eagle, to the bed. If his fellow professors from that over-priced university where he'd hung up his teaching hat could see him now, they'd boot him off the wall of superstars.

"You bastard." Mango hawked spit on his chest. "You broke my heart."

"Bad day, Professor?" I stepped into the room, Fab at my side, her firearm raised and pointed at Mango, who jumped and raised her gun halfway.

Fab boomed, "Drop it. Or you'll be leaving here in a body bag."

"I think I'll hold onto it for now." She called Fab's bluff — well, sort of — and lowered the gun to her side. The two women engaged in a stare-down.

"The only thing standing in the way of you getting shot is me. You even move your arm, and Fab will shoot you." I walked over to the bed and pulled the sheet over Crum, not looking him in the eye. Turning around, I said, "Not sure you remember me, Mango. I'm Madison — the owner."

"Yeah, Gunz's squeeze," she sneered.

"Not me." I held up my hands. "That was another woman, and she left town with a fisherman." Sounded plausible to me. At the time, there *was* another woman, but I didn't ask Gunz any questions, as frankly, I didn't want to know. "I'm thinking there's an amicable solution to this situation."

"I want an apology for all the other women, you dirt bag. One well-placed bullet, and there won't be any more women broken-hearted by your lies and infidelity." One of her long legs shot out and kicked Crum in the foot.

Crum groaned in pain. "I don't do relationships and never promised anything," he whined. "How do you think I've stayed single so long?"

I turned and zipped my lips at him.

"You shoot a helpless old man and you go to jail," I told Mango. "If he's still alive, you may or may not get out. Dead, and you get Sparky." Zzzz. "Hear it fries the hair." I glanced at her blond hair, which was half in a beehive, half hanging down like they'd tussled. "I'm certain you'd hate prison life. Think of it as one-star motel accommodations… or worse."

"I'll beat it out of town and no one will ever find me." Mango was clearly under the delusion that plan would work.

"It may take a while, but the cops will find you. Life on the run isn't as easy as setting up house in another state."

"My arm's getting tired," Fab whined. "If you'd let me shoot her when we walked in, she'd be on her way to the hospital by now. I wouldn't have killed you," she told Mango, "but I'd have shot you in the arm. You'd never be able to use it again." She trotted out her creepy smile.

"Untie me so I can kill her myself," said Crum, who had stayed uncharacteristically quiet.

"One bad idea after another." I tugged at the rope wrapped around his left ankle. Not having any skills in knot tying, I asked, "You got a knife?" The color drained from Crum's face, and I planned to jump out of range if he barfed.

Fab moved behind me, handing over her Walther in another mind-reading moment between us. She made short work of the knots,

327

releasing his ankles from captivity and then his wrists.

Gradually, color ebbed back into his cheeks.

Handing Fab back her gun, I narrowed my gaze on Mango. "This is the second and last time you're wreaking havoc on my property. You show up here again, or anywhere in the Cove, and I'll make sure you end up in jail. You live in Miami, so there's no excuse for you to ever come back."

"What about my retribution?" Mango pouted, thrusting out her double D's.

"You've had enough already. Be happy that Crum has a strong heart. A woman half his age, doing what you did... you'd never find a sympathetic jury." I stepped back so that I had both Mango and Crum in my sight. "I'm assuming you don't want this reported to the cops," I told Crum, "since you haven't requested it thus far."

"As long as she keeps her promise not to come back here, I want to forget this ever happened," Crum ground out.

"Your promise? I'd like to hear you say that you understand and agree," I said to Mango. "What's it going to be? A 'stay out of jail free' card or incarceration?"

"I hate you." She hawked spit at Crum again, but this time, it landed on the sheet he clutched around his waist. "You should be grateful I have a soft heart, you bastard."

I heard a faint choking noise and, being a betting woman, chose Fab.

"Can I move now?" Mango asked sarcastically, then bent down without waiting for an answer. She grabbed a shoulder bag large enough to hold two weeks of clothes, tossed in her firearm, and scooped up a few pieces of stray clothing. She pulled a spandex dress over her ample form, slid into fluffy bedroom flip-flops, and headed to the front door.

Crum stared at the sheet. Knowing he was ill at ease, I slipped behind Fab, who stood in the doorway, eyes following Mango as she headed out to her car. I nodded to Fab and followed Mango down the driveway, hustling to catch up.

"Let's make an agreement between you and me," I said to Mango. "I'd like to end our relationship on an amicable note. I want it clear that you're not to set foot on this property again. If you should forget, for whatever reason you can come up with, I promise it won't end with you leaving as you are today."

"You won't be seeing my bountiful ass again. Every time I come down to these stinking Keys, I get into trouble, and I'm telling you, it's never, and I mean ever, my fault."

I summoned up a sympathetic face… or close enough, anyway.

Mango hit the key fob and opened the door of her monster truck with a grill across the front. She climbed in—no cheater bar for her—

powered down the window, and hung her head out. "Have Gunzy call me," she mewled.

"I sure will." When pigs fly.

Mango squealed her tires down the street and turned the corner, barely braking.

Mac — who'd seen Mango coming, jumped up, and took cover behind a palm tree — stepped out and waited in the driveway. "Crum okay?"

"You see Mango anywhere, here or in town, call Spoon. He's to have her escorted to the county line, but only after she's had the life scared out of her." I made a mental note to check with Stepdaddy and see if he still offered that service. Mother had pretty much tamed his bad boy ways. If not, I'd have to call Snug, and since Mango wasn't one to back down, that might end badly. Also, calling on Snug would run the risk of Gunz finding out, and since his lower friend did all his thinking when it came to women, he'd hop on her again and risk her biting off his whole nose this time. "As for this incident, it never happened and will not be mentioned or gossiped about... ever. And in no way will it be alluded to by snide looks or laughter. Understood?"

"Yeppers," Mac said. "Happy you're handling it this way. I like Crum, and he's a guest favorite."

"Thank you for calling. Crum never needs to know that you're the one who made the call; that way, it won't make your relationship awkward."

"I'm going home. I need a bowl of ice cream."

"Didn't ask—seems quiet here today except for... lucky Crum—but anything I need to know?"

"The place cleared out early this morning. Everyone had plans except Miss January, who fell asleep on the porch. Her boyfriend fetched her inside."

"I'd better get back to Crum's before he and Fab get into an argument." I waved and practically ran back up the driveway.

The door was ajar, and Fab sat on the couch. "Crum's putting his pants on," she said.

The bedroom door opened and Crum came out, in actual pants for once. "I want you to know I was never in a relationship with her. I thought I'd made myself clear that I'm bad at them and hence never get involved." His cheeks bright red, he crossed to the refrigerator, pulled out a beer, popped the top, and downed half of it.

"Crum," I said, in a voice a louder than usual to get his attention. His head bounced up. "This—" I swept my arm around. "—didn't happen. You'll never hear a word about this from either Fab or I."

Fab nodded, and some of the stress left his body.

"Thank you," he said.

Fab already had the door open and motioned for me to follow. Before stepping out, I turned back to Crum. "You hungry? Go to Jake's and put it on the cop tab. If you're not into socializing, call in a to-go order." I closed the door behind me.

"What did we do today?" Fab asked. "In case the guys ask."

"Which sounds better—shopping or tacos on the beach?"

Chapter Thirty-Eight

It started at dinner. Fab was quiet and somewhat introverted, barely listening to the conversation going on around her. At one point, I called her on it, and she blew it off with, "It's been a long day." Red light: Fab was up to something and planned to tell me only after she'd taken some kind of action. Knowing her as I did, it would be late-night and probably illegal.

That wasn't about to happen, so I camped out on the daybed, dressed for action in black sweatpants and a long-sleeved t-shirt, my jacket lying on the end of the bed. I relocated Snow and put my tennis shoes on top, which didn't bother her, as she simply climbed on top of the pile.

Shortly after midnight, Fab crept down the stairs garbed in her ninja outfit.

"Wait while I put my shoes on."

Fab jumped and clamped her hand over her mouth, but not before a small shriek escaped. The other hand gripped the railing. "What the…! Next time, how about a warning? You'd have felt bad if I'd fallen down the stairs."

"Yeah, probably." I shoved my feet in my shoes and tied my jacket around my waist.

"Where are we going?" Not waiting for an answer, I eased the door open and slipped out, Fab behind me.

"You're going to get in trouble with Creole."

"No, I am not, *because* I told Creole I'd be sneaking out to keep an eye on you. I'm to text or call if you're up to something illegal. Can you say the same about Didier, or did you once again slip out of a warm bed?"

"I left a note," she huffed.

"Do you want to marry Didier?" I responded to her glare with, "You have to stop with these antics. If you'd just told him, he'd have volunteered to be backup and you'd be on the road already."

"He's not going and neither are you." She unlocked the driver's door of the Hummer.

"You pull out of this driveway without me, and I'm calling the police and reporting the SUV stolen." I pulled my phone out of my pocket and held it up. "You're thinking I wouldn't do it. Wrong. I will."

"You're the meanest." She unlocked the passenger door.

I slid into my assigned seat and fastened the seat belt. "Guess what? I'll be mean again if you think you're going to drive off and leave me wondering *what the hell*?" I ended on a near-shout.

Fab rubbed her ears and started the engine, backing out of the driveway. "We're going to

Brick's office."

I tapped my non-existent watch. "That's speedy of you. Took you an hour to answer that question."

"Did not."

"When you're done sulking, I'd like to hear why we're going to Brick's. He call you this late?"

She blew down the highway, seemingly lost in thought, fine-tuning her plan for what was about to go down. "I'm going to search and bug his office."

"Wow," I mouthed silently. If she didn't have such a serious look on her face, I'd have thought she was pranking me.

"You remember the last time we were there? After eavesdropping on his phone call, the snippets I heard left me with too many questions."

A shiver went up my spine. I didn't want to ask questions, but Fab wasn't a worrier, and that worried me. "You said at the time you thought the conversation was about Sacks."

"I think he knows who killed Marshall. At first, I thought his motive in helping Alta was because he believed in her innocence. Now, I think he used me to verify there were no leads to the real killer."

"If that's true, why use you? He could've done all the footwork himself—the fewer people that know, the better."

"Unless he wanted a scapegoat—as in me. He wouldn't be the first in the recent past to make me his prime target."

"I know he pushes the boundaries of friendship in asking for you to do all kinds of dangerous things. But since the two of you started out, you've never turned down a job, no matter the risk. Frame you for murder? Brick always puts Brick first, but if he gets rid of you, who would do his dirty work?"

"I'm sure he'd sob crocodile tears, sorry he'd involved someone so unstable." Her words were tinged with sarcasm.

Exiting the freeway, we headed to the main commercial area. The street was lit up with neon sales, hawking anything you could possibly want. Not a lot of traffic, but enough to make me wonder if there was a bar or two nearby.

"You make a left off this street, and someone will see us. You planning on parking and walking?" Whether the boulevard was busy or not, I didn't like the idea of such a bold move, especially since a cop car had passed us in the intersection, which meant there'd be more patrolling the area.

Fab's laugh conveyed, *Have you lost your mind?* "Guess you didn't know there's a back entrance with not a single security camera."

"All I know is the property backs up to a twelve-foot brick wall. Granted, I haven't walked the lot from corner to corner."

"I rode along with Brick once when he needed to get off the property unseen—some unsavory associate hunting him down. He needed time to negotiate a mutually satisfactory deal." Fab snickered. "Unbeknownst to him, I've used it a couple of times for the heck of it. He bought the right-of-way, extended the wall, and no one's the wiser."

"It's hard to believe the man has a brother who's a detective. He's got a reputation as someone not to mess with, but no whispers of anything illegal." The thought of Brick finding out about this little venture sent a shudder through me.

"Brick let it slip once that his brother had saved his ass a couple of times. He didn't say illegally, but it was implied."

"I'm promising you now that he'd better not be planning to finger you for anything you didn't do. I'll send Snug and Toady after him. Both men would enjoy serving him up as hors d'oeuvres to alligators."

"Does your boyfriend find your totally creepy side sexy?"

"The same question could be asked of you."

We laughed.

After going about a half-mile, just when I'd begun to think this shortcut wasn't so short and wonder where we were headed, she made a left into a residential area.

"Please, tell me we're not cutting through

someone's backyard or swinging through the trees to clear the fence."

"Once you climb the tree, getting over is the easy part." She laughed. "*You* are staying in the car, behind the wheel, which will make for a clean getaway if anything goes south, and I'll text where to pick me up." She made another left, into what appeared to be a driveway and wasn't, then a right into an alley that ran along the back of the property line.

The road ended at the car lot. Fab drove in far enough to turn around, then pulled back out just enough that the SUV couldn't be seen by anyone standing on Famosa's lot. It also meant I wouldn't be able to see anything.

"Are you going to tell me what you'll be doing?" I asked.

"I'll fill you in when I get back."

"Anything, text me. That includes if you're taking too long. Won't the alarm go off when you pick the lock?" I asked.

"I have a key and the security code, and no, Brick doesn't know."

"Be careful," I said as she closed the door. I climbed into the driver's seat and hit the door locks. I wasn't expecting any trouble, but it helped soothe my nerves and lessen the unsettled feeling.

* * *

My phone pinged, and I hurried to click on the message from Fab. "I'm about ten steps from the car and didn't want to scare you." I pressed the button to unlock the doors and climbed back over to the passenger seat.

"That was too easy," Fab said, getting in. "Didn't even have to disarm the security cameras—someone already did it and forgot to turn them back on. Bet Brick doesn't know, and that worked to my advantage by not slowing me down."

"Well, don't make me drag details out of you!"

"Did I find a notepad that said, 'Frame Fab'? No. There wasn't a file, a piece of paper with Sacks' name on it, nothing. I did find guns and a pile of cash. I bugged his office and phone. The one thing that caught my attention was that, on his calendar, the day after tomorrow is circled several times in red. What do you suppose it is? I'm coming back then and getting here early. I want to know." Fab wound her way back to the main street and pulled out in the opposite direction from Famosa's.

"That could be a big time-waster."

"I don't care. I don't have any other options," she said testily.

"Then I suggest that we get to Brick's home early and follow him from there, since he might not be going to his office." I'd pulled a bottle of water from the back while waiting and now unscrewed the top, taking a long drink. "He'll notice if you try to follow him in this car. He'd probably also notice my run-down truck hot on his bumper. I suggest that you do a swap with Didier—a Mercedes might escape his attention."

"Like your idea."

Chapter Thirty-Nine

When Fab and I returned to the house and opened the door, Creole stared at us from the daybed, signaling with his eyes as Didier's head popped around the corner. He wasn't a happy man, but before he could unleash a tirade on his fiancée, she ran to him, throwing herself in his arms. She whispered in his ear. Didier took her hand and, without saying a word, started towards the stairs, then paused and said, "Good night." The two disappeared upstairs.

"Didier about drove me crazy," Creole huffed. "He barged into the bedroom with barely a knock, demanding to know where the two of you went. You might want to tell Fab that he didn't appreciate being left a note."

"He never stays mad at her for too long. They'll have made up by morning."

Creole stood and scooped me into his arms. "This great idea just popped into my head, and we're not doing it in the living room."

"Oh darn."

The twosome were gone by the time we came downstairs in the morning, sending a text that they'd be back late that night and for me to be ready to leave early the following morning.

* * *

When Fab turned onto the Causeway over Biscayne Bay, I groaned, hoping that we weren't headed to Fisher Island. Instead, she took the turn to Star Island, drove over the bridge, stopped in front of a security panel, and lowered the window and stuck a card into the slot. The guard in the shack was on high alert, tipped back in his chair… asleep.

"Let me guess, another gift from Brick?" I asked.

"Back when he had me stake out one of his neighbors. Turned out the man was using his place as a grow house. I got the evidence, and a week later, the man moved. Haven't needed it since, but figured if this one didn't work, I have my other card, which is supposed to open any security gate in Miami. After its malfunction the other day, I had it updated. To gain points with Madeline, I had her card updated, too. So, next time she goes out to lunch with her friend, Jean, they have new neighborhoods to explore. I made her a list of the best ones."

"That was very sweet of you."

Fab slowed in front of a house with electric gates. The house, although visible, was set back on the property, making it a waterfront. A long driveway circled around a fountain, Brick's SUV parked at the front door.

"It looks like a regular house sitting in an affluent neighborhood."

"It was a ten-million-dollar fixer-upper."

"Now, there's a bargain."

"They didn't spare any expense fixing it up." Fab scanned the property over her steering wheel. "Went to a party there once. Brick wanted to fix me up with his cousin Dimwit—handsy fellow until I told him if he touched me again, I'd knee him in the groin. A few minutes later, I snuck out the side door. Funny thing, I never got another invitation."

My face pasted to the glass, I checked out the houses as we drove by. "This island has a number of security cameras; we need to avoid them and park someplace where we won't look out of place." That ruled out the properties that bordered Brick's, as they afforded no privacy.

The sun rising made it easier to see that there were a few places to park and go unnoticed. Halfway down the block, Fab u-turned and slowed two houses down from Brick's. Both houses mirrored his and sat back on the property, away from the street. She chose a house that had gates across the driveway and a wall that ran the length of the property. She parked parallel to the wall, under a tree with branches that hung down, both offering much-needed privacy so the SUV wouldn't garner attention from anyone inside.

"As long as neither of these property owners leaves before Brick, we shouldn't face any awkward questions," I said. "You have a 'just in case' story? We're running from the cops? The engine blew?"

Fab groaned. "Memorize this—you got sick, and we're leaving now since you're feeling better."

I fake barfed.

"Have one of those handy, and they'll be glad to see us go. It needs to be a little louder. Cover your mouth, and it will sound less like a cat coughing up a wad of hair."

We leaned back in our seats and peered over the dashboard.

"I told Didier everything, running down the details and not glossing over anything. And apologized for not getting it in order, but he said not to worry, he got it figured out. That made me love him more; he listens and knows me well enough to fit together my ramblings into something coherent."

"Let me guess, no argument about using his car." I ran my hand along the leather seat. Like Fab, Didier kept his car in pristine condition.

"Once I assured him there wouldn't be any confrontations, he was fine with today. He did say he wished I stayed in the car on every job. He kissed me, slapped me on the bottom, and told me to stay out of trouble."

"I reassured Creole before he left for his class that we were only following Brick around. He thinks this is a time-waster and hopes your suspicions are wrong because he's afraid Didier will kill Brick."

"If this day turns up nothing, then case closed on Marshall Sacks. We've uncovered no evidence, and according to GC, the case against Alta is weak and the cops don't have anything that couldn't be construed to point the finger at anyone else. GC noted his preference for cases that had hard evidence and left no doubt as to the guilt of the defendant. He did suggest that Alta take acting lessons to learn not to come off not as snotty as she is in real life."

"Brick?" I pointed at his SUV backing out of the driveway. "Unless he lets his wife or someone else in the family drive."

"Not happening. He did that once with a nephew; got it back thoroughly trashed." Fab started the engine, eased away from the curb, and maintained a discreet distance. "Brick's late today; normally he's at his office by now."

She stayed several car lengths behind him, followed him through the streets south to the Coconut Grove area, and into the driveway of the Bayside Yacht Club. He parked and, without a glance around, headed to the docks, turning to the right, down one of the rows and walking out of sight.

"Now what?" I asked.

"I'm following him."

I grabbed her arm before she could jump out of the car, but she shook off my hold.

"Don't worry. I'm good at sneaking around."

She shut the door before I could ask another question or remind her that she'd promised to stay in the car. I glared at her back as she raced across the grass and through the gate to the main dock, paused for a second, and then began running again, taking a right and disappearing from sight. The marina had several long docks, with shorter ones off to one side or the other. I got to four before I couldn't see any farther.

Although Fab had left the keys in the ignition, I didn't play with the seat or put my feet on the dashboard, knowing if toe prints were discovered, I couldn't blame Fab. Creole would laugh his head off, but Didier's reaction... he certainly wouldn't be laughing.

Checking the time every five minutes wasn't helping my anxiety level. Even if Brick caught Fab tailing him, he wouldn't be stupid enough to hurt her here; he'd know there'd be more than one person who'd want him dead. If this turned out to be the proverbial goose chase, he'd probably believe whatever excuse she came up with. The best one — another case.

An hour later, Brick sauntered up the dock, a man without a care, once again not a glance around. Fooling around on his phone, he paused to stare at the screen, then hustled back to his car.

He exited the parking lot, not in any particular hurry.

Just as I was about to get out of the car, Fab appeared on the main dock, coming from a different direction. *How does she do that?* I needed tutoring in sneaking around. Though, if Mother got wind of my request, Fab would be teaching both of us. If Fab gave homework, I could entice Creole to help me work on my skills. The thought had me smiling.

"Which way did Brick go?" Fab asked as she got behind the wheel.

"He drove out like a man without a worry and went right. Any problem finding which boat he ended up on?"

"I would have, if it hadn't been for a friendly boat washer who happened to be working on one of the yachts. For an extra fifty, he let me sit on the back, out of sight."

Fab pulled out of the parking lot and turned left—the opposite direction as Brick. She was uncharacteristically quiet as she went back to the interstate, heading home. "I'm about to tell you something, and I don't want you screeching in my ear."

"Don't want to promise—might be something worth blowing your ears out," I needled her. "Or we could wait to see how long it takes for me to figure out whatever it is." I smiled at her snort.

"Marshall Sacks is alive."

I didn't quite jump, but at the very least, I

twitched and shook my head, certain my ears were clogged and I'd misheard. "Are you certain?" I knew she was, but I had to ask. "That's good news for Alta... isn't it? Did you actually see Marshall?"

"Naked from the waist up, sipping soda... this early in the morning." Fab made a face.

"It's not possible. Must be a twin brother... something. There was a police investigation. An autopsy. No way," I said emphatically. "Guess this means Alta will be getting out of the pokey soon."

"Marshall's obviously been alive this whole time, and Alta is sitting in jail, so I'd say she's right where he wants her."

"Why let Alta twist? I thought she and Brick were friends. That's the reason he wanted you on the case, wasn't it?"

"Are you done yet? I'm going to investigate and get answers to every question that you're getting ready to throw at me."

"I'm afraid to ask how."

"Stake out the boat and bug the interior. I'll get video and audio files, because without them, Alta might go to prison for life. Or worse, depending on the motive the prosecution sells the jury. I'm not standing by and letting that happen to an innocent woman, even if I don't like her very much."

"What about Brick?" I had to ask—this wasn't just any man she was messing with.

"The heck with Brick. It would haunt me if I did nothing. If I said let's ignore it all and go to lunch, could you forget?"

I covered my face with both hands and let out a long breath. "I get your point, but talk about blowing the lid off Pandora's Box... If you're found out, my guess is that you'll make some powerful enemies and they won't sit back and hope you never expose their secrets."

"One powerful enemy — Brick. He can never find out that I'm the one exposing all the lies. Ever. I don't even want the guys finding out. And you won't have any part of it either."

"For a smart woman, you seem inclined to make the same mistakes over and over. When Didier finds out that you put all our lives at risk with no forewarning, he'll leave you for sure." Dismissing her frown, I said. "Have you looked around? Great boyfriend pickings are slim."

"Didier will understand."

Her whininess annoyed me. "Unfortunately for you, you told me. I know now. Creole and I don't keep secrets... not for long, anyway," I amended at her raised eyebrow. "Cut me out?" My voice was shrill. "I don't freaking think so. If whatever you're planning goes south and Brick can't find you, next stop: me. Besides, where can you get better advice than from Creole? He's got experience dealing with pieces of... like Brick and his ilk."

Keeping secrets had to end. It was not a go-to

option, and frankly, I was tired of having to warn Fab what a terrible idea it was time after time. It must have escaped her memory that Didier and the Sacks were friends and he'd want the truth to come out, let the chips fall where they may.

Fab broke the silence as we merged onto the Overseas, not far from home. "I've come up with a plan."

To my credit, I didn't groan or make some other inappropriate noise.

"I'm going to tail Marshall for a few days, and once I get irrefutable proof that he's still alive, I'll send it to the authorities and Alta's defense team. And there's always the media. They love stories about rich people in trouble." Fab expectantly waited for a response.

"This is why I make the plan and you execute it. Days? I don't even want to hear what whopper you'll make up to hid your absence." I ignored her glare. "You're going to need a boat of your own to carry out this plan, one conveniently parked on the same dock. And backup." *No brainer.* "This isn't a one-woman operation."

"Are you done?"

"No. I'm not." I stared out the window, anxious to get back to the Keys, where it was more green and less concrete.

"Too bad. Boat Dude told me that Marshall leaves the boat every day, so I can be waiting in the parking lot."

"Who is this guy? He washes the boats, poaches a stateroom, and watches the coming and goings? You don't know that he's dependable just because a cash transaction was involved."

"He works at the club full time doing maintenance and contracts out on jobs when the boat owners snap their fingers. He pointed out two boats whose owners rent them out as vacation rentals."

"Does Boat Dude have a name?" I sniped.

"Boat Dude." She laughed at my look of disgust.

"I suppose, while touting his credentials, he leered and stripped you naked with his eyes. You dude magnet."

"Stay on topic," she admonished. "Your job is to find out who owns the boat at the very end and rent that one—today!" She handed me her phone, where she'd pulled up a photo showing the stern of the yacht in question with a nice close-up of the name. "The other's in there, too, if my first choice isn't available."

"Yes, ma'am. Anything else?"

"Food and drink and necessary supplies for several days. And we'll need disguises."

"Done. You're also going to need to contact GC. You'll be making use of his skills." I leaned back in my seat, happy to see the sign for Tarpon Cove.

"You call him." She shot me a cheesy smile.

"Find out if he can tap Marshall's cell phone. Not sure how he'd get the number, unless there's a way to get it off Brick's. I'm now convinced that Brick was talking to him the day I eavesdropped, and you can bet he wasn't on any payphone."

"Like everyone else, GC thinks Marshall blew to bits in the bay. Wait until I tell him, 'Surprise, not really.' Maybe GC can shed some light on how this scam went down, and under a lot of noses. This took a lot of people to pull off." I needed to make a list of questions before I called the man—Fab's and a few of my own. "Marshall Sacks is so high profile, he can't stay in Miami and go unnoticed indefinitely. Wonder what his plans are now that he's orchestrated his death."

When Fab rounded the corner, Creole's truck was parked across the street. She pulled the Mercedes in next to him, the driveway already blocked with my and Fab's cars. We got out of the car and walked across the street, pausing in the driveway.

"Do you need anything else today?" I asked. "I'll get on the boat reservation and call you later."

"Where are you going?"

"I'm taking Creole to Roscoe's for our favorite hamburgers and then back to his house for a walk on the beach." I ignored her retching noise. "Heads up, I'm telling Creole. I suggest that you arrange a meeting of the foursome. Get ready to spend tomorrow going over every detail of your plan. I suspect there will be more than a few changes."

Fab groaned.

"Who else are you going to trust?" Knowing I wouldn't get an answer, I continued, "The three of us are risking just as much as you, whether we're on the team or not. Working as a team, which I suggest, will be the best way to keep everyone up to date."

Fab, in her usual style, didn't commit to anything. "You'll be back in the morning?" she asked, opening the front door.

"If *anything* comes up, we'll both have our phones on."

The living room was empty except for the cats curled up together on the daybed. Voices drifted in through the open patio doors. I crossed to them and peered out. Creole and Didier were sitting poolside, drinking beer.

Fab pushed past me. Stopping at the refrigerator, she called out, asking if they wanted a refill.

Before Creole could answer, I crooked my finger.

Creole grinned and stood. With a few strides, he stood in front of me. "What's up?"

I took his hand in mine. "See you two tomorrow," I said to Fab and Didier. Creole willingly went with me to the front door. When it closed, I said, "I've got plans for you and me. First Roscoe's—we need nourishment—and next stop, your house. You can show me how that ceiling-fan sex that Fab is always bragging about works."

Creole laughed, scooped me into his arms, and ran across the street to his truck. "Let's hit the drive-thru for our burgers."

Chapter Forty

Creole and I agreed to a drama-free day spent at his house with nothing on the agenda. We allotted an hour to catch up on business, and then agreed to ignore our phones unless it was Fab or Didier. Creole was the first to finish, coming out on the patio, where I'd claimed a chair and side table as office space. "What are you up to?" He pointed to my cell.

I checked the time on my phone—I had five minutes left. "Tracked down one of those vacation rental places that offers all kinds of different choices, the most intriguing being a tree house for two. Rented the boat—a yacht, the listing says—across from Marshall's and over one, which will make Fab happy, except we can't check in until the day after tomorrow. It's got two nice staterooms." I winked.

He flexed. "Like what you see, babe?"

I licked my lips.

Creole turned serious. "There's nothing that I like about Fab's plan to prove Marshall Sacks is still breathing. She blew off my suggestion to call the chief and hand it over to Miami PD."

"Involving the chief would be my first

suggestion, but only if it's with one-hundred-percent assurance that Fab's name won't be leaked. She has the same concern about Alta's new defense attorney. Just found out she dumped Cruz—big mistake, but she didn't ask me." I reached over and uncapped his water, finishing it off. "It's one of the reasons that she's feeling paranoid these days, and she's not the only one. She's also been worrying over the question of whether Brick is setting her up, and for what? Murder?"

"Doing all the legwork ourselves doesn't necessarily keep Fab's name secret. Once the chief turns over the file to the district attorney, they'll be hounding him to speak to his source. They'll want to question that person, in addition to verifying every photo and video."

Signaling that I was done with work, I set my phone on my notepad and pushed it away. "This Sacks character has some hardcore connections, and I'm thinking a few are inside the police department. The body was misidentified. How does that happen by mistake?"

"That's one more question for the coroner, along with where the body came from. There's always someone that can be bought off, but..." Creole whooshed out a long breath. "Getting caught has consequences not worth the money. Not to me, anyway."

"And with all your reservations, you still signed on for backup." I leaned over and skimmed his lips with a kiss.

"Only because you're involved." Creole's eyes turned stern. "Just know that your safety is my first priority."

"While you're looking after everyone else's safety, don't forget your own."

"I told Didier, if he couldn't come up with a good disguise, to check out the costume shop in town. Since Marshall's a friend, we don't want him recognizing Didier or Fab. And if Brick makes another appearance, all of us need to duck out of sight." Creole stood and pulled me to my feet. "We're going for a walk on the beach."

* * *

The next morning, I kissed Creole good-bye, with a promise that I wouldn't be gone long. It was my plan to stop at the house, grab my tote, and head back out. But Fab, sensing my intent to leave her behind, snatched up my keys, dangling them off her finger, and stomped out to the driveway ahead of me.

"I'm going with you whether you like it or not," she snapped. "I'm the designated driver, not you."

"Only you think that," I grouched, snapping my fingers at her to unlock the passenger door. "I'll remind you again that The Cottages isn't your favorite place, and that's where we're going." Once I closed the door, I turned away

357

and stared out the window.

"I've got to get out of the house," she whined. "Didier's driving me crazy. Right after you sent the text confirming the boat reservation, he went into planning mode. One list after another. You only got a reprieve because Creole threatened to kick his butt if he interrupted your alone time for anything other than an emergency."

"That was yesterday. Planning must be over by now."

"You'd be wrong. Didier had Creole on the phone when I left, and they were mapping out the stakeout as if it were a military operation. I'm the private detective." A foot stomp could be heard in her voice.

"Didier's the worst—you need to toss him to the curb. Get a boyfriend that doesn't care what you do, one that never worries about your safety. You get maimed or die, he'll be sad for a nanosecond before moving on to the next chickaroo." I liked that Creole cared about my safety. For all his grumbling, he rarely said, "Don't do it," just, "Don't get hurt."

It didn't bother me that Creole was involved in the planning. I was certain he wouldn't ask me to climb the ropes for some bogus reason. I laughed at myself—wrong kind of boat. Luxury yachts had steps. One perk would be that hanging out on the back of a boat, breathing in the fresh air, beat the front seat of a car. In this case, there'd be plenty of food and no planning for how to pee in the bushes without being seen. What could go wrong? Another stupid question that I immediately retracted, lest it be construed as a challenge.

"Surprised myself," Fab said. "I told Didier the whole truth and nothing but… for the second time in a row. Maybe it's becoming a habit."

"Yeah, maybe." I turned to the window, not wanting to hurt her feelings with an eyeroll. "Careful." I pointed. "Dude on the bike has been drinking." He swerved into traffic again before hanging a right. I twisted in my seat, watching as he peddled down the street. Over my shoulder, I said, "Creole thinks you ought to get the chief involved."

"So that's where Didier got the idea." Fab pounded the steering wheel. "This case involves Brick, and I know most of his tricks, so who better than me? The more people that know…"

"Creole says there's no guarantees that your name won't leak out." I shuddered at the thought. "If this doesn't convince you to dump Brick as a client, nothing will." I crossed my fingers.

Fab careened around the corner, backing into Mac's driveway.

Mac sat on her porch, binoculars in hand.

I got out and waved. "Peeking on people is probably a crime."

"It's not like I'm looking through bathroom windows." Mac studied the apartment building next to The Cottages. More than once, Mr. Pee-er on the second floor had garnered an audience as he squirted out the window. "In order to get a good shot, I'd have to climb a tree. That could be harmful to my body." Decked out in her unique style—sequined skintight jeans, muscle shirt, and bright-yellow rubber boots—she ran her hands over her ample hips.

The three of us walked across the street and stood in the driveway, surveying the property. Thus far, it was quiet.

"Why are we here?" Fab asked as she checked out each cottage for little things most wouldn't notice, such as the blinds moving. "You never did say."

I ignored her and asked Mac, "Any fires? Don't tell me I need to go door-to-door."

"I've got everything under control." Mac boxed. "For right now, anyway."

I turned to Fab. "You behave while I'm gone," I said, then walked away. I counted: 1...2... and didn't get any further, as Fab showed up at my side, Mac behind her. "Why is Miss January slumped over in her chair? Where's her favorite sweater, the ugly one?" I nudged Mac and asked Fab, "What's the boyfriend's name?"

Fab rolled her eyes.

"Butthead," Mac whispered hoarsely. "Probably prefers Nestor."

"I'll need your help to get her upright." I tugged on Mac's arm and walked up the steps, standing in front of the snoring woman.

"Butthead's home," Mac warned me. "He'll have a flippin' fit."

"Change of plans. I'll make some noise, and he can storm out and do the heavy lifting." I whacked the bottom of the screen door with my tennis shoe-clad foot. "Miss January, you okay?" I said, loud enough for the neighbor across the drive to peak through the blinds. Probably took up her post when she saw me in the driveway.

The front door banged open. "What are you doing?" Nestor growled.

"You dent the wall, you pay for the repair and not do-it-yourself," I growled back. "Miss January needs a little straightening. Where's her sweater?" I ran my hands down her arms. "She's cold."

"Get your f—" Nestor managed to stop himself. "…hands off her." He attempted to shove me out of the way.

"Get your hands off Madison," Fab roared. "Touch her again, and I'll shoot you."

"Next time, try minding your own business," Nestor ground out.

"Miss January is my business." I matched his glare.

"Change your attitude, *Nestor*." Fab barked. "I'm more than happy to move your butt to the curb, and if you don't think I can, I know for a fact that running from flying bullets will get you moving."

Before he could respond, Kevin appeared in shorts and a t-shirt, a tipoff that it was his day off. "Problem here?" Brown eyes bored into Nestor.

Without a word, Nestor scooped up Miss January and went back inside, kicking the door closed.

"Something about him," Kevin grumbled. "Ran a check, but it came back clean." He motioned to me with his head. "Want to talk to you." He started towards his cottage and slowed, waiting for me to catch up. "Your groupies are following us," he muttered. "You need to tell them that they weren't invited."

"Go check on Crum... and be nice to him. I know you can." I grinned at Fab. Her instant irritation didn't go unnoticed. "That way, we can leave sooner."

Fab flashed a mutinous glare and grabbed Mac's arm, dragging her along.

"What's up, officer?"

"Nice thing you did for Crum. And offering not to tell anyone." Kevin came to a halt, positioning himself so he'd be the first to see if anything went down in the driveway. "It took him a while to shake off his humiliation, but in the last couple of days, he's been out and about. It being trash day was probably also a motivator. On the plus side, he wore more clothes than usual. He had on a shirt with his skirt." Kevin half-laughed.

"It's nice that you're apparently looking out for him?" It amused me that his cheeks turned pink. "I'm liking your new, softer side."

He snorted. "Crum doesn't deserve for his kinky private life to be fodder for public amusement, public humiliation. He's a horse's ass sometimes, but he's a decent guy. And he's a role model for us younger guys, knowing what we can get up to at his age."

My cheeks burned at the thought of a property full of eighty-year-old men chasing women and bringing them back here.

Kevin morphed back into cop mode. "The best thing would've been to call in law enforcement. That way, Mango would in jail where she belongs. But I understand why you didn't. Might have made the same decision myself, if it'd been my day off."

"It wasn't a completely altruistic decision on my part. It had more to do with my property. This wasn't my first introduction to the volatile Mango, and I figured that if she was hauled off in cuffs, she'd come back and The Cottages would be a smoldering ruin before she left." That happening would be like losing a piece of my aunt.

"The woman is high-strung," Kevin said.

"That's putting it nicely. She goes off like a rocket if a situation isn't going her way, and that it doesn't have any basis in reality doesn't hinder her in any way. I issued a warning that she's not to set one of her stilettos on this property again or I'll have her escorted to Alaska."

Kevin growled at that. "If she sets foot on this property, you call me; it would be my pleasure to arrest her."

I noticed that his eyes shot fire. "You know her? As in… you know…?"

His flushed cheeks gave me my answer. "When you first meet her, she's fun and easygoing, always up for an adventure."

My guess was the attraction had more to do with that fact that the woman exuded sex appeal and the adventure was sexual in nature.

"Mango's all innocence, a good-time girl, insisting on no strings. That's an act. Once I got myself disentangled, I chalked it up to a bad choice and moved on."

"You're lucky you still have all your body parts; one man I know had to have a piece sewn back on."

Kevin flinched.

We both turned at the sound of Joseph's door banging open. Svetlana under one arm, he lurched out of his cottage.

"He's got a big smile; what's he up to?" I asked.

"I'm not going to spoil the unveiling of his great idea," Kevin whispered, even though it wouldn't matter, as we weren't in hearing range.

"I should have known that someone else was inhabiting your body for the nice-guy talk.

Somehow, you got rid of him and the real you is back."

Kevin laughed. "Oh no, not going to spoil the surprise. *This one* you have to hear for yourself."

"Got some news," Joseph crowed as we approached. "Svetlana and I are talking about having kids."

Fab, who'd just walked up, said, "Talking?" She started laughing. When she recovered, she said, "Children? You must be drunk." And laughed again.

There must have been something nice I could say, but what escaped me. Joseph had to know it was an impossibility; the only thing I could think of was that the cancer had affected his brain. "You have health issues." I kicked Kevin, who jumped, and whispered so no one could hear, "No wonder you didn't tell me."

"I told Joseph that he and Svetlana should practice child-rearing on Kitty, once she's back, and see how that works out," Mac said.

"I... hmm..." I wanted to say "ick" but refrained. "Where is Kitty?"

"You're going to be sorry you went there. Such a sad story." Kevin wiped a non-existent tear and laughed.

"Crum discovered Kitty in the trash and fished her out," Joseph said in disgust. "She looks like she has a skin disease, and her stuffing is coming out again."

"I overnighted her to California, and she's

being operated on tomorrow," Mac informed us. "Next time you talk about getting rid of me, remember this. Who else could you hire that meets your weirdo challenges and never says no?"

"We'll have a sit-in to save your job." Kevin winked at her, which elicited a giggle.

"Before you ask, I did some investigation into how it might have happened," Mac said. "We know Miss January would never do that. I tried to interest law enforcement here, and he laughed." She wiggled her chest at Kevin. "Fiver on Butthead."

Kevin just stared and had nothing coherent to contribute.

"Not taking that wager," I said. "When Kitty comes back, put her in the office. Miss January asks after her, invite her for a little tea party. Substitute vodka and she'll forget why she's there." We'd managed to steer the conversation past the idea of Joseph procreating—I hoped he was drunk and we'd never hear another word on the subject.

Kevin finally recovered from his visual inspection of Mac's chest. "Sometimes, these impromptu visits of yours are damn entertaining." He waved and cut over to the gate that led to the beach.

Mac had told me once that the guests liked it when I showed up... for the same reason Kevin just cited.

Joseph settled in a chair, Svet in his lap, picked up his beer off the ground, and took a long drink.

I turned to Fab. "Crum okay?"

She nodded. "He's plotting a new business venture."

Just great. "We're working on a case for the next few days," I told Mac. "So I won't be around. I know you can keep this place under control. And you can always reach me by phone."

Chapter Forty-One

Fab, Didier, and Creole discussed their plan one last time before we separated and got into our cars. Didier didn't miss a detail — a PI in training. I wasn't totally attentive, as I'd read the plan more than once and knew my part would be limited, as would Creole's.

We arrived at the marina in Creole's truck and Didier's Mercedes, knowing that neither vehicle would attract Brick's attention should he decide to pay his friend another visit.

Both got out of their vehicles in worn jeans, faded tropical shirts, beards, hats, and reflector sunglasses. Didier had embraced his role and laughed at Fab when he tried to hug her and she stepped back, nose in the air.

Fab dressed in all black — workout pants under a knee-length skirt, a long-sleeved t-shirt, and signature tennis shoes. I'd adopted the same look, but colorful, more Bohemian, and with running shoes.

I split away from the group and found the dock master's office, a one-room shack at the beginning of the center walkway. A beer-gutted, greying man dressed similar to the guys waited impatiently in the doorway, picking his nails. He handed me a key and a packet of instructions and locked the door behind him, disappearing in the opposite direction.

It had been agreed that Creole and I would stay at the boat until the first sighting of Marshall, to gauge if our backup was needed. We saw action the next day, as Marshall left the boat in a hat and sunglasses and managed to blend in in a way that wouldn't attract any attention.

"Finally," Fab said in exasperation. Jumping up, she grabbed a small backpack, throwing it over her shoulder. She snatched up a pair of binoculars and watched as Marshall made his way up the dock and over one row, using that gate to exit. He got behind the wheel of a Mercedes in the first row. "Wonder who the Mercedes is registered to?" she asked no one in particular.

Creole didn't give Marshall much of a head start before he jumped over the side of the boat and followed the man, planning to tail him wherever he went.

Didier climbed down the steps. Fab followed, and he held out his hand, which she took, hopping to the deck. They split up and went in opposite directions, she to bug Marshall's boat and Didier to parking lot duty, to warn Fab if he came back suddenly.

I raced upstairs to the pilot chair, which

369

afforded a view of all of the docks and the parking lot, and kicked back, on alert for anyone we didn't want to run into.

Fab had the boat bugged in almost no time, or so it seemed, which had me wondering how many times she'd done it in the past. Or was it just that easy? She paused on the dock, pulling out her phone. Didier turned, waved, and jogged back to the boat.

My phone rang as Fab and Didier climbed back on board.

"You can put me on speaker," Creole said as soon as I answered. "The arrogance of this man. He thinks whatever his plan is, it's so airtight that he didn't even bother to look over his shoulder. He picked up a woman—close to his age, well-dressed—and they just entered The Beach Grill and took a table next to the sidewalk."

"A woman?" I said.

"Get some pictures," Fab said.

"Got some good ones already. After I follow him back, I'll get the identification number off the car, in case the license tag is 'borrowed' off some other vehicle. Just texted the license number. Get your GC friend on it."

"Be careful," I said.

"This job isn't dangerous unless we're made, and then all bets are off. The big question is, how far would Marshall go to hide his secret?" Creole asked.

The question hung in the air. No one commented.

Several hours later, Marshall and the woman in question returned. Fab and I recognized her from our background research on the man—his ex-wife and heir, Meredith Sacks.

Fab donned a pair of headphones and listened intently. Joking, she said, "I didn't put a bug in the bedroom."

Creole grabbed my hand and pulled me down next to him on the back bench. Leaning against the side, we had a view of the docks. "It will be interesting to see what tack the district attorney takes when he gets this surprise package. He's not going to drop the charges until the police and prosecutors authenticate everything. They'll need to check that the video itself is real—that the dates and times are correct and after the explosion, and that the video hasn't been changed with some high-tech editing program."

"They're getting ready to go out again." Fab jumped to her feet, picked up her camera bag, and motioned to Didier. "Now, I can get video to back up my claims."

"Just a reminder—capture other things in the video that can be used to establish when it was made. Include customers and employees that can be interviewed about today," Creole reminded her as she jumped over the side, Didier behind her.

371

Chapter Forty-Two

Creole and I spent the night on the boat and left the next morning, since there'd been no activity after Marshall and his ex-returned from dinner.

The following evening, Didier called and relayed to Creole that via the bugs on Marshall's boat, Fab had overheard them making plans to sail to the Caribbean and around the islands. The date of departure was tentative because they were awaiting the arrival of their new yacht. There was a sense of urgency in the air, as we all knew that time was running out.

Fab and Didier were gone for several days but kept in touch as they built a file on Marshall. Fab was happy that she and Didier worked so well together, and she confided they'd gotten closer than ever. Finally, she called an end to the surveillance, knowing that if she didn't have enough evidence to get Alta Sacks out of jail now, then nothing would be satisfactory.

Fab had videoed Marshall's every step, and Didier had snapped photos both with and without Marshall's ex. The Sacks ate in restaurants, shopped, and walked the beach with the air of locals enjoying the tourist town. At one point, the couple veered into a jewelry store, where Marshall bought Meredith a diamond bracelet.

After stopping at the office to get their evidence together, Fab and Didier returned home. Since it was another warm evening, a light breeze ruffling the palms, Creole and I had opted to sit outside by the pool, sticking our feet in the water. Fab and Didier joined us there.

"Is faking your own death a crime?" I asked.

"Not if you don't try to collect on the insurance, but framing someone for your murder is," Creole said. "Since I haven't been privy to everything Marshall's been up to, I'd say at present, the one holding the most liability is Meredith Sacks. She's looking at jail time if she collected on the insurance or any other policies that would require a valid death certificate for her to receive the proceeds."

"Certificate or not, at this point, it's easily proven that she knew Marshall wasn't, in fact, dead," Didier said.

"I don't suppose we'll ever find out who was cremated." I made a face, hoping the man had died of natural causes before being blown up in Marshall's scheme.

"What does Brick get out of this, except jail time?" Didier asked. "He'd risk his cushy life for a friend?"

"Brick thinks he can do what he wants and other people will pay the penalty, not him," I said in disgust. Fab nodded.

"It's a stretch to think that Brick can somehow incriminate Fab for the crime." Creole downed the rest of his beer, standing to get more from the patio refrigerator.

"The females in Brick's life appear to be expendable—Alta, Fab. One he's letting sit in jail for a crime he knows she didn't commit, and the other, he may be trying to finger for complicity in the same crime," I said. "Maybe his bright idea is to give the defense more than one suspect to present to the jury."

Creole was back, drinks in hand. There was a brief silence as he handed them out.

"Fab." Didier tugged on her hair. "Promise that you're going to stay away from that man." He cut off her response. "Don't lie and then run off behind my back."

Fab threw her arms around his neck.

"Getting rid of Brick doesn't mean the end of your PI work," I reminded Fab, as she tended to think the opposite. "I've made a list. It's only got a couple of names on it, but it's a start, and with any luck, they can supply the adrenaline rush you love so much. The old clients that you got on your own—not through Brick—you can accept or reject on an individual basis."

"Who are these *new* clients?" Fab asked.

Didier poked her in the ribs.

"Is that sarcasm?" I squinted and wanted to laugh at her disgruntled look. "There's a strip joint in Homestead that needs their security updated and an old folks home that needs the same thing." I smiled sweetly.

The guys laughed.

"I don't believe you," Fab huffed.

I clasped my hands over my chest. "The home is mostly men, and we all know the special rapport you have with the older age group."

Fab made an attempt to splash me with water, but Didier grabbed ahold of her arm.

Creole laughed in my ear. "Why is it when someone has a problem, your first inclination is to come up with a solution?"

"If I can't meddle in my best friend's life, then whose?" I winked at Fab.

Chapter Forty-Three

Fab lay on the couch, Snow by her side, and I was stretched out on the daybed, Jazz lying crosswise across my body, as Fab told me—after the fact—what she'd done. I didn't waste my breath telling her I'd rather know as soon as she concocted one of her plans. Just that morning, she'd finished getting the videos and corroborating pictures of the Sacks case together and passed the boxes, each individually addressed, off to some dubious fellow to hand deliver one to the district attorney, one to Alta's attorney, and the last one to the lead detective on the Sacks case.

Not long after she'd gotten confirmation of delivery, and before I could start haranguing her with questions, our phones rang. Fab flipped her phone over, showing me Brick's face. I mouthed GC. She relocated Snow and headed to the patio to take the call.

"Sacks is about to be on the move," GC said. "He just got a call that lasted less than a minute. He hung up, saying, 'We'll be waiting,' then told Meredith, 'We gotta get out of here. Someone figured out I'm not dead and took it to the police.'"

When I first contacted GC about needing additional surveillance, he demanded to be kept in the loop and up to date on everything that happened. Fab had told me that more than once, he'd pointed out a detail she'd overlooked.

Fab was shoving her phone in her pocket as she came back through the patio doors. "Brick demanded an appearance in his office—now. Didn't give a clue as to why. From the tone of his voice, he's agitated about something."

Since I'd failed to get Fab's attention to tell her that I was still on the phone, GC ended up hearing everything. "More happy news," he said. "Famosa showed up while Sacks was freaking out about the call, found the bug, and went ballistic. Communications abruptly ended. I'm assuming he smashed it or blew it to bits."

I'd put the call on speaker, so Fab heard most of what he said.

I hurriedly told her about Sacks skipping town, in case she had questions.

"I'm not sure why I hesitated to tell Brick that I quit and mean it this time, but now I'm happy I didn't. This visit could be about Sacks, Brick's office, or something else. Maybe I'll get lucky and he'll slip up and reveal part of Sacks' getaway plan."

"Who knows how much time we have until he takes off?" GC mused. "Call your snitch on the docks and fork over more cash to keep an eye out. Have the man call the second Sacks leaves — a picture of the getaway vehicle garners a bonus."

Any more questions? I mouthed to Fab, and she shook her head.

"One more thing. When you meet with Brick, be calm and confidant, and remember direct eye contact sells a lie," GC said.

"Fab never listens to me when I remind of her that." I made a face at her.

She rolled her eyes.

"Be damn careful." GC disconnected.

Fab was already on the phone, talking to her dock connection, adamant that he not take any chances. It impressed me that she never asked anyone else to take unnecessary chances.

"You're lucky the guys aren't here — they'd never let either of us go to Brick's alone. Another thing. You're not going to be alone with him for very long. I'll give you a few minutes, and then come up and make a scene of some sort. Don't know what yet. Hopefully, something comes to me before I make my entrance."

"Fifteen minutes max." Fab smiled with relief. "Make it award-winning, so he kicks us both out."

* * *

Fab flew up the highway to South Miami. I

figured we were both thinking the same thing: "Who tipped off Sacks?"

With Famosa Motors in sight, I texted the guys a brief update on the situation with Sacks and let them know our location and that we were about to enter the building.

"You come up with a scene yet?" Fab asked as she waited to make a left into the driveway.

"Yes, and I'm not telling you, so you'll be surprised by my antics." A trip to Brick's office didn't usually leave me feeling fearful for my friend. "You be careful. I don't think he'd call you to his office for a showdown if he suspected you of planting the bug, but don't be afraid to shoot him if he's foolish enough to draw first."

"We're not staying long... hopefully," Fab said in a small voice that conveyed her worry. "Five minutes."

I snapped my fingers. "Trot out your snooty, condescending French girl—she's always good in a tight spot."

Fab pulled up in front and parked. "No customers?" Looking around the lot, I spotted a couple of car salesman with coffee in their hands. She got out and waved to them before going inside the building.

As the seconds dragged by, my tension ratcheted up. I didn't wait for the full five minutes, minus the time for me to get up the stairs. I walked under the roll-up doors and made eye contact with Brick's flame-haired

Amazonian assistant/bodyguard, Everly, as she stood and assumed a butt-kicker stance.

"Hold it right there." She stepped around the counter. "Turn your ass right back around. Mr. Famosa doesn't want to be disturbed, and certainly not by the likes of you."

Brick's angry voice floated down from above.

I glanced up and noticed that Fab hadn't taken her favorite post on the window ledge. "Too bad." I headed to the stairs.

"Stop right there," she barked and moved her hand behind her back.

"Drop your hand." I wiped the smarmy smile off her face by pulling my weapon from the back of my waistband and pointing it at her before she got to her gun. "Brick give you instructions to shoot me?"

"You horrid bitch, you know you've been banned from this property," Everly spit.

"News to me." I glared. "I'm going to overlook your unfortunate choice to pull a weapon on me as long as you sit back down and go back to doing whatever it is you do. Painting your nails?"

Anger radiated off her body as she walked backward to her desk without a word.

I didn't take my eyes off the woman as I made my way over to the stairwell. Given the opportunity, I had no doubt she'd shoot me in the back and come up with some lame excuse that Brick would back up. As I neared the bottom of the steps, Brick's shouting got louder. Then silence. I jumped up the stairs two at a time.

Fab was seated in a chair, her back to me. I paused to catch my breath, then stepped into his office, not bothering to wait for an invitation. "Having a bad day?" I asked cheerfully and moved over to Fab.

Apparently just finished chewing someone out on the phone, Brick whirled around in his chair and, at the sight of me, slammed the phone down. The Smith and Wesson Magnum holstered under his arm caught me off guard. I'd never seen him display a weapon.

He glowered at me, leaning forward over the desk. "You threatened Everly," he bellowed.

It took willpower to stand my ground as he shot out of his chair. He stopped halfway around his desk, reminding me of a guard dog who hadn't had a meal in a while and was barely restrained by a leash.

"She drew first. It's not my fault I'm faster." I should have tried harder to keep the note of smugness from my voice. "You expect me to stand there and get shot when all I wanted was some candy? You still have the candy dish stashed over there, don't you?" I pointed to the credenza that ran along the wall.

He assessed me with angry eyes that made my neck hair stand on end. "I don't like you," he told me.

Gee, thanks, but I know that already.

"But I'm about to offer you a golden opportunity to redeem yourself and get back in my good graces."

I did a mental eye roll.

"Someone is trying to screw me, and a message needs to be sent that such an action would be bad for the person's health."

Me? Message sender! Not happening, even if I had any respect for him.

He opened a cabinet door, retrieving a bag of candy and tossing it at me. "Since Fab's pregnant, I'll need you to do night guard duty."

Skittles! Ick! Good thing I was looking down, glaring at the candy choice. When his words penetrated my brain, my eyes bugged out of my head. *Pregnant!*

"Sorry, but you'll have to continue to dislike me," I told him. He and I both knew I couldn't care less about how he felt about me and that his job request had never had any chance of success. "I'd have to ask my boyfriend. But I can save us from waiting for the answer—it will be no, and I always do what he tells me." *Wait until I told Creole that last part; he'd laugh his head off.* Besides, blaming him sounded better than *Hell, no.*

"Get out," he roared and pointed to the door.

Not without Fab. I held out the bag of Skittles, and when he didn't take it, I dropped it on his desk. "I don't like these. Can I choose my own?"

Brick was on the verge of bolting the rest of the way around his desk to throw me out bodily, and I'd be lucky to get off with a tumble down the steps. Fab stood, put her arm around me, and squeezed hard. "Who knew a woman got so tired when she's pregnant?" She yawned behind her hand. "We'll talk about this again," she said to Brick. "Think about using one of my guys." She pushed me toward the door and out into the hallway as she spoke. I turned slightly, just in time to see Fab mouth, "Sorry," to Brick, who practically had flames leaping out of his head.

"I'm not pregnant," she whispered when we got to the bottom of the stairs. "I morphed into you for a second, and that's what came out. Better than the obedient girlfriend story." She snorted.

Fab bypassed the shortcut out the side door and headed back into the showroom. She stopped in front of the reception counter and crazy-girl smiled at Everly, who glared ice picks at her, then me.

Fab leaned slightly over the counter, not quite in the woman's face, but close enough. "You *ever* threaten my friend, verbally or with a gun or any other weapon, I'll hunt you down, and you'll be nothing but a memory for your friends, if you have any. Don't think I won't find you, even if you decide to make your new home under a rock. Capisce?"

Realizing that Fab expected an answer, Everly said through thinned lips, "Got it."

Fab grabbed my wrist, and we hustled out

under the roll-up doors.

Once the car doors closed, Fab hit the locks. "The best plan is to go back home, no detour to the boat. I wouldn't put it past Brick to have us followed. He called because he's livid over finding the bugs in his office and wants me to ferret out who planted them. Unbeknownst to me, he runs regular checks for bugs, and that's how he found them."

As she drove out into traffic, I kept an eye on the rearview mirror for a tail. I'd asked her about the information she'd learned from the bugs she put in Brick's office, but she'd passed it off as nothing. Totally boring.

"From his reaction, you'd have thought his manhood had been hacked off. He's not used to someone getting one over on him." Fab laughed.

I wasn't as opposed to that idea as I should be.

"Brick's bright idea was a stakeout. What's with all the stakeout requests of late? I had him about talked out of that idea, convincing him that whoever set it up knew they'd been found out and would be foolish to come back. Then you walked in the door." Fab laughed and hit the steering wheel. "Good job. What surprised me was that he offered you the job. I know for a fact he has other investigators on call."

I admired Fab for emerging looking unscathed from what had to be an intense meeting with Brick. "Any mention of Marshall?"

"Waiting for any word of Marshall had me on

edge, but it didn't happen." Fab whooshed out a long breath. "I can't stop thinking that I'm the only one on his radar and this command performance was because maybe I let something slip. But if he had proof of any kind, we would've had an ugly confrontation."

The Keys sign reminded me I needed to text the guys and let them know we were headed home.

On cue, Fab's phone rang. She answered and hit the speaker.

"Good thing you answered or I'd be on my way over to that bastard's office," Didier snapped. "Got your text. Creole and I were already in Miami, and we raced over to the docks and got here minutes before Marshall and Meredith left. She passed us, racing up the dock, and left on foot. A power boat named *Leisure* pulled up at the other end of the dock, Marshall tossed in a duffle bag and jumped on board, and he and the driver were gone."

"Apparently, Meredith wasn't ready for life on the run," I said.

"I dialed 911, but it was too late," Creole said, his exasperation coming through the phone line.

"Creole and I both want to know how the meeting with Brick went," Didier said.

"The meeting was reasonably civil," Fab said. "It started out with too many questions about my new business, which I sidestepped. As you can imagine, he's not happy that I branched out.

Then he got to the reason he demanded the meeting—the break-in at Famosa. How could a mere mortal get past his security? Not a word about Marshall."

"We'll be back at the house in a few hours; we're going to hang out here and see if anyone shows up," Didier told us.

"Be careful," Fab said before hanging up.

"Now what?" I asked. "Marshall left by water, and with no one following, he could go anywhere."

"Don't you find it interesting that as soon as the evidence that proves Marshall is alive reaches the hands of authorities, Marshall disappears?" Fab mused.

"For a man who moved around town without a care, he's running scared now. Probably wondering how someone caught up to him."

Fab signaled and made a turn to the east. "We're going to the boat. Order pizza from that chain pizzeria we all like; that will lessen the guys' irritation that we're not very well-behaved. Certainly not as much as you told Brick you were." She laughed. "I deserve an award for not reacting to that one."

Chapter Forty-Four

"Coming back to the docks was a good idea after all." Fab pointed over the steering wheel at Marshall's Mercedes, which had been loaded on the back of a flatbed and was now turning out of the clubhouse parking lot. Fab's eyes were glued to the truck as it passed her. At an impatient honk from behind us, she pulled into the lot, u-turned, and followed the flatbed.

My phone rang, and Creole's face popped up on my screen. "Where are you going?" he asked as soon as I answered. "Clearly not back home."

"We brought pizza."

He laughed. "Which will be cold by the time you get back from who knows where. I was scanning the parking lot when you two did your U-turn, and Didier and I were flipping to see who'd go after you two."

"We're following Marshall's car. I'm guessing, since Fab hasn't shared her plan, that she wants to know if the Mercedes ends up at Brick's. I know I do. Hopefully, this road trip doesn't end up in Georgia."

"Be careful and stay in touch," Creole said.

I made a kissy noise and hung up.

"Whoever is helping Marshall is on their game, having the car hauled away before the cops show up. Assuming they do. Who even knows if they will?" I leaned forward in my seat, snapping pics of the truck's license plate. "Would be nice to get a picture of the placard on the side of the truck."

The truck had bypassed a couple of turns headed to the Interstate, and instead, we were backtracking the way we'd come — back in the direction of Famosa Motors. Which could be a coincidence. Or not. The flatbed turned onto a side street that ran parallel to the main boulevard in a seedy commercial area offering an array of services for used trucks and cars. He slowed, signaled again, and backed into a used car lot.

I turned as we passed the truck. "Barfy's Towing." At Fab's raised brow, I insisted, "That's what his sign says... maybe."

Fab doubled back, slowing, and since street parking was prohibited, she pulled into the dirt lot that served as parking for a roach coach. The aluminum shutters had been rolled down, and it was closed for the day. It gave us a diagonal view of what was happening across the street.

The tow truck now parked, another man came out the front door of the manufactured home being used as an office. The man watched as the driver unloaded the Mercedes onto solid ground.

I snapped a few pictures of the pay-by-the-week car lot. "This is boring. And before you ask,

I'm not coming back tonight to have a peek at records that may or may not exist."

The lot employee jumped behind the wheel of the Mercedes and drove it around the back. The tow driver got back in his truck and drove out without so much as a wave.

"Interesting, no paperwork." That had all the hallmarks of a Brick deal.

Fab managed to hit all green lights back to the boat. She parked at the far end of the lot next to another SUV that was a foot longer.

We were climbing the steps when Creole shouted, "Damn."

Didier pulled a large pile of poker chips across the table in front of him.

Creole stood and took the pizza boxes from my hand, taking them into the galley to nuke them and handing them back, one at time, to be put on the table, which had been set with paper plates and towels.

Fab handed a sack of beer to Didier, who opened it and smiled.

"You just missed what could've been some real excitement but turned out to be a big nothing," Creole said, pulling me up a chair next to him. "Local cops showed up, headed straight over to the yacht, and climbed aboard. Not sure what they did, but they were gone in less than three minutes."

"Wouldn't they need a search warrant to go on board?" I asked.

"So you do listen when I talk about doing things legally." Creole smiled at me. "They can climb on board to knock on the door. If it had been me, I'd have called out, which we didn't hear either of them do. I'd also have asked questions of any boat owners I could find hanging around." He turned to Didier. "Did I miss anything?"

"The part where we were the only two hanging around, and they didn't try to talk to us." Didier shook his head.

Chapter Forty-Five

Creole's doorbell rang, which meant that Didier and Fab had arrived since no one else had the address.

I pushed off Creole's lap, and he got up and checked the security feed.

"You must have had a talk with Fab," I said, "since she's not kicking the door in. What did you do, threaten bodily harm?"

Creole shrugged like an innocent man, which meant some sort of one-upmanship confrontation had gone down. "Let's hope they brought something good for dinner."

"We know it won't be hamburgers."

Fab professed to hate burgers but always ate every bite, complaining the whole time.

I was a step away from opening the door when a barrage of kicking began on the other side. It could only be Fab, and it meant that she'd figured out how to bypass the security pad at the fence. So much for promises.

Creole's eyebrows shot to his hairline. "Can I shoot her?"

"They've got food. Now smile." I opened the door to Fab's grin and Didier's chagrined look.

"Remind me to give you one of my business cards." Fab smiled at Creole. "Your security system could use an update."

I turned and grinned at Didier, who winked in return and linked his arm in mine. We went out to the patio, leaving Fab and Creole to snap a few words in French at one another behind us.

Didier set two shopping bags from the Seafood Kitchen, a new restaurant in town, down on the table. He brushed my hand away. "I've got this."

Earlier, I'd gotten out the dishes that I'd bought Creole and set the table out on the patio. On one of my recent trips to the store, I bought various sizes of pillar candles and put together a centerpiece that included seashells and a piece of burlap ribbon.

Creole wrapped his arms around me, peering over my shoulder. "I'm on bartender duty."

"The refrigerator is restocked; I made sure that there's plenty of beer choices and filled the wine rack. I grabbed glasses and left finding the corkscrew to you."

"The wine's breathing, smarty."

"Fancy wine," I teased as Creole pulled out a chair for me. I flicked up the corner of the container that Fab had just set on my plate. "Yum. My favorite." I picked up a piece of shrimp and bit into it.

"It's not hamburgers. But good job." Creole winked at Fab and got a snort in return. It was an unusual night where all of us were drinking the same thing. He filled the wine glasses and was just starting to sit down next to me when his phone rang. Checking the screen, he headed back inside the house.

"I can show you how the speaker button works, so we can all listen in," Fab called to him.

Creole turned and shook his finger at her with a "behave" glare that I recognized. Mine usually came with a hint of a smile.

Fab stuck her nose in the air.

Didier and I grinned at one another.

"Fabiana, it's amazing the man hasn't wrung your neck despite our friendship," Didier said.

"Hey, everyone, hurry up and get in here," Creole called from the doorway. He turned on the television and flipped it to a news channel. On the screen was a video of a boat exploding, the news anchor reporting that it was the second in recent weeks. Creole shoved his phone in his pocket. "That, friends, is the *Leisure* blowing to bits."

Fab figured out the significance first and blurted, "The boat that picked up Marshall and headed for the Atlantic?"

"According to my friend, the bodies of two men were fished from the water," Creole informed us. "I called in a favor, and in addition to the latest explosion news, my friend was calling with an update. There hasn't been a whisper around the halls of the Miami police department of Marshall surviving the original boat explosion. He found it odd, given that the evidence we provided that the man is still alive is damn convincing."

"Any chance he was on that boat?" Didier asked, pointing at the screen.

Creole flicked off the television when they moved on to another story and waved us back out to the patio, where we reclaimed our seats at the table.

"The bodies from this recent incident are at the coroner's, and there's a lockdown on the file, which is unusual. My friend's got an in there, and we'll hear as soon as the findings come back. If one of them is Marshall Sacks, I'm sure the tests will be run again."

"That would be weird — fate or something — if he was on board. Do you suppose there'll be a second funeral?" I asked. That lightened the somber silence that had descended around the table.

* * *

After dinner, Creole dragged the chairs closer to the fire pit, facing the water. "We've got wine to drink." He grabbed up a bottle, refilling our glasses. "And Fab's going to update us on her meeting with Brick."

"I'll bet he knows about this latest explosion and whether Marshall was on board or not," I mused. "Wouldn't surprise me if he doesn't need to wait for the coroner to know what the results will be."

Could this case get any weirder?

"As you know, Brick forced a meeting on me today," Fab said.

"I had to restrain myself from shooting him." Didier's eyes flashed with anger. "He deserves payback for browbeating the two of you and constantly trying to coerce you into illegal activities."

"I think we've thoroughly corrupted you," I said. Didier was the only one of us that didn't make it a habit to holster a gun somewhere on his body before leaving the house.

"You tell them." Fab smiled at Didier, conveying that she was happy with whatever he'd done.

"Fab loaned me a derringer, which I strapped in an arm holster." Didier flexed his muscles. "If only I'd had a camera to capture the look of surprise—more like shock—when Brick first spotted me off to one side. Then his eyes zoomed in on my cannon. He attempted to intimidate me, engaging in a stare-down, which went nowhere. To my amusement, he looked away first."

"Your lighthouse recommendation was a good one." Fab tipped her wine glass to me.

Brick had called early that morning, his anger vibrating through the phone. "I need you to follow up on some leads. Someone screwed me, and I'm hoping it's not who I think it is. Come to my office now," he ordered Fab.

I shook my head at Fab frantically. She'd put the call on speaker, and those neck hairs of mine were screaming no.

"I'm feeling a bit queasy right now," Fab said.

I wanted to clap at the whiney tone she used; it was one I hadn't heard before.

"In my office. Now," he ranted. "Women have babies every day and function just fine."

Mr. Sensitive. I'd bet cash he never talked to his wife like that when she was pregnant with one of their brood.

"I — "

"I'm waiting," Brick blasted and hung up.

"I wonder what he wants. Whatever it is, I don't like it. You're not going," I said adamantly.

"I'm going to deal with him now. No need for you to put yourself in the line of fire of his nasty comments." She stood and left the kitchen, going upstairs.

Over my dead body.

I stood and ran into the entry, picking up Fab's purse and snatching her keys out of the side pocket where I knew she kept them. I grabbed my keys, shoving both pairs in the pocket of my jean skirt, and raced back to the island, where I retrieved her phone, hitting redial.

Brick answered, "What?"

At the same time, Fab reappeared and stood in the doorway.

"This isn't Fab. It's Madison." I hit the speaker.

"What in the hell do you want? You've got a lot of nerve, calling me. You've got two seconds before I hang up."

Fab ran across the kitchen, reaching for the phone.

I turned out of her grasp. "Not so fast, you're going

to want to hear this. You're expecting Fab, and she won't be showing up because I hid the car keys."

Fab and I flinched at the loud bang. The line went dead.

"You took my keys?" Fab asked in annoyance and rushed back into the entry, grabbing her purse.

"Guess who I learned that trick from?"

The phone rang, and Brick's face appeared.

"Give it to me." Fab held out her hand. "If I don't talk to him, he'll find that suspicious."

I handed it over.

"Fine," Brick barked. "It's been a while since I've been around a pregnant woman, and I should've been more sensitive."

I rolled my eyes. He didn't sound the least bit sorry... or any other similar emotion.

"Two o'clock, I'll be at your office," he said. "And I'll need the address since I haven't been there yet."

I shook my head wildly, scribbled an address on a notepad, and shoved it back across the countertop.

"We can discuss it now," Fab suggested.

"In person is better."

Fab rattled off the address, at the same time poking the pad. Once they disconnected, she asked, "Jake's?"

"The lighthouse. Which is why you need to call Gunz; he'll let you use it if you ask. Never give out the real office address to anyone except your riff-raff contractors, who I trust more than Brick. You're never at the lighthouse, and no one in their right mind is going to mess with Gunz."

"That would be a big mistake. They'd end up like that man whose wife dispersed her husband's remains through a wood chipper."

I squeezed my eyes closed. "Pretty sure that's death-penalty eligible."

"He was dead."

"That's probably a good thing."

"The missus had him cremated, and that's how she spread the ashes."

"I don't want to hear any more of your heartwarming send-off stories. Make the call." I got up and got as far as the front door when it opened and Didier came in, smiling. "Good, you're home. You can escort your girlfriend. Don't start," I said, pointing at Fab. "I don't care if you're thinking I'm a crappy friend, I'll get over it. You are not going by yourself." I disappeared upstairs.

"Ever since the break-in at his office," Fab went on, "he's been totally paranoid. Says his files were ransacked and someone has sensitive information. He wants to know what they're going to do with it."

"You didn't come back to the car with any files that night, so I'm assuming he made that up or there's a second person. Perhaps, the same person who turned the cameras off before you got there."

"All made up." Fab was adamant. "My guess is he's waiting for me to slip up. He always operates under that 'keep your friends close' rule."

"I'm guessing you came up with another excuse. Something good, I hope?" Creole asked.

"Before she could respond, I rudely interrupted," Didier answered, the corners of his mouth turned up. "Told Brick no way in hell or when it froze over, whichever he preferred." He hugged Fab to his side.

"Bet he emitted an angry snarl on that one." I mimicked the man, which had everyone laughing.

"I suggested that he find someone else, since I wouldn't be working for a while," Fab said. "He didn't take that well. He abruptly stood up, and his parting shot was, 'I've got another meeting. When you get your head screwed back on straight, call me. Best pre-wedding advice I can give you is don't marry him. Big mistake.'"

"Let's hope that's the last we see or hear of him." Creole said.

"I followed him to the door and reminded him that I was pregnant. His eyes softened a bit, and he actually smiled. I don't think he'd hurt me unless he had proof positive I bugged him."

"Can you believe he never said good-bye to me or acknowledged me in any way?" Didier huffed out a humorless laugh.

"So, that's the end of working for Brick?" I asked.

Fab shrugged, as if to say *we'll see what happens*.

"Absolutely," Didier said emphatically.

Chapter Forty-Six

It was a week later when Creole got a call from his informant and went to meet the man for an update on the Sacks case. On his way out the door, I reminded him of our late lunch plans with Fab and Didier at The Brewery, a restaurant that the couple had chosen, which to our relief, was not fancy.

Finally, the dinner dishes were cleared away and another round of drinks ordered. The guys both chose beer samplers consisting of four different types—the names written on a black display board—while Fab and I finished off the bottle of wine.

I banged a spoon on the table in an obnoxious manner and felt a tug on the back of my hair. I couldn't decipher Creole's reaction without turning around, but he wouldn't be upset as most of my antics made him laugh. "I have a toast I'd like to make. To Creole." Leaning over, I smiled at him and kissed his cheek. "Congratulations, love. He's passed all his medical and physical evaluations and been deemed one hundred percent," I announced.

Fab snorted. "Guess this means you're not a psycho on the loose. That's good to know."

Creole laughed.

Didier, not so amused, frowned over the rim of his glass.

"There's more." I tipped my glass at Creole. "You tell them."

"Got my PI license. If you two need backup, I'll make myself available."

"What—" Fab jumped. "Ouch."

"Was that your leg? Sorry." I pasted on an insincere smile.

Didier turned his eyes on Fab, who frowned and sat back in her chair. "You going into the business full time?"

Creole shook his head. "Just thought it was good to have, considering the trouble these two attract. Despite what some people think, doing things legally makes for less paperwork, not to mention less likelihood of ending up in jail."

"Make sure I get one of your business cards," Fab said.

"You are really annoying tonight." I half-smiled.

"What is it you like to say?" Fab tapped her cheek. "Hmm... oh yes... That's why we're such good friends... we can be annoying together, or some such thing."

Creole and Didier laughed.

"To our foursome," Didier toasted.

"There's more news. This will be more to your

liking." Creole winked at Fab. "Marshall Sacks is really dead." He paused for a few seconds to allow that to sink in. "The second explosion killed him and the skipper, Gary Greene. The boat was a rental, and all the paperwork was in order for the Greene fellow."

"Who died in the first boat explosion?" Didier asked.

"The coroner's trying to figure that out now. Misidentifying a body almost never happens. I'm not going to say never, but damn close," Creole answered. "It would take a series of errors for the coroner to do that. The professionals who issue death certificates take them very seriously."

"What happened to the information that I had delivered?" Fab asked. "Anybody the least bit interested?"

I shared Fab's annoyance and frustration, knowing how hard she worked to get the information together.

"They took your information very seriously and were in the process of verifying it all," Creole assured Fab. "If you were thinking they'd come out and make a statement, they won't, because they won't disclose anything that makes them have to answer questions that would make them look incompetent. If it became public knowledge, it's likely the coroner's office would come out with an announcement saying they'll be investigating internally to find out why and how the mistake was made."

"I've been thinking about how they might make such a mistake," Fab mused. "It actually wouldn't take much. A technician could easy switch a DNA sample from the dead body with a sample from Marshall. But the best opportunity would be if Marshall made sure that the comparison sample, the one cops would've taken from his house, was actually DNA from the dead guy."

"This isn't an 'Oh, well, mistakes happen.' They're going to want to know not only how it happened, but who the earlier victim was," Creole assured us.

"I take it Alta will be freed from jail?" Didier said.

"I'd say that depends on the evidence they used to book her." Fab arched her brow at Creole. "Am I right, detective? If they can actually prove that she planted the bomb that caused the first yacht to explode—which they asserted in her bond hearing, resulting in her extended stay in jail—then the answer would be a big no. She'd still go on trial."

"It's rumored that the evidence isn't as airtight as the prosecutor once thought," Creole said. "Since Alta was charged with murder after the first explosion, now that it's been determined that the man was still alive after the explosion, authorities would have to drop at least the murder charge."

"How is it that the news media isn't all over

this case?" Didier asked.

"It's possible to keep some of the information from the media, but certainly not all of it. I expect they'll get ahold of the full story eventually."

"So, Marshall orchestrates this plan in an attempt to get Alta out of his life and make sure she spent the rest of hers behind bars?" Didier shook his head in disbelief.

"That's what the lead investigator is looking into. He suspects that Sacks had something bigger to hide and has expanded his investigation to include his business interests," Creole said. "Depending on the results of the investigation into the second explosion, it's likely there's still a killer out there."

"Wonder what Brick knows?" Fab said.

"Great minds." Creole tapped his temple. "I called his office and got his assistant. Passed myself off as a buyer hoping to acquire the latest Ferrari. I finally got out of her that he's in Europe with his wife."

"Brick doesn't take vacations unless the wife insists," Fab said.

"Brick's all about Brick," I said. "I'd like to know why he'd get neck deep in something that could land him in jail."

"That's why I told my friend to suggest to the lead investigator that he widen his scope and include Brick's financial records. One thing I know about the man — he's all about money."

* * *

A few days later, GC called. "The charges against Alta were dropped. She was released at midnight with no fanfare."

"No lights, cameras, news mentions?"

"I've got one last tidbit for you before I hang up on you."

"So, you acknowledge that you have hideous phone manners."

"Do you want to know or not?" he grumped.

"What is it you say? Don't waste my time with dumb questions?"

"I've never—"

"You would if you'd thought of it."

He laughed. "Would you like to venture a guess as to who Alta's ride to freedom was?"

I sighed loudly into the phone.

"None other than Meredith Sacks, wife number one. They hotfooted it out to Fisher, where they've been holed up in the manse ever since."

Chapter Forty-Seven

"Alone at last," Creole said in exasperation, slamming the door, crossing to the couch, and setting me down.

"It probably has something to do with Fab barely getting the car in park before you had the door open and were dragging me across the seat. I scarcely had time to catch my breath before I was upended over your shoulder. So rude."

"All I heard was laughter, so I'm thinking the duo isn't nursing hurt feelings."

I had waved good-bye to Fab and Didier, and they both gave me a thumbs up as Creole shut the truck door.

"Don't move." He pointed his finger at me before disappearing into the closet, coming out with a foot-long black velvet drawstring bag and a rolled-up beach blanket. He reached for my hand and pulled me up against his chest, leaning down and brushing my lips with his.

"Ready?" he asked.

I eyed the bag and had to restrain myself from touching it. Reading my thoughts, he moved it out of reach. He smirked and hooked his arm around me, steering me toward the patio door and down the steps to the beach.

The sun hadn't set completely, a sliver out on the horizon. The water sparkled and quietly lapped the shore. He came to a halt in our favorite spot and tossed down the blanket, which landed in a heap. We each grabbed corners and straightened it out.

He pulled me down next to him, brushing my cheek with a kiss. I turned, and he captured my lips, cupping my face and deepening the kiss. He broke off, leaving us both breathless, and pressed his forehead to mine, looking into my eyes. "I don't want to get engaged."

We're breaking up! I held my breath, letting it out slowly. I'd be damned if I'd cry. I shoved him, and he fell back, but not enough that I could get out of his embrace. "Get off me," I ordered. "You could have told me at the house, as in my house, that we're breaking up."

"What in the hell?" he roared. "Where did you get that idea? I've wanted you since the day I laid eyes on you."

"So, you brought me out here to say what, 'Let's shack up'? I don't understand."

Creole kicked the sand, sending it flying in all directions, running his hands over his face. "Damn it. *I. Practiced.*" He stood, grabbing his bag. "Don't go anywhere. Don't think I won't chase you down the beach, and I'll win." He poked his chest, then turned and walked away.

"What the heck?" I whined and said to his back, "I don't want to be out here by myself."

After taking a few steps, he shrugged and turned, coming back and standing at the edge of the blanket. "Do over," he stage-whispered.

"What?" My brow rose.

"Hey, babe." He bowed and sat down facing me. A chagrined smile on his face, he nudged my legs wide enough to settle in between. He untied the mysterious bag and withdrew a bottle of champagne, two glasses, and an oblong box.

"Could you reassure me that we're not celebrating splitting up? And that this…" I shook the box, hearing a faint shift. "…isn't my 'get lost' gift?"

He glared and said sternly, "Do you remember me just saying, 'Do over'?"

I grinned, not the least bit contrite, and slipped the bow off the box. *A bracelet?* Instead of shaking it again, I took off the lid. "A USB drive?" There was no mistaking my confusion.

He picked it out of the box and laid it in my hand. "Remember when I told you you'd be the first to know about the project I've been working feverishly on? Here it is. I wrote a cop thriller. Tomorrow, I'm sending a copy to an interested agent."

"I'm going to know a bestselling author." I threw my arms his neck.

He chuckled. "We've got to get it published first."

"I'm impressed." I leaned in, kissing him hard on the lips.

He placed the glasses in my hand, popping the cork.

I watched as he caught it in one hand. "Now that was impressive."

He winked and filled the glasses, then burrowed the bottle in the sand. He clutched my hair and gently tugged my head back, saying softly, "Look at me. I'm going off-script and ad-libbing."

Lifting my eyes, I stared into his cobalt blues.

He held his glass out in a toast. "I love you." He clinked the rim of my glass and scooted forward, wrapping his legs around my backside. "Will you marry me?"

"But you said—"

He pressed his finger against my lips. "Marry me."

"Yes." I sank against his chest, and he tightened his arms around me.

He loosened one hand and reached behind his back, extracting the bag, this time pulling out a small black box.

"You got me a ring?" I squealed.

"That's one thing I did right." He grimaced. "That old saying about practice making perfect... I had my speech memorized, all flowery and romantic, and I didn't remember a word." He opened the lid. "If you don't like this, we can go pick out something from the jewelry store. This was my mother's wedding ring." He pulled out a cushion-cut emerald, surrounded by a row of diamonds, set in platinum.

"It's so beautiful." Tears slid down my cheeks. "And your mother wore it. I love it, and I'm honored to wear it.

Creole slid it on my ring finger. "It fits." He grinned.

He tightened his hold around my waist, leaned down, and gently touched his lips to mine. I responded hungrily, pressing my body against his and crushing his mouth. When we finally broke apart, I dropped my head into the crook of his neck, clinging to him breathlessly.

"I still don't want to be engaged," he whispered down at me. Sensing my confusion, he went on. "We'll elope."

When I recovered from the shock, I squeaked, "Elope?"

"I'm thinking me and you, barefoot on the beach. Not sharing the day with hundreds of people we don't know."

"But we'd miss a good brawl. You know Westin family shindigs—we might even make headlines: 'Fisticuffs break out at local wedding.'"

"That's what I love about you, always making me laugh."

"I'm glad you're in a good mood." I laughed back. "Love, love your idea of getting married on the beach, the waves lapping our feet. There's just a slight problem. I'm not telling Mother that she's being gypped out of a wedding for her only daughter, so I'll leave that to you. And it needs to be done in advance. If we wait until we get back, she'll never speak to us again." I added, "Let's not forget Fab and Didier. We're not going to be very popular."

"So, not tomorrow?"

I shook my head.

He let out a long breath. "We'll keep our engagement secret for now and tell people this is a…" He thought for a moment and kissed my finger. "A friendship ring."

As Creole looked on, annoyed, I threw my head back and laughed, imagining the look on people's faces when we tried to sell that yarn. "Now that we're tying the knot, you'll have access to my good advice 24/7. Not that you don't already, but now I'll be by your side. Da, da, da…" I threw out my arms and wrapped them around his neck. "Confide in Mother what you want, and she'll make it happen so that everyone is happy."

"How about the day after?" He wrapped his arms around me, tightening his hold. "I love you."

"I love *you*."

PARADISE SERIES NOVELS

Crazy in Paradise
Deception in Paradise
Trouble in Paradise
Murder in Paradise
Greed in Paradise
Revenge in Paradise
Kidnapped in Paradise
Swindled in Paradise
Executed in Paradise
Hurricane in Paradise
Lottery in Paradise
Ambushed in Paradise
Christmas in Paradise
Blownup in Paradise
Psycho in Paradise
Overdose in Paradise
Initiation in Paradise
Jealous in Paradise
Wronged in Paradise
Vanished in Paradise
Fraud in Paradise
Naive in Paradise

Deborah's books are available on Amazon
amazon.com/Deborah-Brown/e/B0059MAIKQ

About the Author

Deborah Brown is an Amazon bestselling author of the Paradise series. She lives on the Gulf of Mexico, with her ungrateful animals, where Mother Nature takes out her bad attitude in the form of hurricanes.

Sign up for my newsletter and get the latest on new book releases. Contests and special promotion information. And special offers that are only available to subscribers.
www.deborahbrownbooks.com

Follow on FaceBook:
facebook.com/DeborahBrownAuthor

You can contact her at Wildcurls@hotmail.com

Deborah's books are available on Amazon
amazon.com/Deborah-Brown/e/B0059MAIKQ

Made in the USA
Coppell, TX
01 August 2024

35476188R00233